Eirrin. Love of the greater gods, *Eirrin*. It's liquid music the name was. A name that called up, that *meant,* the world's bravest and fairest men and women, thick-maned horses, red and brindle cattle, rivers like molten silver with gold shining in their beds, and great forests old as time. Poets and craftsmen Eirrin produced, whose work vied with that of nature; learned men and women of supernatural wisdom and power. Splendour, and wealth, and delights. *Eirrin.* All barred to him—because of the treachery of kings . . .

In vengeance and bitterness and hatred did the reiver Cormac savage the shores of Gol's kingdom. Mothers frightened miscreant youngsters with stories of Captain Partha, Captain Wolf, the scarred raider with eyes cold and grey and glittering as the metal of his sword. Cormac *an-Cliuin* he was: Cormac the Wolf.

CORMAC MAC ART

More Swords-and-Sorcery from
Ace Science Fiction. . . .

The CORMAC MAC ART series, based on the legendary Irish hero created by Robert E. Howard, written by Andrew J. Offutt, the popular author of heroic fantasy.

Also by Andrew J. Offutt:

- KING DRAGON (Illustrated)
- CONAN THE SORCERER (Illustrated)
- CONAN THE MERCENARY (Illustrated)
- And don't miss Andy Offutt's tales in Robert Asprin's wildly popular swords-and-sorcery anthology series: *Thieves' World, Tales From the Vulgar Unicorn,* and *Shadows of Sanctuary.*

Also by Keith Taylor:

- BARD

THE TOWER OF DEATH

ANDREW OFFUTT & KEITH TAYLOR

Fantasy

ace books

A Division of Charter Communications Inc.
A GROSSET & DUNLAP COMPANY
51 Madison Avenue
New York, New York 10010

THE TOWER OF DEATH

An ACE Book

First Ace printing: August 1982
Published Simultaneously in Canada

2 4 6 8 0 9 7 5 3 1
Manufactured in the United States of America

THE TOWER OF DEATH

Introduction:
The Cormac Mac Art Cycle

Robert E. Howard began the recounting of the fifth century Irish hero's exploits in *Tigers of the Sea,* which Ace has reprinted. They and the keeper of the REH papers and the Howard literary agent then asked me to continue the cycle (*none* of which was printed during Howard's lifetime).

My first three novels followed *Tigers* chronologically. The fourth went back to recount the treachery-born events that led to Cormac's becoming outlaw, then exile from Erin. Later forced also to flee Alba. Caledonia/Scotland, he bitterly took to the sea as a reiver or reaver: pirate. He met the giant Wulfhere the Dane in prison. Later still Cormac became the only Gael aboard *Raven,* a Wulfhere-commanded ship crewed by Danes. Some of their exploits formed the four stories in Howard's *Tigers.*

This is the fifth of the novels I have written, but the second in chronological order. It precedes *Tigers* by a few years. Herein the mac Art is younger—indeed, he lies about his age because of that embarrassment of youth we have all experienced. An exile, he has not forgotten her he left behind: Samaire. He loved her as he loved their mutual land: Erin or Eirrin.

He is a grim and sombre fellow. He is to become less so only in later years, when he re-meets Samaire and gains purpose and goal—and Irish shores. With Keith Taylor, this chronicle returns to that Cormac of less optimism and more dourness, and a different part of the world. Cormac is the exiled pirate among foreigners, crafty and untrusting.

Howard clearly indicated that mac Art's activities were hardly confined to the area of the British Isles. Rome had withdrawn from Britannia after four centuries of interference and domination. Britons were dying to invading Saxons and Jutes and Angles who would give the land its new name: Angle-land or *Angle-terre:* England. (Strangely, some Britons had fled from the continent whence came the conquerors. There they founded lesser Britain—Brittany—and clung to it.)

On that continent, the legacy of Rome's pomp and paraphernalia of governance were more evident. The land was already in division among many lords. Soon there would be a king in Italy! Though Frank-land, France, did not exist, the Franks were on the rise with their terrible throwing-axes so like a pre-charge artillery barrage. The Roman title *comes* remained. It would become the French *comte,* which we call count. And though no Count has ever held demesne in my Kentucky, this state is divided into 120 count-ies.

A new age was aborning, in Europe. With the importation of the concept of stirrups, the age of chivalry —*cheval*-ry or horse-ry—would grow out of the chaos left by Rome's fall, and endure until some fool went and invented gunpowder. (Surely not Hank, protagonist of Mark Twain's sf-hf novel!)

In the A.D. 480s, Cormac and Wulfhere were raiding along the coast of what would become France, and soon they had to cross the treacherous Bay of Biscay to northwestern Spain—and honest employment!

Keith Taylor knows about twice as much about that area at that time as Andrew Offutt. That's why he is needed as cohort in this novel and its direct sequel, *When Death Birds Fly*, and the others we have outlined, leading all the way to Wulfhere's homeland, Danemark. Without Keith Taylor, this novel would be about half as good.

We have never met. We live precisely halfway around this planet from each other. Yet there are few lines in this book that are pure Taylor or pure Offutt. When we collaborate, we collaborate. (How? Expensively, between here and Australia!)

Sir Keith has worked out and sent over a fascinating astrological compilation for both Cormac and Wulfhere. Maybe it is pure imagination and maybe it isn't. What do you think their signs are? (Well actually, no, I didn't say that we are believers—or that we are not.)

The zodiacal signs of these two troublesome seawolves are of no concern to Emperor Zeno over in Constantin-opolis, or to his *comes* of Burdigala, the Count of Bordeaux. The Dane and the Irisher have been raiding all too successfully, and are about to be in big trouble.

—Andrew Offutt
Kentucky, U.S.A.

PROLOGUE

"D'ye command war-galleys or wash-tubs? And are they fighting men at your orders—or babes messing their swaddling linen?"

Harshly the demand was snapped out, and harsh was the mood of the speaker. Count Guntram of Burdigala* had lately come in for scathing rebuke on the grounds that he'd let his master's law be flouted. Not a man to suffer in silence was milord Count, or to deny his underlings their just share of the king's anger. In truth he had just vented but a tiny measure of his frustration on the stolid officer before him.

Athanagild Beric's son looked back at the count levelly.

"My men are warriors, by God! As for the ships—" Athanagild shrugged and the movement brought a twinkling flash from the silver-gilt brooch that pinned his long green cloak to his shoulder. "My lord has inspected them himself. There are not enough, and they are old, and no others abuilding. You said it yourself, so don't tell me I'm scrabbling for excuses."

Guntram scowled and his face worked, but he told the officer no such thing. The man was right. Rome was a

*Bordeaux

4

dying Colossus and the world it had created was coming apart all around the deathbed.

The count turned, still scowling, to stare out the unshuttered window at the courtyard of his mansion. The softly playing fountain, the colonnaded walk, the tiled roofs; all boasted silently of Roman architecture, and at least a hundred years old. The fountain leaped and shimmered prettily—and if it stopped Guntram of Burdigala knew it would hardly be worthwhile trying to have it repaired. The matter of warships was comparable.

But no, he mused, not quite; the matter of constructing and repairing warships was not *quite* the same.

Proculus, head of the municipal curia (who had brought two shrewd members of that body with him) coughed. Guntram turned slowly back, wearing a sour and challenging expression.

"My lord *Comes,*" Proculus said primly, "it is not that shipwrights cannot be had. There are enough and to spare, it would seem, to knock *merchant* vessels together." He stressed the one word with distaste, while blandly ignoring the men of commerce also present in the chamber. "Fashioning warcraft, no doubt, is a different matter, and the men able to do it fewer—"

"And most of them," Athanagild put in, for he commanded the royal fleet based in the Garonne, "would liefer work for shares in pirate loot."

The *comes* or count banged a sword-strengthened fist on his oaken table. Objects jumped, and so did his secretary, who was sorely needed since my lord Count could neither read nor write. The count did not notice how he'd disrupted the poor man—or paid no mind, at any rate.

"*Pirates!*" he roared. "By the heart of Arius, I've gone through reports of *pirates* all morning until I'm fairly sickened. That shipping isn't safe is ill enow. That these northern thieves have dared pillage ashore is enough to make me—me, a man who followed King Euric into battle after battle—wish for Judgment Day!"

"Their numbers alone make them difficult to destroy as rats, my lord." The smooth, rather soft voice came from Philip the Syrian, a swarthy man and pockmarked. He blinked heavy eyelids. "The noble Commander Athanagild must cope with Breton corsairs, Saxons and Jutes out of Britain—*King* Hengist notable among them —aye, and their cousins settled in the Charente, upon his very doorstep as it were—"

"*And* the Frisians," Count Guntram snarled, "*and* the Heruls, the Danes—that whole damned boiling sea of North Sea robbers! Not to speak of the Scoti who sometimes take the notion that our coasts are the very place for a happy little junket, and Vandals up from the south to try their luck! Hooves of the Devil! I live here too, merchant! Their numbers are *greater* than rats!" The count's big hand, which bore heavy gold rings and dirty nails in almost equal numbers, lifted to stroke his pepper-and-salt beard. His face softened to an almost ludicrous contrast; his little bright blue eyes glittered.

"Nay," he said almost softly, "with pirates on the water in such numbers, I know not why you are not ruined. I'd like to know how you manage."

Philip's eyes, dark as garnets, flickered and went suddenly as hard. His brocaded tunic and soft Cordoban shoes, no less than the shining gems scintillant on his person, did indeed suggest that he was managing very well indeed. The other merchant, Desiderius Crispus, in a simple dress-tunic long out of date and a wholly false air of patrician hauteur, looked more austere. And the count was too well informed to credit that sham.

Philip said, "If I may speak for us both, my colleague?

6

I believe, my lord *Comes,* that it is because the bulk of our trade goes by land or river. For myself, what goods I ship are brought from the east to Narbo Martius, and then hither. I should not dream of trusting my wealth on the western seas at matters ar now."

"You slimy, lying serpent!"

Guntram gripped the underside of his much-abused table and heaved it over. Ink, reports, quills and fine blotting sand were scattered like trash. The secretary, who had been seated at one end, rolled backward and betook himself out of the way. A corner of the table had banged Proculus on the knees; the phrases he hissed between his teeth as he rubbed were hardly in keeping with the dignity of his position. He stared silently at the count as if wishing the big soldier were small enough to stamp.

The Count of Burdigala was amove; he seized Philip by the throat and choked him until his bulging eyes saw the stark face of Death. Then Guntram flung him down among the papers and ink to get his breath.

"D'you think I'm a fool?" Guntram roared. "Or that my spies waste their time? From *Narbo* is it, with tolls and levies each mile of the way? Pah! And you," he snarled, rounding on Desiderius. *"Traitor!* I'll not bore ye with all I know. It was full eighty swords of Spanish forging, the best there is this side of Damascus, that found their way into Hengist's grasping hands—not so? Not so? And paid for in gold from a looted *church!* Ahhh! And you, Philip of Syria. Captain Ticilo may not be your man for speaking publicly of, but I know what he did in Massilia last year, and what Vandal galley gave him escort the length of the Spanish coast. *And* raided Lusitania on its way home, to such profit that it must have had advance information to guide him. What last I heard, Lusitania is part of our Gothic realms as much as this city—which means, Syrian, that these dealings

7

were no common sharp practice or thieving. They rank as *treason!*" He looked at Proculus. "Be that not so, sir?"

"Beyond doubt, if there is proof," the municipal prefect said, with stiffness. "It would merit the severest death the law can award."

Philip had not risen from his knees; Desiderius now joined him there.

Both merchants wailed for mercy. They had been moved, they avowed nigh fearfully, to do what they did out of desperation for the losses these same pirates had inflicted upon them. If the menace could be abated, the seas cleared or rendered so that a merchantman had so much as even odds, would be their dearest wish come true. Let the Count of Burdigala but state his desires. And so forth.

Guntram was not listening. Proculus had his ear at the moment, and Proculus was waxing condemnatory. He straightened, lean in his robes through with a growing pot. His thin-lipped mouth was twisted. Pain from his smitten knee and disgust at the exhibition he'd been forced to watch were in equal measure the cause of it.

"My lord Count," he snapped, "this disgraces me! Here is neither a court of law nor a wharfside grog-shop —though just now, one might well take the one for the latter. Let these men be arraigned for their crimes in due form, and let the civic questioner be the one to lay hands on them. I give you good day."

"Hold!"

Guntram's crisp order stopped Proculus in his tracks. He gazed at the bleak-faced count, frozen in motion.

"My sons are beyond that door," Guntram of Burdigala said, all in one deadly tone. "They have swords, and will cut to pieces any one who leaves afore I have told him he may. *Anybody,* sir. An ye have complaints, you can make them later, in that due form you love so well—but by God you'll stomach it for now! This is urgent business, should it chance that ye've not yet grasped it!"

The prefect looked stricken. No fleshy, high-coloured, wine-loving old Visigoth he faced now, baffled by law and literacy and intent only on secure comfort in his declining years. Nay, this was Guntram the war-man who had reddened his sword on a score of battlefields in doing his part to turn back Attila's Huns and conquer Hispania. The cheerful ruthlessness on the old soldier's face was warrant that the threatened murders would be performed.

Proculus gathered what dignity he could, and returned to his place in that temper-littered room.

"Better; tha-at's better," Guntram said, nigh purring. "Now attend, all of you. I spoke of an inland raid. The report is amid this litter somewhere . . ." Guntram looked hopelessly round himself. "Well, the gist of it is that a pack-train carrying oil, white salt and fine glassware from Italy, was ambushed and robbed on a *forest road* . . . full twenty mile from the coast! The robbers were Danish pirates; their leader was recognized. There cannot be two men of that size, accoutred so, and with beards so red and axes so huge. For that it was on *me* the king's anger fell. The stolen goods, y'see, were meant for the royal court. An I cannot deal a sharp blow to these pirates within the year, there may be a new Count of Burdigala . . . and a new commander of the fleet." Guntram's eyes wandered to Athanagild; Guntram glowered about at them all before he went on:

"Certain it is that there will be two less merchants in this city! And the new man, whoever he may be, will have words whispered to him about the municipal curia . . . bribes and such, you know; the king cheated of his taxes and the like. Think on it. Given our king's the sort who's apt to dismiss an old soldier who served his father

9

thirty years and feels his wounds every night—to dismiss such a one over the matter of the royal table salt, what can you expect? Eh? And it's written proof I have, and witnesses, mark me! Your fates depend on mine, *all* of you. You had better be convinced of that."

Guntram had gone to purring again; was worse and more menacing, those men thought, than his shout and bluster.

"I'm with you, my lord Count," Proculus assured him. "A loyal subject should do all he can to put down pirates. But how can I be of aid to you? I am no sailor or fighting man."

"You can help with counsel," he was told, "and ere we're done there may well be a few little legal matters that need smoothing over. The Syrian was not merely gabbling when he said pirates are too many, but we have no need of sinking them by the dozens. Athanagild! Say that you knew where to find them, just where to find them, man, and what their movements would be?"

The younger Goth's eyes sparkled. "My lord! I'd lay a couple of the greatest among them by the heels. We'd set some examples to give pause to the rest."

"And gladden the king's heart," Guntram said, and he well nigh beamed. "He might then listen to me when I urge him to march his war-host into the Charente, to subdue or destroy those serpentish Saxons there! The damned place is a home away from home for Hengist and his throat-cutting captains! There'd be glory in it for you too, man. You'd have to strike from the sea at the same time."

"Trap your specimen pirates first," Proculus advised with wise cynicism.

"Right you are. *I want Wulfhere and Cormac mac Art!*"

"Merciful Saviour," Philip the Syrian whispered.

Fleet Commander Athanagild grinned broadly.

"My lord Count, your pardon," one of the *curiales* said. "I know little of individual pirate captains. Of these two I have not heard."

"By God," Athanagild grunted, "had you my job, you'd know their names! Or were you trader, or seaman or pirate of any sort. My lord?"

"By all means tell him."

"Wulfhere of the Danes is a giant. He's all of a foot taller than I, with the bones of an ox, a chest like a wall, and a crimson beard to cover half of it. *Hausakliufr* is he nicknamed in his own language—the Skull-splitter, and not for compliment's sake. Battle is the greatest joy of this colossus's life—the plunder's but an excuse. His fellow Danes are hardly a weak-kneed lot, but they outlawed him because he was too dangerous to have around. Somewhat more to the point, there's no bolder or more expert sailor on the northern seas."

"You sound, sir, as though you had encountered the man."

"I've seen him," Athanagild owned, and the words came betwixt clenched teeth. "Aye, and heard him laugh at me through a gale. None would make a better display on a gibbet."

"And the other?"

"Cormac? That one's an exile from Hibernia, one of the few reivers wild enough to sail with Wulfhere. He's dark as the Skull-splitter is red, a master of the sword, and subtle-brained. Wulfhere loves him for his battle-prowess and relies on him for his crafty advice. No snakes in Hibernia, eh? This Cormac mauled our coasts with a Celtic crew of his own, some years agone. One ship these two have, and sixty followers, and with that they've raked Britain and Gaul and Spain as if there were naught to oppose them but wax men with paper weapons."

"I want them!" Guntram said harshly, and was

momentarily nonplussed with no table to bang. "With all their fame, they've but one ship and none to avenge them. What's more, it was these very two lifted the king's pretties from the pack train."

The disparaging scorn in his last phrase rang clear. Too canny to say it out in such words, or indeed in any words, Guntram despised his king. Alaric the Second, King of all the Visigoths, the old soldier considered a disgrace to his father's name. Despite his rage at the piratical activity along his shores—and inland—the young king preferred to buy erotically skilled women from Egypt and the Levant to beguile his nights, rather than warships to patrol his coast. Guntram almost snorted, thinking of it; indeed, his nostrils flared.

Honest Gothic lasses with broad hips for bearing, and no knowledge of degenerate tricks; these had been good enow for Alaric's father Euric—and aurochs horns to drink from. No question, the race was declining. The younger generation would never carry it to century's end, but fourteen years off.

Well . . . business.

"I want them!" he repeated, and glared at the merchants. "And you *objects* are going to help me take them. Do not think elsewise!"

"Impossible, my lord!" Desiderius Crispus cried. "I do not deal with these men, nor does the Syrian. I keep myself informed. Did they barter their loot in Burdigala at all, I would know of it."

"True, it's true, my good lord!" The confirmation burst eagerly from Philip. "Their buyer is in Nantes, in the Roman kingdom."

"Nantes," the count growled. "And the name of their buyer?"

"I do not know, my lord. By Saint Martin, it's the truth!"

12

Though Guntram eyed them narrowly, he did not hector them the further. He'd sharper pins than that to jab these two with.

He said sharply, "Your oath in a saint's name settles it. It must be true. The part about Nantes is right, in any event, and it's fortunate for you that I happen to know. I've had a spy there of late; the same that uncovered your own shifty dealings, so y'see he knows his word. He traced the man through a customs official he found to be corrupt. The Dane and his partner deal with one Balsus Ammian. Know you aught of him?"

"My lord Count, I do." Desiderius said, and Guntram saw his surprise was real enow. "But it would seem . . . not so much as I did think." He watched the count make an impatient gesture; Guntram had not fetched in Desiderius to flatter his choice of spies. "Aye. Balsus Ammian dwells by the waterfront and makes great affectation of being one step from poverty, but in truth he's no less rich than—"

The merchant stopped suddenly.

"Than you are?" Guntram suggested. "Aye, that tallies with my man's description. We talked until late last night."

The merchants' mutual thought was easy to guess: *I must learn who this spy of Guntram's is.* Which, of course, was why he was not present at this meeting they now knew Guntram had planned, and planned well.

"An I find ferrets of yours within sniffing distance of his name," the count said genially, "I'll see your bones picked bare and rattling in the wind. Understood?"

Under those innocently staring blue eyes, they did assurance on him that they understood.

"So. Let's get on, then. These piratical swine have shown that they too keep themselves informed. I mean to tempt 'em with a cargo they can scarce resist. Wine,

13

for the most part, but with a treasure of lighter goods, and none of the dangers of fakery; the lading will be true. It will sail from Narbo, and around Hispania hither. Word will be let fall. The Dane and the Gael, if I judge them aright, will not waylay the ship off the Hispanic coast. They will choose to take it within comfortable distance of their market—and Athanagild will be waiting."

Guntram paused but long enough to glance at Athanagild; the commander nodded with enthusiasm.

"And do you, sirs, know the best part of all?" Guntram went amiably on. "It is you who will public-spiritedly provide the bait, and at your own cost."

The merchants broke into a babble of protest. Proculus silenced them by gazing dreamily at the ceiling and murmuring, *"Treason.* The knives. The clamps. The hot lead."

Count Guntram nodded approval. This Proculus fellow might be snobbish and finicky, but once he got into the spirit of things the man was downright useful.

"But my lord," Desiderius bleated, "they may succeed after all!"

"In which case you will have to take your losses, now won't you? But aye, it's a thought. I should like them to have a nasty surprise awaiting them in Nantes, in the event they do. It requires thought. But you have more to tell me yet. You may not traffic with Wulfhere and Cormac, but you are to betray to the full measure of your grimy knowledge the pirates you do buy from. Either they are taken and executed within the year—hooves of the Devil, within the *season!*—or you, dear sirs, suffer in their places. Well, sirs, I am waiting."

They did not force the noble count to wait overlong.

CHAPTER ONE: Trap for A Pirate

At the mouth of a reedy creek perched a raven with whetted beak and talons flexing. Dark was the predator, with sharp eyes for that which would feed her. Yet this raven was no bird, but a ship. And unlike her namesake, *Raven* was no scavenger of corpses, unless it were the great sprawling corpse of Rome's empire in the west. She was a fighting bird.

Two men stood in her bow in the morning light. Athanagild had described them without error, save in one point only. Yet still he had not conveyed their *presence;* to accomplish that would require a bard aflight on the inspiration of his demon.

Wulfhere was immense, and no less; a man huge of height and thew, with fire-blue eyes under thickets of brow and a beard like a conflagration. Though he was restless with waiting, he moved not save to fondle the great ax he held across the front of his body and, once in a while, to sigh. At such times his scale byrnie expanded as if it were hard put to contain him. That was but illusion, though a remarkable one. On the Danish giant gleamed heavy golden buckles, studs, and armlets. His war-gear was adequate and more. In his belt gleamed the whalebone hilt of the broad-bladed dagger sheathed there, and a smaller ax was tucked through that same broad thick belt at his other hip. Against his knee leaned a shield like a scarred moon of battle.

Athanagild's one mistake had been in saying that the Skull-splitter overtowered him by a foot. It was half a foot only, though the high bull's horns adorning the Dane's helmet made it seem the more; Wulfhere affected the style of his ancestors. But then Athanagild's one sight of Wulfhere Hausakliufr had been from a distance. The which was confirmed by the fact that Athanagild Beric's son was yet alive. Wulfhere was only five inches over six feet . . .

The man at his side was equally still, and seemed more at his ease in that moveless waiting. Leanly muscular in his shirt of black link-mail, Cormac mac Art of Eirrin wore no ornaments on his darkish skin. Strange this was, in one of a race whose men loved to adorn themselves, and never more splendidly then when they went forth to fight. This Gaelic Celt, though, had ceased long since to care for show. He was all stark professionalism as he scanned the nearby sea, casting an occasional searching glance into the reeds behind him. Had they moved contrary to the light sea breeze, he'd have issued a warning. For copper-beaked *Raven* lay in ambush here as in the jaws of a bear—hopefully a sleeping one.

Cormac, Wulfhere, and their crew of Danes lurked in no less than the home waters of the Visigothic kingdom's Garonne fleet. In truth, from where he stood at *Raven's* bow, Cormac mac Art might have hurled a stone into the River Garonne's estuary. Moreover, just the other side of that great estuary nestled Saxon settlements, and Saxon pirate ships along with some few thousand Saxon fighting men under a dozen independent chieftains—and every one was willing to be ĸnown as friend to Wulfhere's greatest enemy, Hengist the Jute, King of Kent over in Britain.

Four nights agone they had lowered *Raven's* sail, unstepped her mast and rowed softly in with muffled oars. Since then they had eaten cold food only, spoken almost never, and then not above whispers. They had endured the mosquitoes and midges. As Cormac seemed scarcely to notice them, someone had murmured low that any gnat biting the sombre Gael knew it would die horribly.

Waiting strained them sore, and chafed men of action. They endured. They exercised as best they could by arm-wrestling on the oar benches, and straining betwixt them with braced feet and backs.

Rather nearby, other men than they were weary of waiting.

On the estuary's northern side, two galleys of the Visigothic royal fleet lay tucked behind a woody point of land. Athanagild Beric's son, treading the deck of one ship, tugged his heavy moustache and frowned at his marines, who were eating their supplies at a deplorable rate. Had he known the men he'd been ordered to capture had been almost within shouting distance for days, unseen and un-dreamed of, Fleet Commander Athanagild might have suffered a seizure.

The while, beating up the coast from Bayonne in the merchant tub *Thetis,* came one Gervase, a plain sea captain. He squinted brown eyes northward, and then at the coast; Gervase was both fearful of Saxon war-boats and hoping for a Gothic galley on petrol.

My luck, he thought morosely, *to meet the Saxon pirates so near safe harbouring!*

An odd sort of voyage, too; the whole distance around Spain, and having to pay toll to the Vandals on the way. Curious. He spat to landward, with the wind. It wasn't long since those towheaded heretical bastards would have taken the whole cargo, and slaughtered the crew for being Orthodox. A lot of them still would, and did. But Gaiseric was the man who had made their sea-power, and he was a decade in hell.

The Vandals were not the terror of all the Mediterranean any longer, but only the western half . . . and learning that one did not kill a cow for its milk. Still, they were unchancy, and it had been good to see the Pillars of Hercules fade into distance.

It was strange, though, the way the backers had insisted on this route. They had brassed up so readily, too, with the Vandal's toll. Not like them at all. From Narbo to Toulouse by road, and then down the river to Burdigala by barge, that was the proper route! Simpler and the Devil of a lot safer.

Aye, but the royal court was at Toulouse. The Gothic king might have decided to buy the lot—at *his* price. Likely enough the backers had decided the Vandals were a better risk. In any case the danger money was coming to Gervase for it.

Had he known that his backers and the Count of Burdigala had of a purpose set him out as bait for pirates, he might well have dropped in a fit at the same time as Athanagild. Both men were thus protected by lack of knowledge.

At the creek-mouth, a fox barked twice.

Sudden fierce eagerness filled Wulfhere's Danes; not often did foxes bark from treetops. One of their own, called Halfdan Half-a-man for his short stature, swung nimbly down from branch to branch to soggy earth and made for the ship. An oar swept out over *Raven*'s strakes. The blade grounded on the creek-bank and Halfdan walked up it, a stocky personification of delight. He took shield and ax without having to think on it the while he moved forward to give word to his chieftain.

His grin told the news ere his tongue could form it. "It's the one! Or if not, there be two corbitos for Burdigala under brown canvas with a pale three-sided patch!"

"How does she ride?"

"Heavy! By Aegir the bountiful, there's wine in her hold, as ye were assured! And outrun *Raven* such a round-bellied seagoing walnut could not, even were she riding light!" Halfdan smacked his lips. "We will drink tonight."

"Ahh," Wulfhere gusted, in a bliss of anticipation. *"Push out, then, ye thirsty sons of Dane-mark!* Reward is ours!"

Cormac said naught, and his grin was a bare skinning of teeth as he drew his sword. Dark and smooth-shaven was his face, of a sinister cast not amended by the scars upon it, or the cold narrow eyes grey as his weapon-steel. His visage was fitly framed in the cheek-pieces of his helmet, a hard leather casque strengthened with plaques of black iron. Its flowing horsehair crest was the nearest thing to ornament he had on him, and even that to a purpose; was a lasting taunt to Hengist's Jutes, for the White Horse was the badge of their royal house, and they fought under a standard of white horsetails.

Held vertically, oars thrust down into the creek-bed, poling *Raven* forward.

As she slid lithely out to where she had more water-room, the poling men seated themselves and ran their oars out horizontally. Their two-score benchmates did the same. The blades dipped raggedly, cut into water, and fifty strong men pulled back against its resistance.

Raven sprang forth on a bright sea glittering with scales of hot gold.

Knud the Swift, in the stern, called staves for his

comrades to row by, and they rowed hard. Water peeled back white from *Raven*'s copper-sheathed prow. It hissed by the strakes. Oars lifted shining, swept back, dipped, and men drove them forward again, revelling in the free use of muscles too long cramped. Work? Naught of the kind! A touch of healthy exercise to get the kinks out before they bathed their weapons!

> "Brightly flash the oar-blades,
> Washing in the whale's bath,
> Dipping in the salty
> Ale of Aegir's daughters.
> Better is the brew there,
> Casked in yonder cargo,
> Where the wine of Eastland
> Waits for Wulfhere's killers.
>
> "Ye that row to steerboard,
> Raise your oars and rest them,
> While the wights a-portside
> Turn us to the grappling.
> See, the southron sailors,
> White with terror-madness,
> Hunch like hunted conies
> With the stoats among them."

In truth, it was not such a large brag. The crew of *Thetis* was more than two to one outnumbered, and every man able plainly to see it. Nor might they have stood against the wild slayers out of the north, even at level odds. As for an attempt at flight . . . *Raven* was making three ship's lengths to the fat corbito's one. It was unfair, so close to home—and mad and raving mad the pirates must be, to be trying it! Demons from the reddest pits of hell they seemed, a-glimmer with metal scales and bosses and horned like Satan, their dark ship a dragon fit to carry such creatures.

The voyage had been hard and weary, and this to be its ending! Unfair.

Raven was so close now that Gervase could see the Danish leader's face, aye, and his henchman's, too. Gervase knew them at once. Not a seaman on these coasts but had heard of the ruddy giant with his ax and burning beard, and the dark-visaged sworder in black mail.

The heart of Gervase turned cold. Yet at the same time he felt hope stirring, for it was said that these twain were not given to wanton slaying of the helpless. And helpless he was, and all his crew.

Captain Gervase licked his lips and shouted through cupped hands, *"Quarter!"*

Wulfhere loosed a roar of laughter. "O-ho-ho-ho-ho! Quarter ye're asking? Oh, little man, little man! You cheat us of a good fight!"

"Not such a good fight as that," Gervase called wryly back, considering the aspect of his men. "But such as we can put up, unless you promise us our lives, we will give you. And more than that!" he added in sudden inspiration. "We've casks and casks of good wine below. Do you board us bent on slaughter, I'll take two men and smash them open myself!"

The Skull-splitter ceased to laugh. "Ye be a monster!" he bellowed. "A black-hearted monster!"

Cormac mac Art laughed. It was untrue that he never did so, and he did like grit.

"Let him have his way, Wulfhere," he advised. "I've a notion how this can be turned to our account. Let me be having his ear."

"I had rather let you have his whole head," Wulfhere grumbled.

"Ahoy, trader! Do but these things and we grant ye life. Be ye running your tub ashore, and that swiftly, then set your crew to loading your cargo aboard us. Swiftly, ye hear? Swifter than the like was ever done aforetime! And remember the price, do ye fail!"

Gervase looked once at the dark, scarred face, and turned to scan again his disheartened crew. None but a madman on the breast of the sea would have opted for resistance.

"Done!" he said.

And done it was. A spear's cast from the nearby white beach, *Thetis* let down both iron anchors and *Raven* grappled to her. Cormac was first on her deck, with four men eager at his back, among them Knud the Swift and one warrior with hair black as the Gael's own, a rare sight among northerners.

"The lighter stuff first, and most costly," said Cormac. "It's silk ye have aboard, and rare gems and spices. There is ivory too, balsams and jewellery that's after being looted from Egypt's king-graves. It's unwise ye'd be for attempting to deny it. Show me."

Betrayed! Gervase thought bitterly. But who could have done it in such detail? None surely, but the factor who directed the lading. And Gervase promised himself that he'd see the man torn by bears—if he survived this day.

For the pirate's list was true to the item. The bolts of cloth the sailors threw down to Wulfhere were not all of silk; some were Egyptian cotton loomed so fine and shining that the difference was not evident at a glance, and nigh as rare as silk, here in the west. They were stowed in the bow, with the boxes and packets that came also from Alexandria, the incense and pepper and the all but priceless sugar.

And Wulfhere, thirsty Wulfhere, had scarcely a glance for any of it.

"The wine!" he demanded.

The wine was brought forth. Sailors levered oaken casks from their cradles in the hold, and trundled them to the hatchway. Ropes were knotted about them with a fearful care to make them secure, and brawny men drew them on deck, flashing uneasy sidewise stares the while. The casks were lowered over *Thetis*'s side and received with joy by the wild crew of *Raven*. Swiftly those men lashed their prizes firmly to bench-ends with a proper eye to balance and distribution so that *Raven* should continue to ride the sea well.

All was accomplished with a will and speed that no stevedore on Burdigala's docks had ever approached.

Since *Raven* was both a leaner vessel than *Thetis*, and shallower of draught, she could not take the entire load. Still, by canny stowing the Danes made a fair shift towards it.

No more than an hour later, the Danish galley carried twenty-three casks of red Falernian; three were lashed crosswise in a row in the stern with ten more on their sides along each row of oar benches, so positioned as not to impede the oarsmen—and them sitting appreciably closer to the sea than they had been.

Cormac and his four sword-comrades added their weight to the load.

"Now if ye'll be casting off our grapnel-irons," he said, "it's farewell we'll be bidding ye, with due thanks for your hospitality—and a caution not to raise your anchors whilst we be in sight."

Gervase nodded glumly. The grapnels were prised loose to thud down aboard the galley. The Danes raised an ironical cheer as they pushed off from *Thetis*'s plump side. Gervase's square wind-burned face darkened; anger got the best of caution.

"Laugh when you're out of Count Guntram's reach!" he yelled after them.

None aboard *Raven* had Latin but Cormac and Wulfhere, and only the former was fluent. No Latin was required, however, to recognize the name Guntram. The Danes replied with laughter, boos and rude gestures. Then they settled to rowing.

Gervase, watching them go, gripped the timber of his ship's rail till his knuckles showed the colour of the bone beneath.

Raven's oars marched smoothly, like the jointless legs of some strange water-centipede, yet this time they imparted speed but gradually. Out and out across Garonne-mouth moved the pirate craft, turning for a nor'westerly course.

Not the least of Gervase's warring feelings was wonder that he lived.

His passions were to be further moved, and that in moments. For while the corbito rolled at anchor, he saw —beyond the departing *Raven,* on the estuary's north side—shapes move and emerge. With bulging eyes he recognised them as biremes of the Garonne fleet. They too had their masts unstepped and their decks clear for fighting.

Master Gervase struck his fist on the rail in explosive joy.

That was his first response, but then he was not the swiftest of thinkers.

Two warships! *Raven* captured or sunk! The cargo recovered! Such pirates as survived hanging on a gibbet, after appropriate tortures!

Then it struck him.

They must ha' seen the whole business, from first to last! Why—blight 'em with boils—from where they lay, they couldn't ha' helped it!

Why didn't they appear sooner?

The answer became obvious as soon as the question was posed.

24

They wanted the pirate heavy laden. Easy meat. They let us be robbed for that—and killed to a man for aught they knew, had we not received quarter!

Our fine overlords. Our bloody Gothic protector!

Gervase's hands had slackened. Now they gripped anew, with the insensate pressure of vises. A vein beat and coiled in his temple like a frenzied blue worm. The battling furies in his heart found expression in eight words.

"Carve 'em like mutton! Give 'em hot hell!"

Which side he meant to encourage was known only to his god.

The Danes saw the warcraft appear with no dismay, and even no particular surprise. The very madness of waylaying a ship at the mouth of the Garonne, when Cormac had suggested it, had made it irresistible. They had known the risk. Wulfhere had shouted for very delight, called the Gael sword-brother, and dealt him a clap on the back to have staggered a lesser man. He was unaffectedly happy now as he had been then.

"Will ye give look at that?" he rumbled. "Wolf, we are not to be cheated of battle after all."

Cormac answered only a nod, but he was not unhappy about that prospect.

The biremes rushed on, driven each by two banks of oars to *Raven*'s one, and thrice fifty rowers to *Raven*'s three score, and them sentenced criminals urged to their work by ropes' ends—knotted. Each warship had a barnacled bronze-tipped ram jutting from her prow below the water-line, and a hundred Gothic marines on her deck.

Tough-handed war-men they were, in hard leather cuirasses studded with iron, and round iron caps, armed with buckler and *spatha,* the thirty-inch single-edged Gothic sword. One in three was equipped too with short bow and full quiver. Ordinarily the Danes would have laughed at such, for they were archers the masters of any in the southern German tribes. Now though they had spent four days in ambush in hostile country. The weather had been wet, very wet, and so were their bowstrings, even the spares.

Cormac's slitted gaze ran the length of the biremes, for he saw them broadside-on as they raced to intercept.

Mounted on each afterdeck was an engine such as he'd not seen till now, a dart-thrower resembling a huge crossbow. The Greeks had used them ere Rome's empire arose, never mind fell, and Cormac had vaguely heard of them, garbled as ancient sorceries. He'd thought the techniques lost, and well lost. Someone had worked at reviving them.

Someone, he thought, *is concerned about us.*

Marine archers lined the rail of the leading warship. Their bowstrings hummed, and thirty arrows hurtled at *Raven.* Of that first volley, most fell short, hissing as the water took them, and none found a home in flesh.

"Out to sea!" Wulfhere thundered. "Let's find how these Goth lubbers take rough water!"

Crew and ship were as one; *Raven* turned due west. Iron-muscled backs and limbs put explosions of energy into rowing. But the galley was heavy laden, and while her change of direction had postponed the meeting, the Gothic biremes were gaining at every oar-stroke. The leader would be running beside them soon, and within arrow-shot, and then the Goths would loose volley after volley.

But—Cormac grinned hard—*an we win beyond that sheltering bulge of land to northward first, the Gothic aim'll suffer!* Wulfhere was right.

The dart-thrower banged.

Cormac saw a bolt long as he was tall spring over the

26

sea. It flashed above the heads of his straining rowers to pierce the water for a fathom ere it lost force. The Gael did not see, but starkly imagined, its four-bladed iron head. Such a thing would split *Raven*'s overlapping strakes as Wulfhere's ax broke mail.

The dart-thrower's crew was winching back its cable now for another shot.

"Behl's fiery eye!" he said between his teeth. "Were our archers in fettle, we'd be dropping ye all stone mortal slain about your engine!"

The bireme ploughed on. Now it lagged a ship's length behind *Raven*, now half, and now it edged in, foot by foot. The archers loosed again.

The war-shields hung along *Raven*'s foaming thwarts were some protection, and helms and byrnies more. These arrows, though, were shot to fall from above. Some skewered brawny arms or calves. One man had the sudden sight of a feathered shaft pinning his hand to his oar; burning pain followed. Another felt naught, for as he bent forward in a stroke, an arrowhead drove through his offered neck between helm and byrnie. He was instantly dead. His oar trailed useless, fouling others.

Knud the Swift justified his by-name by leaping to the bench, heaving the corpse aside and seizing the oar-timber. Three benches behind him, the man with the nailed hand coldly broke off the arrow-shaft and freed himself.

"Relief here!" he growled.

And the gap of water separating bireme from clinker-built northern galley grew straiter.

Wulfhere had gone thoughtful, hefting his giant's ax. The head was large as his two hands together, and weighed all of seven pounds. The Gothic helmsman stood in plain sight—but no, the Skull-splitter decided,

27

besides being loath to part with it, not even he could hurl this particular ax quite so far. He drew the smaller one from his weapon belt.

It was a short-hafted Frankish weapon, meant for throwing, of the kind that bore the name of that fierce, treacherous tribe—a *francisca*. He'd practiced long hours with it and knew to the nail's width its properties in flight.

"The helmsman, Cormac," he said. "If I bring him down, can ye remember that ye be seaman these days, and not tending pigs in Eirrin any longer? And give the right order?"

"It's a seaman I was ere ever I saw your mattress of a face," the Gael said.

Wulfhere, grinning, brought the Frankish ax back over his mailed shoulder, edge upward, and braced a wadmal-clad knee the size of a shield-boss in the bow. The missile-ax made two full turns over thirteen paces, he knew, therefore one in half that; and for targets beyond or between such ranges, one must impart more spin or more drag so that the weapon struck with edge flying foremost.

The blue eyes in their mesh of weather wrinkles judged the distance with experienced calm.

A further flight of arrows hummed, sped almost straight up now, so close were the adversaries. Wulfhere heeded them no more than had they been a swarm of gnats. He'd cautioned Cormac to do what was necessary, knowing that he might be dead himself. His hairy, thick-muscled arm swung forward.

The Frankish ax glittered through five full turns in the sea air . . . and sank, as into a turnip, through the helmsman's temple.

He'd scarcely begun to fall when Cormac barked, "Up oars to steerboard! Turn, *turn hard about! Towards the Goth!*"

One heartbeat's pause of pure amazement—and then the crew obeyed. Straight up from the water rose the line of oars on Cormac's right, while the rowers to port-side doubled their already bone-cracking efforts, so that a couple of oars broke off short in strong hands. *Raven* turned in perhaps but three times her own length, while her timbers made cracking protests. The bireme's ram came thrusting through seething water to gore her—but the helm was untended, veering, for a bare sufficiency of confused moments aboard the Goth.

Raven had come fully about, swifter than the Goths had deemed possible in a ship her length. Her copper-sheathed prow now aimed directly at the bireme's port line of oars.

Blind and captive below decks, urged on by thrashings, the bireme's rowers took her to disaster.

Athanagild Beric's son, bulging-eyed on her bridge, screamed, "Back water! Back water!"

But there was hardly time to say it, much less see it done.

Raven had lost impetus in her turn, and lacked space to gather it anew. It was the bireme's own hungry speed did the work.

Her double bank of oars shattered on *Raven*'s prow and beneath her keel, as so many rowan wands under a coulter's blade. The broken ends whipped back within the hull to do gruesome carnage among the rowers. Backs broke, ribs went in pieces, brains flew from their enclosing skulls in gobbets of pink and grey mud.

Marines on deck went sprawling. Some stayed on their feet by clutching the deck-rail, as did Athanagild on his bridge. He stood appalled, maddened, infuriated. Again he beheld Wulfhere Hausakliufr, and this time far closer, but untouchable, arrogant, like a tower of iron a-quiver with mirth. He laughed in their amazed Gothic faces as he passed.

"Go home to your mothers!" was the advice he gave them.

"Loose! Loose arrows!" Athanagild screamed at his archers. "Feather me that great hog! Kill him! *Kill him! A hundred solidi for the man who does!"*

Wulfhere heard, and remained standing in the bow long enough to be sure he was almost the sole target for the next flight. Then he ducked beneath the dragon-head beside Cormac, and covered them both with his shield, off which a shaft or two rattled. Most rebounded from the hammered copper that armoured the prow, or hissed in the sea, which made it an arrow-flight wasted.

"Loose again! Kill the rowers! Curse you, *ready the dart-thrower!"*

Modern artisans proved hardly equal to those of former times; the dart-thrower's mechanism had jammed after one shot. Upon gaining that bit of news Athanagild raised his fists and addressed Heaven in raving blasphemies. His god, that one Cormac called the Dead God, took no note.

Meanwhile, the Danish galley had made a close turn around the crippled bireme, and was running for the open sea once more. Athanagild's archers rained arrows on them with grim method as they passed, so that fourteen men were wounded and two more slain. As *Raven* had but forty oars functioning and the second bireme was close upon her, all in all no one was any longer amused.

They left land-shelter for an ugly cross-chop brewed by Ran, who spread nets for ships, in one of her bitchiest moods. Less poetically, the inimical sea here was due to the jut of the Armorican peninsula to the north, and the mass of Spain to the south, lending their complications to the heavy swells from the Western Ocean. *Raven* began to buck and wallow like a drunken walrus; the

Visigothic ship drew nearer.

Cormac went aft to watch, covering the steersman with a shield.

Another huge iron-headed dart plunged into the sea, a spear's length astern. Three flights of arrows followed, and at the third, Cormac gasped and sank down. Wulfhere, amidships, saw and hastened aft.

"Cormac! Have they killed ye, man?"

"I'm—winded," the Gael bit forth. He grinned. "The mail, and this leather sark and padding under it, kept the point from my hide. Them and their little four-foot bows!"

"Ah," Wulfhere mourned, lest the other accuse him of waxing sentimental, "it's a bad day and growing no better. I dared hope then that we'd be rid of ye."

Raven mounted a swell that slopped brine inboard. Then the sea vanished from under her, and she dropped her belly into the trough in a way that slammed teeth together and rattled spines. Men got desperately to work, bailing.

"Wulfhere," Cormac said, "It's too heavy we be. Man —the wine must go."

"WHAT?"

"The wine," the Gael repeated. "It must go."

The big Dane's dismay very nearly equalled Athanagild's. Cormac's cold voice cut through his expostulations, his protests and all loud anguish. They were wallowing like hogs in muck, and less happily by far. The Visigoths were having their sorrows, but soon they'd be so close that even their bowmen could not continue to miss—unless the reivers lightened ship. At the same time they'd be littering the sea with the menace of bobbing massive casks to trouble pursuit. They'd float, though not high; immediately below the surface, most likely. It had to be done.

31

Wulfhere turned away. Cormac cursed hotly; the Skull-splitter's strength was needed for the work, and he chose to mope!

The Gael called Hrut Bearslayer to him. The silent carl, not quite right in the head from a sword-cut thereon, was the one man of the crew whose bulk and strength equalled Wulfhere's. He was single-mindedly loyal to Cormac besides. Word was passed along. The oar-men, working in pairs, unlashed the casks and tipped them over the side. Cormac and Hrut between them disposed of the three in the stern. They rolled and tumbled away behind.

Cormac, watching, saw one shatter on the bireme's ram, and another, lifted by the swell, slam and break on the craft's carvel-built side. Planks were sprung. The sea was abruptly sweetened and darkened, while some lookout cried a warning at the Goth's masthead . . . and mac Art was satisfied.

The more so for *Raven*'s now riding the waves lightly as a bird.

The water remained savage, but the crew was used to dirty weather. They were often out in it by choice, as naught made better concealment—and the weather itself was now fair enough, save for this gusty, unpredictable wind. The bireme, carrying a hundred weapon-men who did not row, and all their gear, fell behind. *Raven* was away and at large.

Erelong, the Gael went forward to where Wulfhere gloomed at the waves like a man-shaped thundercloud. Cormac shook his head in exasperation, and set a hand on his friend's burly shoulder.

"Ah, Splitter of skulls . . . the world has not ended! It's the best of the plunder we have yet, and tonight will see us in Nantes, guesting at the merchant's table. Ye ken well he has a cellar the gods in Tir-nan-Og might envy, and that even your vast self cannot drink dry. Not to be mentioning his daughter, and there isn't a feater bawd on these coasts."

"Cormac," Wulfhere said, not turning.

The Gael sighed, and shrugged, and left him to mourn. The ship must be looked after, even if the great souse's heart was breaking. The mast must needs be stepped again, here on the choppy sea, and sail raised. Was a task fit for the chastisement of Loki, and enough to make him, were he present, wish to be back in his dry comfortable cave with the vipers. *Then* they might ship oars and beat northward under canvas.

They left the sea reddened in their wake, with blood and richest wine.

CHAPTER TWO: Two Pirates, A Trap, and Clodia

As Burdigala to the Garonne, was the city of Nantes to the Loire. And, blessedly, it was part of a different realm. Philip the Syrian had called it "the Roman Kingdom," and with cause.

Its ruler was Roman by birth, education and loyalty. Master of Soldiers he'd been; his title now was Consul of the Empire, bestowed on him by the Emperor Zeno, who sat in Constantinople and had nothing that mattered to do with him. In law he was an official, representing Zeno. In practice he was independent, and the barbarians who had overrun the rest of Gaul were nothing if not practical. They thought of him as a king, and called him a king—*Rex Romanorum*.

His name was Syagrius. Consul Syagrius; King Syagrius.

He no more approved of pirate forays along his shores than did Alaric of Toulouse.

For this reason, Wulfhere took his galley up the Loire with secretive care, and anchored her two miles from the city. The plunder was loaded into a fishing boat he had paid for, grudgingly, as he was robber by profession. It was Cormac's advice, crafty and well-reasoned as usual, to do this remarkable thing. It was certain as aught could be that the fisherman who received their coins would not run bleating to the law. The law would question him by increasingly strong methods as a matter of course. That was assurance enow of his shut mouth, and less like to attract attention than his death or disappearance.

In darkness the fishing boat came to the waterfront of Nantes.

Its precious load was covered with sacking and old fish-nets. The three who rode in it wore long enveloping cloaks of coarse wool, under which they carried their helmets. One was a flame-haired giant; another was dark, scarred and leanly muscular; the third likewise black-haired, the single Dane of such colouring in Wulfhere's crew. Black Thorfinn, he was named.

They moored the boat before a dockside warehouse. One end of it had been made into living quarters and a grog-shop, where any might come and go with a ready excuse, if not always without suspicion.

Wulfhere and Cormac were too striking to show themselves even in such a place, and made their way to a less public door. There they knocked in a certain rhythm. A balding Gallo-Roman in stained tunic came to let them in. He did not look at all a financial match for Philip or Desiderius Crispus, which was as he liked it.

"Cormac," he said in greeting. "Skull-splitter."

"Our very selves. And Thorfinn ye'll not be knowing. He has no word of Latin, Balsus, but give him to drink and he will not pine for conversation. He's here to help with our load."

More than that, he provided excuse for them to talk among themselves in Danish if they wished. The advantage was that Balsus Ammian would comprehend not a word. Cormac's early life had not left him a trusting man.

"Plunder," the merchant said, closing the door and replacing the bar. He found the word about as enticing as gout, to hear him, but his dark eyes gleamed. "It is a bad time for trade, Captain, but aye, we can discuss it." To the brutal-faced hulk attending him he said, "Back to your bouncing, and tell Clodia we have guests warranting our best. Hungry, thirsty guests new from a sea voyage."

The chucker-out's nose had told him as much. With a grunt, he went through to the grog-shop, whence were borne odours of sausage, ale, wine, tar and sweat on gusts of argument, laughter, bawdry and alleged song.

Balsus led the way up creaking stairs to a room hung with cheap tapestry and rugged with sheepskins. Its odour was musty, but the pirates had sat in far worse. The lamps Balsus lit from his candle, puffing, burned scented oil. Cormac wondered idly how much could be got from rendering their host, and him wheezing like a walrus ashore after a rise of stairs. . . .

They threw off their wadmal cloaks, and seated themselves with a creak and chime of battle-harness. The chairs held firm, even Wulfhere's. They had been in this house erenow.

"Well, Captain," Balsus said, "I'd never ask you—no, no, far from me the thought—to talk business neither drunk nor dined. You are famished, not so?"

A nod from Cormac and a vehement rumble of Wulfhere's belly assured him it was.

"But a hint, an intimation while you eat—perchance a sample?" The hand of Balsus flashed in air, fingers partway curled into graspy claws.

Cormac, who yet carried his helmet in the crook of his

arm, produced from it a wooden casket, and something else. That something glinted in the lamplight with gold and lapis lazuli and breathtaking jeweller's art.

It certainly took their fence's breath, and his face showed agony at the need to handle it casually. The bauble dangled, turning on its fine chain, from his graceless fingers, the sigil of a writhing winged serpent. His skin seemed to tingle at its nearness. It had not the look of mere ornament, though it was that, and wrought by a master; it impressed as a formal talisman.

"Might it be? Cormac watched him closely.

"It's forgetting the casket ye seem to be," the Gael murmured, and set down his helmet beside his leg.

"Time and to spare," returned the merchant, dissembling too late. "One doesn't wish to be hurried. By Saint Augustine! Frankincense!"

The aroma pervaded the room above that of the lamps.

"And more of the like yonder," Cormac told him. "Spices, gums, jewels, and rolls of silk still dry in their covers. Our finest haul yet, so let us be having no more natter of how bad is trade nowadays. Your hands do betrayal on ye, man. It's downright palsied with eagerness they are."

"H'm. A splendid haul, yes. Not to be denied, but such—distinctiveness—brings its own problems, good my sirs. Makes it all but impossible to dispose of, do you see?" The fingertips of Balsus now massaged his palm.

Cormac stared back at him, unwinking. His hard-boned face looked more sinister than ordinarily. Wulfhere, no fool, did not try to match that intimidating performance. He simply looked benign, and patient with his fellow man's gaucheries.

Into the room and the moment, breaking the tension, came Balsus's daughter Clodia.

A shrewd, spirited presence she, possessed of red-brown eyes and dense red-brown hair, with hips a-sway and skirt a-rustle. The tray she bore upheld an ale-jug large as a bucket, and four pewter tankards. Had been a goodly feat of strength on her part to bring it upstairs, but she knew it would last, in this company, one avid breath after it was poured.

The healthily-constructed young woman set it down on the table with gusty relief.

"Captain Wolf!"

She perched on his knee, took Cormac's face between her hands and kissed him with knowledge and willingness enough to melt the grimness from his mouth. Nor was Cormac over susceptible. She knew him from the days when he had led his own crew of reivers from Eirrin, wherefore she and her father called him "Captain" even yet, for courtesy's sake—a fancy to which Wulfhere was not mean-minded enow to object.

"And our walking menhir all shaggy with lichen!" she added, bussing Wulfhere with equal warmth. "You need not tell me. My beloved father has been trying to cheat you again."

She poured the heavy brown ale. The three did not so much drink as breathe it in. She poured again, this time including her father in the round, and that finished the jug. Clodia put it aside.

"Garth"—this was the chucker-out—"will be waddling in like a goose with a keg in his arms. Sausage and cheese and a roast sucking-pig will come after; the man who ordered it will be desolate to hear that it fell in the fire, but we'll feed him costless on something else—ohh!"

Her eyes had fallen on the Egyptian sigil. She picked it up with a murmured, "Beautiful," and was about to slip it over her head when Balsus snatched it away. He did more. He struck her fiercely and snarled a curse.

Seeing Cormac's eyes upon him, coldly speculative, he muttered something about "the jade's getting above herself."

The Gael knew well there was more. Balsus Ammian's daughter had a business head as good as his own, and better judgment of men. Not only for her services as barmaid did her father have her attend such meetings as this. No. Something about the pendant itself had aroused his touchy possessiveness. Balsus must be deeply moved, else he'd conceal it better.

That, Cormac thought, *will increase our profit from this night.*

He wondered what the bauble's significance might be.

Clodia had retreated to Wulfhere for comfort, which he charitably provided with a hand up her skirt. Her tears quickly dried, she fussed and wriggled and slapped him lightly without making aught of real efforts to get away; she did glance sidewise to see the effect of this byplay on Cormac. He was paying not the least attention; no care on him if Wulfhere were to set her astride his lap and go him to work in earnest.

The edge removed from his thirst, Cormac poured down his ale at a slower rate. His custom was not to touch wine until business was settled, and until they had food in them, their trading would not even be discussed. But there was news to be had that did not bear directly upon business, and Cormac had always an ear for news.

Balsus dropped the winged serpent on the table beside the casket.

"Handsome," he said casually. "Yes. But as I mentioned, trade becomes ruinous. And there are bribes. The custom-house must document, for lawful credibility, such goods as I buy from you . . . the which is naturally not done for love. Its chief grows more and more demanding. I've cut back his profits, and chanced the sale of more common goods without telling him, but what you bring tonight is not of that class. 'Tis conspicuous—such as none but kings or great nobles can purchase. Such folk are finicky over forms of law, if not their letter.''

"We can spare ye the danger and worry," Cormac said bluntly. "It's kings and great nobles there are in the west of Britain whose fathers never bowed to Rome. These are not, I promise ye, finicky with forms of law. It's no such foolish questions as where we got it they'd be asking.''

"There now, father, see what you've done!" This from Clodia, leaning on Cormac's shoulder. "This customs official Nestor is greedy, true—but he takes what he can get, and sweats and shivers o' nights, I shouldn't wonder, lest the Consul get wind of his . . . private transactions. What can he do but complain? Nay, he's that eager to tumble me he scarcely even does that—the fool, hankering to mix business with venery!" (Which was Cormac's own opinion on the matter, and the reason he had not tumbled Clodia in the years of their acquaintance.) "I doubt he so much as suspects he's been cheated.''

Someone found that cue too apt for resisting.

An object, impelled up the stairs by a casual toss, arced through the doorway left open for the promised ale. Its distinct sodden thump on the floor drew their eyes, which widened, Balsus's and Clodia's in profound horror. The object rolled to a terminus and tilted a face of starkest agony towards them.

Balsus croaked involuntarily, *"Nestor!"*

Cormac did three things, and on the instant, and so near simultaneously that the difference was not a practical issue. He shoved Clodia violently away lest she cling to him in shock. He sprang to his feet, overturning his chair. He ripped sword from sheath with a harsh metal whine.

And one action more he took. Stooping, he snatched his helmet and covered his square-cut black mop with it.

All this was done whiles Wulfhere and Thorfinn were rearing upright, in an explosion of hair-trigger response too swift for the eye. Then Cormac was ominously, totally still again, a strip of edged pointed steel in one hand and readiness to kill in every line of him. Yellow lamplight shone on his mail and helmet.

Men seethed into the room, ten or a dozen, disposing themselves either side of the door.

Cormac recognized them as Franks.

Ax-armed they were, in long leather vests and close-fitting trews; with the backs of their heads shaved bald, most of the remaining hair drawn up in a thick tress on top of the head and the rest combed forward in a fringe over their brows, they could be from no other tribe.

No half-civilized Goths or Vandals had they here, but untamed killers out of the forest marches.

"Let nobody," a voice came from the dark beyond the door, "move a finger."

The speaker sauntered in. Lithe and handsome, indeed over-handsome, begemmed and perfumed and shaven, his dark brown hair exquisitely barbered in Roman bangs, he was a picture. Limpid hazel eyes were scarcely needed to complete it; despite their colour, though, they had even less warmth in them than Cormac's. Too, they were as watchful, if not so slitted and deep-set.

Wulfhere looked infinities of scorn at him. The Dane's horned helmet stood on the table. Coolly, deliberately, he set it on his shaggy head. The stranger betrayed no irritation.

"A defiant fellow," he said affectionately. "A fearless, overgrown rat in the woodwork of the kingdom! You are going to squeak like a mouse between the claws. I have some clever iron devices that will reduce you to manageable size, a nose here, a finger-joint there. *And* your glowering, dark-visaged friend."

None answered him. He lifted the head of the customs official by the blood-splashed hair.

"This fool could tell you, were he not forever dumb. But perchance his expression says enough. He did not die graciously . . . and he *did* suspect."

Thump went the ghastly thing on the table. Clodia started. The stranger lifted a brow in appreciation of the sight that made.

"Your late friend Nestor contracted a fever last month, and thought it was plague. He called for a priest right enow, and he couldn't babble his confession sufficiently fast. The priest broke the confidence of confessional to gain favour with his bishop, Remigius of Reims . . . and in my turn I owe the bishop a favour, now. There is always proof to be had when one knows where to look for it. The king was pleased . . . behold in me the new customs assessor of Nantes!

"My name is Sigebert. It will be better known for this night's work—a fortunate one for my future, eh? The new broom sweeping briskly, as they say. One fat traitorous merchant and a trio of sea-pirates on the first night of my office, all for torment! I judge your profession aright, do I not? Methinks I can even guess your names, or two of them. The Count of Burdigala might pay well to have you handed across the Loire into his hands. My king would approve the transaction, I am sure."

Sigebert loved, Cormac noted, the sound of his own sweet voice. Aye, and in particular when it was explaining how clever he was. Cormac despised the man, but he remained silent.

Sigebert raked the woman from hair to feet with sparkling eyes.

"You need not suffer, my dear," he said politely. "Unless of course you're of firm mind to join your father and this low company you've fallen into, whither they are bound. Let me advise you: welcome me instead to Nantes in appropriate fashion."

Clodia shuddered. Her father, no doubt, would have pleaded for leniency, but he was too terror-stricken to find his tongue. Such was never a fault of Cormac's, and he felt that Sigebert had orated long enough.

"Be not a fool, man," he said. "I suppose none of your soldiers is after having a Latin education? They do not look it."

"They apprehend not a word we are saying."

"And I'd lay wagers that it is not by chance. Well, then—take ye Nestor's private arrangements unto yourself, as ye have his house and station. Accept our bond that we will deliver ye full accounting of all we . . . find, asea, and a third share in the profits. They ought to suffice for such splitting, with the Nantes customs assessor to pass us intelligence. And that ye may look better than him who preceded ye, to be sure, we'd be looting no Roman craft. In such wise it's happy and wealthy we'll *all* be!"

Sigebert considered the swiftly sketched proposition. Watching, the Gael began to believe he had talked his way out of this trap.

He knew Sigebert's kind. There were Franks in some numbers at the court of Soissons; their kingdom lay to the east, where they had been settled as federates of the Empire. The polite fiction was that they were still its subjects. Franks made up a large part of King Syagrius's army. Much rarer were polished courtiers like this one, but they existed, wearing Latin speech and Latin education like their jewels, and Sigebert had seemingly learned Latin calculation as well. It had not changed him.

Under costume and manners this Sigebert was Frankish to the marrow: treacherous, bloody and cruel.

Thus too had Clodia assessed him, with no difficulty. She knew men. When she thought of having to please this one abed, and gave thought to what that might involve, claws of panic terror ripped at her mind. She could not help shaking.

Sigebert's gaze kept roving to her whilst he considered. He obviously enjoyed the outward signs of her fear.

He made up his mind.

"No. Wealth and happiness? They are more to be hoped for from my lord the king than a pair of foreign reivers. *Take them!"*

Like fierce hounds unleashed, the soldiers bayed forward.

Wulfhere's ax sprang aloft, light as a withe in a child's hands. The foremost Frank hurtled back again, breast caved in, a scarlet ruin of a man. He fouled the legs of two of his mates. As one stumbled, he felt the cold sliding intrusion of Cormac's point in his throat. A short Frankish ax banged on the Gael's helmet, turning his head. Fuzzy lights crossed Cormac's vision. On a born sworder's instinct, and all the training and experience that had been his portion since, he struck backhanded.

A drawing stroke with the edge it was, and it opened his assailant's side through leather and flesh to the spine. Entrails bulged out like a host of escaping snakes, and steel grated on bone.

Clodia seized the moment's opportunity to hide the

Egyptian sigil in her hospitable bosom.

Her father, less greedy or less calm in emergency, thought he saw an opening and barged for the doorway. The flat of a Frankish ax clouted him negligently on the side of the head, impelled him through the frame and dropped him senseless a pace or two beyond it.

And Wulfhere killed another man, and Black Thorfinn the second that had fallen before him.

Cormac twisted lithely aside from a hurtling ax-edge, dropped to one knee beneath a second, and drove the point he favoured over the edge under a leather tunic and deep into a Frankish groin. The man made a high whistling shriek like a snared rabbit, and folded double on his way to the encrimsoned floor. Wulfhere's ax clanged and crashed, and there was company for Nestor's severed head.

In bare moments, Sigebert had been left with three men standing. The smile had vanished from his mouth to be succeeded by something like horror. He drew his sword from its gilded sheath.

Black Thorfinn met his weird then. With a raucous battle-cry in his teeth, he cut at Sigebert. A soldier interposed his buckler. Thorfinn's sword shrieked along the rim; his point, by a freak of chance, snagged the corner of Sigebert's mouth and ripped upward through his cheek, to slice the ear from his head on that side.

The same soldier swung his ax. It split the scale byrnie to chop through Thorfinn's ribs and open his lung.

The Frankish lordling staggered, but did not fall. Red howling agony filled his head. He saw the man who had hurt him. By naked instinct, he thrust home.

Thorfinn, stricken already, his armour gaping, had half a foot of steel rammed through his navel. The irony was that never but in pain-maddened frenzy would Sigebert have used a thrust at all. Swordplay was entirely with the edge, and of all men only Cormac mac Art seemed to appreciate what the point could do; the Gael used it deliberately and constantly. He had learned the art's efficacy long ago in Eirrin, of a fine weapon-man. A dead man, one of too many dead bloodying the Gael's life-wake.

Thorfinn fell, gasping. Sigebert stumbled through the door and half-toppled downstairs, screaming for the men who surrounded the place. The three remaining soldiers retreated as far as the head of the stairs, dragging the inert Balsus with them.

Cormac slammed the door and dropped its bar.

"Out of this!" he grunted.

"But my father!"

"Stay here, then."

Clodia chose not to do that. She wrenched open the door on the room's far side, and the reivers followed her out. They left a bloody shambles behind them, as often they'd done afore, the lamplight shining on gore and cloven metal. Then the door closed after them.

The trio stood in a musty darkness in the main part of the warehouse, on a crude railed gallery that ran about it on three sides. The floor below was stacked with ship's goods: barrels, bales and bundles; canvas and thin dressed leather for sails and pitch for caulking; oil and candles and salt meat, rope and cord and twine. And concealed among it all, as leaves in a forest, such trade items as were never bought for sailors. They would be found and confiscated for certain, but there was no time to resent that.

At the warehouse's far end were strong double doors —with more Franks waiting hard by them, the blaze-eyed Cormac guessed.

Within reach though was rope in plenty, and Wulfhere's ax knocked a hole in the roof with a couple of careless blows. He boosted Clodia through it first, as she was the lightest. Cormac followed, mounting on the Dane's vast shoulders. The while Wulfhere made scathing remarks about his weight, his clumsiness and the unclean state of his feet, so offensively near his captain's nose.

Cormac vanished nimbly through the hole, braced his feet on the beam Wulfhere's ax had exposed, and lowered the rope.

Like the beam itself and Cormac's steely muscles, it creaked as the Danish giant climbed out of the warehouse. Mother-naked and bone dry, Wulfhere weighed nigh two and three-quarters hundred pounds. In full war-gear he went far over three hundred, and it was not just anyone, any body, who could play his anchor-man.

As he had come up last, he went down first.

Cormac gripped Clodia, growled, "Wulfhere! *Catch!*" and tossed her unceremoniously from the roof. She squeaked, biting off her scream.

The young woman was solidly made, and her impact in Wulfhere's arms from such a height drove even him to his knees. He let her slip to the ground, giving her a pinch for luck.

Cormac knelt for a brief space on the roof, listening from that vantage to the noises borne on the night air.

Sigebert was shrieking his wrath and pain yet, somewhere at the front of the building. The citizens of Nantes were raising a racket in the background, while soldiers in the warehouse came blundering after their lawful prey. Cormac wished fiercely there'd been time to fire it about their ears. With a jerk of his head, he slid down the rope.

Aground, he sliced the rope through with his sword as far above his head as he could reach. Mayhap the Franks would miss seeing it now—at any rate, the first time they passed the spot. And if they missed it then, it was like they would obliterate their quarry's tracks in the mud with their own trampling feet.

The three legged it.

The dark twisting alleys of the Nantes waterfront were as well known to all the trio as *Raven*'s deck to Cormac and Wulfhere. To the eastern Franks, they were an unknown maze.

"Now, girl, we part," Cormac said. "By the great Lord of the Mound, we got ye clear of yon trap, but we've not adopted ye! Go your way."

She gulped. "I dare not. You s-saw what manner of man is that Sigebert. He'd have used me; now he will torture me besides."

"Then do not be letting him catch ye. There's all the world open to ye."

"Not for a woman alone. The Devil, Cormac! I've nowhere to *go.*"

"Aye, Wolf," put in Wulfhere. "The lass has the right of it."

Cormac swore savagely. "The soft-headed great gomeral ye are! So then; come with us, girl, if ye can be matching our pace. But it will tax yourself. Blood of the gods!"

He spoke not another word till they reached the ship, and few then. A black Gaelic melancholy akin to madness was upon him, with its immediate cause in the loss of the boatload of plunder, the richest they had taken yet.

But the loot, as loot, meant little.

What it had symbolized to Cormac, he was hardly aware himself. He was exile, outlaw and pirate, and these dark facts had the casual treachery of kings for their direct cause. It was not strange that they had marked him. Lacking any home but *Raven*'s deck, or any safety but that to be found in his weapon-arm and his companions', he lived for the day each day, trying to forget the past and with no confidence at all in his future.

Yet the Gael of Eirrin was young. Cormac mac Art had less years on him then his looks made credible. Younger he was than he had let even Wulfhere know, or than the mighty Dane would have believed. In outward seeming he had become more Spartan than Celt, though his race's fanciful, extravagant temper had not quite been ground out of his soul.

He was not beyond dreaming of a return to Eirrin in wealth and power, to claim one unforgotten girl whose face still troubled his sleep.

(Years had passed. She was girl no longer, but woman, and married woman, he was painfully certain.)

Nor had wealth or power come his way on the reiver's path. He'd scars and red memories and a reputation to show for it, naught more. The haul at Garonne-mouth had been the richest ever to fall into his hands, and now, like others, it had slipped from between them. Not in itself, but as a foundation to build on, that booty might have made him at last able to buy justice at home—and that justice in this world usually had to be bought, Cormac knew well.

He ground his teeth in a fury of frustration as he fled through the Gaulish night. The womanish presence was distinctly unwelcome, merely a further burden.

Clodia kept pace with them. They were fighting men in their heavy battle-gear, and she unburdened. They had come through a long wearing day; she was fresh. These helped lessen the men's advantage of longer legs and harder condition, and above all she matched their pace because she dared not do otherwise.

The young woman ran, with skirt lifted about her

thighs, its ends tucked through her girdle. Pale legs flashed. She ran through streets and convoluted lanes, swam an inlet the men were tall enow to wade (and in their iron, were constrained to) and then plunged further through mud and reeds.

Clodia reached the ship staggering; her breath had the sound of tearing cloth.

Behind them wavered a line of torches, and hounds were baying.

"Get under weigh!" Wulfhere commanded. "By the shields of Asgard, we have half Nantes breathing up our backsides! We stepped into a trap, companions, and someone will pay for it. But do we bide here, the paying will be done by us!"

Cormac heaved himself over the thwarts, streaming water. Clodia, wading out, stepped in a sink-hole and screamed.

"Help mee! Abandon me here and you murder me!"

An oar pivoted her way. She seized the blade, and felt her legs pull free of the sucking mud. Cormac, his black mood increasing if such were possible, stood impassive. Wulfhere turned from giving orders, showed his teeth in something not a smile, and raised a hand with the fingers tensely clawed.

His meaning: *Thor strike you, shut her up!*

With a curse, Cormac leaned far out and grabbed Clodia's skirt. It was the nearest thing to his hand, its ends having come loose from her girdle, and she having got one knee precariously over the oar.

He dragged her, sliding, along the oar-shaft. She stuck briefly, and then tumbled aboard with her sodden skirt ripping up the seam. Her legs were stockinged up to the thighs in slate-coloured, ill-smelling mire.

Clodia looked about as erotically fetching as a half-drowned kitten, and her language withered the reeds for thirty paces around.

50

Raven's square sail rose on its long yard, to fill with the land-breeze. She began to move. The line of torches dropped away astern.

Cormac watched the bright smears fade in the night almost with regret, for he'd have relished further fighting in that moment. It would have been more enjoyable than thinking, for what had he to think upon that was good?

The grey pallor of false dawn was showing when *Raven* cleared the Loire's mouth. Clodia huddled as small as possible. She was among cut-throats and slayers who might do as they pleased to her, with only their leader's word to restrain them. Most Viking captains would give her to their men, and afterwards to the sea. She did not look for that from Wulfhere, yet neither did she suppose he'd pamper her.

It's slavery in a foreign land for you, girl, she told herself grimly. Yet it was preferable to what would happen to her father. She sniffed—and looked thoughtfully at the Gael.

"Warships!" someone howled.

It was naught but the truth. Out of the half dark came the shapes of two Roman galleys, with war-men tough as the Visigothic marines, and better disciplined, on their decks. Jolted out of his bleak introversion, Cormac stared while his thoughts took urgent form, like layers of pearl, around the word *again!*

Planned, he thought, *all planned,* and the vow of blood-vengeance formed in the back of his mind. For now . . .

They could not fight and win.

Southward down the coast lurked aroused, alert and blood-hungry enemies.

Westward along Lesser Britain's shores, they would inevitably be run down when dawn appeared. Nor was dawn far off.

"Cormac?" Wulfhere said tranquilly. "Methinks they truly have us this time. We will taste mead and ale in Valhalla this day; or do we fare to Helheim, we'll go there escorted with due honour. Not even you can trick us out of this."

"Had we time, I'd bind ye to a wager! *Southwest* is our way, sea-wolves! Cut across the open water, and if they dare follow they are not Romans, but seamen! Be ye with me?"

Jaws dropped and crewmen muttered. Some raised cries of protest.

Better to die in clean battle, they said, bathing their weapons, than lie cold in the arms of Ran! For only fools did other than follow the shore on their voyaging, clinging close as sea and shoals permitted. From choice, they never ventured far out to sea. Like all former invaders, the Germans who crossed the water to Britain did so where it was narrowest.

Concerning the wide gulf lying north of Spain, it was more feared than the open Atlantic itself, for the winds and currents that unpredictably stirred it. The Cantabrian Sea, it was called by Roman geographers; to seamen who named it out of their own experience, it was the Bay of Treachery.

Raven had not ventured far from land even when dodging the Gothic biremes, and at that the water had been wicked. Cormac now urged what was frighteningly worse.

Clodia was appalled.

She had never been on the sea in her life, but she had heard sailors talk in her father's wine-shop, and seen how they gripped their drinking jacks when they spoke of Treachery Bay. An she needed further proof that it was terrible, she had it when bloody-handed pirates, to whom the death grip of battle was something to joy in, showed trepidation at the thought of braving it. That they gainsaid their captain's blood brother aloud gave her courage to cry her opinion.

"Madness!" she yelled in a voice that cracked in a squak. "Mac Art, this folly of yours will murder me—murder us all! Your men have—"

Cormac rounded on her with a snarl. The Saxon knife he'd once taken from a man who had no further use for it glittered in his fist. The other he clenched in her red-brown mass of hair, drawing back her head so that her white throat was offered to the blade.

"Twice now," he said conversationally, "have ye insisted we be bent on your murder, wench! Now ye'll be closing your mouth and keeping it so, or this little blade and I will see to it that ye'll have been a seeress who predicted her own death!"

He released her. She staggered, tripped and sat down. Her eyes were chestnut-round. Cormac turned to the men on the benches. Them he addressed with biting scorn.

"Ye heard that? A woman who never felt a deck under her feet, and she sounds no worse than ye soft-bellied cod! *Wulfhere's Killers!* Ha! Look at him there, ready to vomit for shame! What say ye, Skull-splitter? Shall we swim the Bay and leave them to snivel at the Romans?"

"Never," Wulfhere assured him. "We have *Raven,* and we hold her. I say we cross Treachery Bay, and toss overboard any who dispute that. Let them do the swimming! Ordlaf?"

Ordlaf Skel's son the steersman, who had not joined the outcry, spat over the stern. "I'll succeed, chieftain. And even should I fail, there'll be none able to twit me."

Wulfhere boomed happy laughter. "I'm served by one man, at least! You hear, codfish? Oh-ho-ho! It will be an adventure! Who is there that doesn't fight? But this thing was never done afore, that I've heard of! Now bend your backs, or you will be having to fight ere the Romans reach you, and with *me!* But do make it a speedy decision. Yon galleys be not standing still!"

His persuasiveness carried the debate.

Thus it was that the top-heavy Roman warcraft saw *Raven* vanish whither they dared not follow. Even then, the pursuers did not guess the resolve that was aboard the pirate craft. The Roman commanders assumed she had put back to the coast in the hour before dawn, and wasted their day searching bay, cove and channel for her. By then she was far out on the heaving grey sea, with low-pitched grumbling on her benches, and prayers to Lord Aegir and the Thunderer.

Clodia was lucky, and over-lucky, not to be sacrificed to the sea people.

CHAPTER THREE: The Bay of Treachery

Grey.

Grey sea under grey sky.

And *Raven* pressed betwixt the two on a surging horizon while the sky grumbled and now and again bellowed like a beast jealous of its territory.

The ocean swells grew out of Ran's breathing belly like monsters prowling the grey world. Slowly they gathered, rising, rolling. To those who watched from the little ship tiny on the sea as a fruit-fly at an imperial banquet, it was as if they had the leisure of all time to watch them form. Then the swells were fulfilled. They peaked like wet mountains beneath the keel, the sun striking lights from them like mica in granite. For a stricken heartbeat the crew of *Raven* looked down a glassy tilt of forever.

And then they slid down it. Faster the ship went, and faster still, tobogganing insanely—to the next wet mountain that bulked up even as a grey colossus. Should the steersman fail to keep her head aright, *Raven* would wallow and do her best to gulp in half the Bay called Treachery—and go swiftly to the bottom.

Ordlaf held her. He plied the weighty steering-oar
with neither panic nor hesitancy. Even so, *Raven* took
water. Men were kept bailing all the while, and all the
while more water sluiced over the deck and into the
bailing well. No; was hardly the best of jobs. But then
neither was Ordlaf's. Nor was Wulfhere's, for he was
master of *Raven* and thus responsible.

All this, while the weather stayed fair.

The girl from Nantes attached herself to the end of
one oar-bench, as a limpet to its rock. She quickly
became abominably seasick. Her lovely complexion
went all greenish and she suffered the humiliation of
retching and chucking until there was naught left in her
stomach. After she loosed the first spasm inboard,
someone seized her by the neck and flung her to the wale
like a puppy not yet trained.

"The fish want it," she heard the Danish pirate say.
"We do not." And the callous dog had himself a feel of
her while he was at it.

Much later, she crawled back to her old position. She
was still miserable, and now there was no relief. Her
stomach was empty, and sureness wasn't on her that she
had not vomited up her guts as well.

Then the weather worsened.

The men from the fjord-sliced north had it that Thor
created thunder by hurling his hammer "Miller," which
struck with a shower of sparks that was lightning;
indeed his keep was called *Bilskirnir*, Lightning; and
that sleepy Aegir was lord of the sea below. But Aegir
mostly slumbered. Not so his wife Ran, who had the
temperament of a she-cat in heat and no toms about.
The Tyrannis of Cormac's people was probably the
same as the nordic Thor. Not so Lir, who was the sea,
and his son Manannan. And was Manannan MacLir
ruled the waters of salt. It mattered not who was right;

56

the Saints or "Christians" said the father of their Dead God ruled land and sea on all the ridge of the world, the pompous jackals, and the Romans of the old way had it that Neptune did.

Perhaps they were all right, aye and the Greeks too with their Poseidonis. Whatever the case and Whoever ruled: He or She was restless.

Now restlessness became anger.

The wind that gave Treachery Bay its name began it, in roaring gusts. It blew at random from eight several directions and all at once. Forty feet tall, the mast creaked and its foot-thickness began to seem frail. The sail cracked and boomed with the winds' unpredictable shifts. At first, Wulfhere tried trimming it accordingly, but his orders were useless ere they could be carried out; a new wind pre-empted. Judging from the darkening sky, worse was acoming.

Wulfhere dolorously bade his men lower sail.

Wind-roughened water seethed about, complicating the ocean-swell. The longship bucked and slammed. *Raven* was become the sea's prisoner. Clodia lost her grip, lurched three paces and fell, banging her hip that was wide and wide for childbearing. She whimpered, knowing she'd bear a colourful bruise. The girl who'd never afore been asea sought some new haven, any place to anchor herself, and again she missed hold. Clodia tumbled across the foredeck with a noise that sounded more like exasperated protest than aught else—though it broke on a note of despair. As if to add insult to injury, the wind screamed angrily at her and hurled a great splash of cold water over the merchant's daughter.

Impatient hands, big hands and leathery-rough of palm and calloused fingers, seized on her and Clodia first squeaked, then made a grateful noise.

It was Cormac mac Art who tucked her under a

battle-hardened arm, and paused to seek and be sure of his balance. Clodia hung there, a dazed, dead weight. In a plosion of long swift strides, Cormac gained the mast. He hugged its solid thickness with his one free arm, again pausing.

Wind blew so hard as to bang him with his own sword-scabbard. Setting his feet on the X of crossed beams that were braced within *Raven*'s sides to support the mast, he lashed Clodia thereto. This task he performed impersonally as he might have seen to a loose bit of cargo.

She'd be safe now from plunging overboard or disrupting working men, and no nuisance in her land-hugger's clumsiness.

Cormac remembered something.

Without ceremony, he plunged a hand between Clodia's excellently blooming breasts. Astonished, the young woman knew the fleeting thought that this was scarcely the time, but she made no objection. She instead smiled, and lifted her wet face.

Cormac's groping hand found the Egyptian sigil, all that was left of his hard-won loot. He plucked it forth.

"Doubtless it's keeping it warm for me ye were, just," he said with flat-voiced cynicism. "Thanks. If drown I must, it's as a man of property I'll be going down to visit the son of Lir."

"You great swaggering boar!" she screamed out, eagerly hitting upon an object for her misery and wrath. "You—you fathom of scars and ill manners! You with your mailshirt cleaving to ye like a second skin with the crusted sweat and blood and stink of the five years you haven't had it off! I know now why your enemies run away in droves! The sole reason your friends do not the same—"

She railed on. It was not true, but he said nothing. She

added several imaginative hypotheses about his friends. Cormac had ship's matters to attend to, wherefore he paused but long enow to drop the winged serpent about his own neck, beneath the battle-gear and cloth. Then he turned away, and Clodia knew with rage that she was already forgot. Hardly comforting; she knew well that she was a savoury, ripe morsel for male lust. And this one couldn't even be bothered bidding her hush, or denying her allegations, or so much as slapping her.

Little cause had she to feel hurt. He'd made her safe, assuming *Raven* survived.

The weather remained foul and the wind continued to veer wildly and shriek like the Ban-Sidhe or Banshee of Cormac's own homeland. Men broke their backs rowing and bailing, and snatched what rest they might between turns. Ordlaf Skel's son manned the steering-oar until he was nigh dropping, and Wulfhere relieved him then, to stand braced like the Colossus of that southern isle called Rhodes.

Again and again the wind shifted direction and tried to creep up behind them like a hungering hyena, or blow *Raven* onto her side.

A howling squawl hit them like a hammer of Thor. It tossed the ship about as if she'd been a chip in rapids, and none slept while that lasted. Had *Raven* turned broadside-on to those maniacal seas, she must have capsized in a moment—as she almost did in any case.

Minutes of high excitement became hours of anguish.

After midnight, they enjoyed a spell of clear weather. Men sagged and breathed through open mouths while with dull eyes they stared at wet boards.

Cormac, passing the mast on his way to rest, was put in mind of Clodia. Hours had passed. He paused to free the sodden bundle with stringing hair gone dark with wet and frost-flecked with brine. The knots binding her to the mast were soaked stiff and salty, hard as lumpy iron nodules out of a cold forge. Annoyance that had driven another man to shrug and forget it made the Gael persist, while a sailor's respect for good cord kept him from simply cutting it. His tough fingers opened the knots at last.

Clodia virtually fell away from her support.

"Thank you, Cormac," she gasped, and she meant it.

Conviction had come on her that, left there longer, her limbs had begun to rot off. A like thought had occurred to Cormac. Yet necessity was on them to raise sail, and Clodia had been in the way.

"Cormac . . ."

His face remained impassive despite the piteous appeal of her voice and face. "Ye live, Clodia. And it's not as my guest ye be aboard." And he went from her.

By scanning the stars through wind-shredded gaps in cloud, and by Behl the sun as he shook off the dark and reigned anew, they discovered that they were far off course. Now Clodia of Nantes knew the reason that men of the sea ever equivocated with words such as *should* and *with luck and good fortune* when they answered the simple question: "How long will it take?" For none could ever be sure. A journey by sea might take two days or ten—or three months, an a ship was blown so far off her course and then afflicted with calm.

Erelong, those aboard *Raven* had contrary winds to fight again. These rose to such a patch that not sail only, but mast as well had to be lowered, else both had gone by the board. The wind shrieked like mad hags babbling inanities and lightning lit the sky with lurid flashes, followed by the crash of thunder.

Thor was angry.

Aegir was awake, and angry.

Ran was angry. And what care had the son of Lir for a girl of Nantes, and boys and men of Dane-mark, and one long exile from Eirrin?

It went on that way for five days.

Save for two other such respites that were all too brief, their time on the Bay of Treachery was consistently as bad as the first day, or worse.

They were fighting a sea that deserved all its fell repute, that hated humans and drowned whales while tearing down cliffs. Its bottom must be crowded with ships and bones, assuming that many had been foolish enough to come abroad here. A lesser ship than *Raven* and her crew had not been seen again save as fragments of ax-honed wood torn by wind, and sodden corpses washed up on far beaches. With weaker leaders, even that crew might have given up from weariness and let themselves rest—in the nets of Ran.

Two of the wounded men died.

Two others, able-bodied companions, were lost in the hell of the sea for a moment's missed footing; in truth, Ubbi was gone because he'd released his grip on his oar long enough to pick his nose.

Four deaths, and they received no comment aside from muttered oaths and a fare-thee-well. There was not even time to think good thoughts of those men. The Danes could mourn their comrades later, so long as they did not join them. And so long as former comrades returned not as liches; Those Who Walk after Death.

During one of the respites, idly talking men decided that Aegir and Ran had naught to do with this awful stretch of water, and the skalds must merely have failed to make mention that here reigned Loki and his ugly get, Hela who ruled the underworld. Clodia was willing to think them right, as she had already decided they were the coldest, meanest, bravest and most competent men under heaven.

On the fifth day the winds steadied, and fell.

Raven rocked gently on the water become glassy plain, and weary survivors of wrathful, treacherous winds basked in the gentleness as in sweet bed-linen. Men sagged, or merely crumpled and slept, or rose and stretched—and then slumped. Up went the sail, and it was hardly less relaxed than the men beneath.

In twilight, they espied a dark coastline. After the cloudy sundown a land-breeze roved out to bring the welcome scents of earth and forest. Yet was too soon to rejoice; as leaders, the Gael and the huge Dane had to decide what landfall might portend. Nor was thinking easy for them, with fatigue on their bodies and brains like thrice-filtered poison.

They spoke with great deliberation and exaggerated care and what, in fresher state, they'd have deemed thick simplicity, the Gael in particular.

"Yon be Hispania," Wulfhere said. "Must be."

"Hispania," Cormac agreed. "And the northern part. Most likely the north-west. Galicia. That is the name they call it by. Galicia." He paused to ponder, and that ponderously. "Have we enemies here?"

"I think not. Ye'll not believe me, Wolf, but this is one coast where I've never done business. Farther south, aye. Never here."

"Nor I."

"Strange."

"Umm." Cormac was bethinking him of former days, when he'd led a band of Eirrin's reivers and men had named him the greatest such sea-wolf since Niall of the Nine Hostages.

Aye, Cormac *an-Cliuin* had plundered farther south than this too, all the way to Africa's sparkling shores and within the very blue, blue Mediterranean. Yet it chanced that he had never put in at Galician shores, not even for naught so harmless as to lift a few cattle for fresh eating. He'd taken nary a drop of Galician booty off a ship, to his knowledge. There could be naught against him here, in this northwest corner of Hispania . . . save his reputation, o'course, should he chance to meet with narrow, finicking men.

He raked through his tired memory for what he knew of this land.

The people here were an insular lot, he seemed to recall, not the sort to care what he and Wulfhere had done in other places, to other peoples. The Galicians were just as separated from other men as the sea-roving tigers of *Raven*. Some German tribe held the mastery here, didn't it? Aye—what was it they were called, now. An amalgam of tribes, an old group united in—

"Sueves!" the Gael said aloud.

"Slaves?"

"Na, redbeard: *Sueves*. The Suevi. The people who rule this land." He slapped his knee, on which the watered, salted leather had gone dry and hard as old bark. "Fine, then! They'll not be hanging us unless on principle, and—"

"Principle?" Wulfhere's tone was truculent.

"We *are* pirates, Wulf! We can make ourselves understood by them. It's a German people they are, or were. I had their king's name, once."

"Ah! One Veremund the Tall. That his height is what a *Dane* would reckon 'tall' I misdoubt, though. Umm . . . the name's all I know of him."

"Veremund. Verem—aye! A king with ideas, I'm told. It's trouble with the Goths he and his people are after having. It ought not harm our credit an we let him know the Goths are after having trouble with *us* . . . and he'll be knowing that anyhow."

"How much trouble," Wulfhere asked, "and how bad?" After a moment he added, "The Sueves with the Goths, I mean."

That Cormac knew, but he also knew his own brain

was working little better.

"There is the meat of it, Cormac. And be they at odds still, or at peace? For all we know, they now be Gothic vassals."

Cormac, silent, laboured at remembering. The conquests and dispossessions that had boiled across the known world in the last hundred years were beyond any man's power to keep straight in his head. The writhe and surge of humanity in this that the "Saints" called the fifth century in the reign of their Lord had been like unto the winds of Treachery Bay. Those in Britain, that Cormac was more familiar with, were complicated enow.

The Gael stalked through his own mind, sorting. Blood of the gods, how many places he'd been, how much he knew of the world! And to think that but eight years agone he'd been but a provincial boy who'd thought he had the world because he'd slain a bear of Connacht, alone and with a dagger!

He said at last, "No, it's no Gothic vassals these people are. The Sueves came down into Spain with the Vandals and the Alans, a long lifetime agone. The Sueves remain, though they were squeezed westward; the Vandals and the Alianis have crossed into Africa and become one people. The Goths, I was hearing, did subdue these Suevi three or so times, on behalf of the Romans. The first time and the second, the Goths have the lesson and then returned to those lands ceded them over in Gaul. Hmp! Roman diplomacy at work, I'm not doubting, and them with no desire to see the Goths grow too powerful."

Cormac squinted darkly at the sky, reflecting.

"The last time matters fell out differently. The Sueves were waxing fierce once again, under a king named Remismund; they had taken Lisbon, this one Germanic tribe! It was that city's own Roman governor himself who oped the gates to them! By then Euric had just become king over the Visigoths, and he marched them over the mountains once more, to rout the Sueves."

"I know about *Euric*," Wulfhere rumbled. "Ha! All know about Euric. He did well, that one."

Aye; by the wild standards of his day, Euric the Visigoth had done well. Remismund the Sueve, knowing himself threatened, was so daring as to make appeal to the Emperor himself in Constantinople. He was ignored. In the mean time, Euric's Goths conquered southeastern Hispania right handily, and occupied Lusitania with swaggering men of ever-shifting eyes. They swiftly tore loose the Suevic hold on Lisbon and enforced Suevic submission, even to making them accept the creed of the Arian Church. Euric the Goth, "terrible by the fame of his courage and his sword," ruled from the Atlantic to the Rhone, from the Mediterranean to the Loire. Nor had he recognized even nominal bonds with the Empire, as had his predecessors. A proud fire-eyed man, Euric, who ruled in no name but his own—and made the world to know it.

And he sired Alaric, Count Guntram's unbeloved liege.

"He did well," Cormac mac Art said nodding. "Sorrow's on him he had no heir worthy of him. King Alaric the Second! Huh! Alaric the Timid is closer to the truth, and that previous Alaric who conquered even Rome itself must be turning in his grave with shame! It's quiet the Sueves remained while Euric lived—but he's two years with the heroes, and the Sueves know well what this King Alaric is. And by repute their king is all that Alaric is not."

Wulfhere slipped fingers into his beard to scratch briny encrustations. "I make water on *repute*, Cormac!

Oft it means naught more than a rumour here, a boast there. Ye sound like Veremund's housepet. Have ye certain knowledge of aught he's done for this *repute* of his?"

The dark-visaged Gael smiled grimly. "Well, it's no great battles Veremund of the Sueves has fought, nor has he taken cities—the which is only wisdom, as he's not ready. Yet all the shrewder Goth lords in Hispania can see him working towards it. The man's after taking pains to deal fairly with the Roman land-owners, Wulfhere, as the Goths do seldom. Veremund even speaks decent Latin; better than mine, and mine is none so bad. It signs to me that he wishes to rule a kingdom, not an enclave of conquerors who stand less than steadily on the necks of a subject people . . . who'd still be there after the conquerors vanished. That he has a golden welcome for skilled smiths and armourers is no rumour, but fact. Stand on it. Always I try to know where such men are going, and—by Behl's burning eye! —so do the merchants. The last time we were in Lisbon, I had it from the governor himself—"

"What?"

"—the governor's daughter herself, late one night, that it's Veremund who's behind the incursions of river pirates on the Duera. Petty stuff, and they but petty rogues who've never sniffed the open sea. Methinks it's meant for a first trial of how far he can go. King Veremund affects to know naught of them, and promises to hang any he catches."

Wulfhere chuckled.

"No certainty's on me of this, Skull-splitter, and ye can be making water on it for wine-shop babble if ye like: But Veremund has sent envoys to the Cantanabrian Mountains over eastward, to sound the people there. He's not like to be receiving firm answers this early in the game, even if such be true. Still, it says something of this Suevi king, that such a story can be told and believed."

"The Goths must be spineless or mad, to sit on their saddle-galled backsides and do naught! I'd have this Veremund's hall in ashes and himself in pieces!"

"As would I. As would full many of the Goths. But they and we are not kings. Their ill luck it is that their king remains far away with his Egyptian whores, and will not be putting his armies into motion. Worse that the very landscape, with mountains sprawled across it like dragons, makes campaigning so hard."

Behind them somewhere, Clodia squealed and a man laughed; Cormac and Wulfhere did not so much as turn.

"Surely aught of unity will never prevail in this land, Wulfhere, as it does in Eirrin—almost—with our—*its* peoples united under council and High-king—almost. Aye," Cormac said softly, almost wistfully, "and with all the learned men and artisans moving freely where they will in the practice of their crafts . . . and them sacrosanct, by law and ancient usage."

Wulfhere was silent, leaning against the inner hull and picking his fingernails with his teeth. Aye, he knew his battle-brother Cormac for one of the prideful Eirrin-born, and such men never forgot. *Not like us Danes,* Wulfhere thought, *who know other men are equal to us . . . except the Norse, and the Swedes, and the Romans o'course, and those damned namby Britons, and of course the idiot Germans who . . .*

"Was Strabo," Cormac was saying on, "who likened Hispania to an oxhide outspread, not only in shape but in hue and relief, all dried and cracked and puckered. Other great differences there are, even where the terrain is flat. The weather for one, and the peoples. These Sueves—they are a fierce independent lot. The Basques are the same. They should be! It's the same stock they are as the Caledonia Picts, when all's said and done—or Eirrin's Firbholgs. Only the Tuatha de Danaan by their sorceries were able to prise loose the Firbholgs' hold on Eirrin. And it was no easy time my ancestors had, in winning Eirrin from the Danan breed!"

Wulfhere noted how his comrade had availed himself of the opportunity to point out the superiority of the people who had exiled him, but the Dane said naught. Were all Gaels of Eirrin such as his shipmate and battle-brother Cormac mac Art, the Eirrish would surely own half the world and statues of Crom and Behl would stand in Rome.

Cormac fell into withdrawn silence. Wulfhere moved aftward. Cormac but gazed at the nearing coast as if that clotted extent of darkness fascinated him.

It did not. It was one more foreign and likely hostile shore. He'd seen many such. Not the least intimation came to him of rare events waiting, or any high promise. At present he was, after all, a very weary man.

From behind him a slap resounded, along with an angry exclamation in a woman's offended voice. The sounds mingled with Wulfhere's belly-deep chuckle and the gentle slap of water along *Raven*'s hull. The Gael sighed. After coming so far at cost of such immense labour and peril, all gods defend them, they had to arrive with a woman aboard! Where did Wulfhere find the inclination?

"Quiet," he bade them, not deigning to turn.

Clodia made complaint, none the less. "But this huge man-mountain *persists* in—"

"*Quiet.*"

"And for why?" Wulfhere demanded. "It's little we have to fear of Veremund's Galicians here asea. River barges and fishing boats manned by native Spaniards are not going to trouble *Raven,* would ye say? Has Veremund warships? I never heard of it. Nor did yourself."

"So. I did not," Cormac made admission. He yawned. "I'm needing quiet while I think—remember that? Thinking? I'll admit Veremund's being shipless is a thought that will mayhap bear following out—another time. The Sueves' fathers knew all they knew of the sea from travellers' tales, as did the Vandals once . . . but the Vandals learned seamanship."

"Of a sort," put in Ordlaf. If Ordlaf of Dane-mark knew of a better helmsman than himself on all the seas, no one was likely to learn it from the lips of any aboard *Raven.*

Ivarr snorted. "These Sueves be dirt-farmers, lorded over by horsemen. High-nosed fools! Five years after they're born, they can never bring their knees within hailing distance again. They'd dine from the saddle if they could."

Men laughed, and encouraged Ivarr added, "Can't bring their knees together, those men. And their women come to the same state not much older."

Wulfhere roared and smacked Ivarr's shoulder—and Clodia's backside, simultaneously. Tight-lipped, Clodia moved out of the big Dane's reach. Coming to Cormac, she clutched his arm and renewed her appeal.

"Please make him—"

"Belay that. *Look!*"

Fire, shoreward.

A dancing bright wisp of flame it was, that swiftly grew. In minutes it was a large yellow glow bright enow to be visible for miles of a clear night.

"Signal," Wulfhere muttered, thinking aloud. "That, or beacon."

"Or a rite of some kind," Ivarr added. "Some

chieftain's obsequies? I'm not sure yon fire does not burn on the sea itself."

"Wreckers," was Ordlaf's suggestion, and a world of loathing he packed into the word.

The others shared that loathing, and contempt. No seaman who had sailed the tricky coasts of Armorica, now known to many as Lesser Britain for the Cornish and Cymric folk who had settled there, went unmoved by the word *wrecker*. The name was an epithet. Wulfhere snarled in his bristling crimson beard.

"If such they be, let's find and kill them!"

"If such they be, old Splitter of skulls," Cormac said, "we will." His tone was abstracted but not a whit less deadly for it. "We will, aye . . . but suppose that be a simple harbour-light. It's no less mad we'd be to let it be drawing us in. Belike we'd be finding ourselves greeted with a royal claim on *Raven* and all she contains."

"Aye, Captain." Ordlaf spoke quietly. "Best go wide of it now, whate'er it may be. Make investigation by daylight."

"For that we'd all fall asleep arowing," Cormac mac Art added, "an we attempt it now."

Raven turned southward upon water like shimmering silk. Men pulled their oars, and pulled again, with no strength in their arms. They had used the last of it, and still they rowed. The shore they neared was wild and shaggy, with no signs of cultivation.

"Put in yonder," Wulfhere said, thrusting his massive head forward like a hound spotting birds. In truth he was squinting into the night.

The sanctuary he had chosen was a wood-fringed cove scarce so large that it could be flattered as a bay. The longship nosed in slowly. Cormac, at the bow, probed ahead for rocks. The cove seemed innocent of such, excepting the seaworn mass at its southern end, which bore a goodly frost of bird droppings.

They backed oars and anchored. No man would go ashore. The ship's fire had been drenched out, days agone, but victuals remained, with an added odour of the sea from their sealskin wrapping. They ate lightly, without benefit of fire. Wulfhere, like his crew, was undismayed by cold food—but he did hark back lugubriously to the wine casks they'd heaved over-side. Cormac groaned. He knew there'd be complaints on that score at random intervals over the next several years. Such obscene waste had gone painfully to the Dane's heart, or more aptly to his throat and stomach, the more susceptible parts of him.

"Still ye remind me of something, guzzler," Cormac said. "That business at Garonne-mouth; would ye not be saying it was too like what happened after, at Nantes? At both places we found *traps,* and them well laid, wouldn't ye say?"

Wulfhere shrugged and yawned. The matter was too far away and too long agone to concern him now. "Ye may have the right of it, Wolf. Does it signify? It's never news, is it, that men of the law don't like us. Mayhap we will take it up wi' that fop Sigebert and his lord another day, though it's from one ear only Sigebert'll be giving listen! I'd surely like a word with that one-eared bastard when he lacks a score of weapon-men about him, were it only for Thorfinn's sake. But these be Galician shores, and our concerns be here."

Cormac grunted, "Aye," and said no more.

They stretched the lowered sail for an awning, lest it rain. Blissful it was to lie down for a night's sleep on tranquil water! Cormac made no objection when Clodia lay beside him and pressed close; indeed, he hardly noticed. After five unresting days on a crazy sea, he'd rather have had oblivious slumber than the embrace of Fand herself.

Clodia was, though, in proud fleshy bloom and ripe,

71

and someone found interest and impulse to stoop and
fondle her boldly as he passed. That resulted in a yelp
and spasm that made Cormac sit up, hurling aside his
covering cloak. A sharp, icy irritability weighed on him.

"Will ye horny sons of mares be still!" he snarled.
"You too, wench! By Midhir and Morrighu, the next
man who troubles my rest will sleep ashore or in the
water where I'll right briskly hurl him. And yourself,
Clodia. Be that understood?"

There were soft hootings, and comments of a scur-
rilous nature emerged from the shrouding dark. Mac
Art paid those no mind.

Once more he wrapped his cloak about him and composed himself to sleep, and this time with success.
Clodia curled against his back, pleased he'd at least
called her by name. She passed an arm about his waist,
and clung. She did not intend that any "horny sons of
mares" should drag her away from him for amusement
betwixt the rowing-benches, an someone awoke in the
night and decided he was sufficiently rested to be up to
it.

CHAPTER FOUR: The Horror in the Lighthouse

Dawn provided colour and detail for a coast that might until then have been Hel or the Hesperides. Sunrise proved it to be neither. Both Cormac and his Danish shipmates stared, silently thoughtful, for this land bore haunting similarities to their home shores.

For Cormac mac Art, the one man of his race aboard *Raven,* and more irrevocably an exile, the similarities roused memories. And they were bitter.

Gossamer morning-mists had already begun to ravel away in the sun. Estuaries, deep and wind-swept like the northern fjords, sliced into a fertile land. Deep, blue-shaded woods of beech and oak stretched broadly. Beyond loomed the greenest mist-shrouded hills Cormac had seen since he'd departed Eirrin the Emerald of the Sea.

Was said the Eirrin-born never forgot, or found true happiness elsewhere on all the ridge of the world. Homesickness took him by the throat like an enemy; homesickness roiled in his stomach. Though *Raven*'s deck was now the one true home he had, it was suddenly hateful to him. The land drew him like a sorcerer's spell of summoning.

"I'll be returning soon," he said thickly.

"Your shield," Wulfhere said.

Cormac slung it along his arm. With a splash and a stumble, he dropped from *Raven*'s thwarts. He waded forward, his eyes fixed on this land as if he were one possessed. He was vaguely aware of Clodia, who was following him close. He did not glance around. He waded ashore.

It might have been worse. At least she'd not bleated any *Cormac, wait for me*'s after him, for the crew to guffaw over. She was even tagging a few paces behind and keeping her mouth shut . . . which, had he seen his own face, would not have surprised the Gael so deep in his memories.

Then he ignored and even forgot her.

Eirrin. Love of the greater gods, *Eirrin*.

It's liquid music the name was. A name that called up, that *meant*, the world's bravest and fairest men and women, thick-maned horses, red and brindle cattle, rivers like molten silver with gold shining in their beds, and great shadeful forests old as time. Poets and craftsmen Eirrin produced, whose work vied with that of nature; learned men and druids of supernal wisdom and power. Splendour, and wealth, and delights. *Eirrin*. All barred to him.

All Eirrin barred to him. Because of the treachery of kings, and a deliberately provoked quarrel.

Cormac mac Art of Connacht had been meant to die of that provocation and ensuing duel. Instead, he had slain. Considering when and where he had done death on another Gael of Eirrin, his slaying had been well-nigh as bad as him slain, or as disastrous to the boy he'd been. He who provoked did so during the Great Fair; Cormac slew him during the High King's peace, which was inviolate. For such a crime the laws did not award other punishment than death.

Cormac had fled away, in misery, ere he could be taken and executed. By then he knew treachery had been done on him by a rival, and by a king—and surely too the High-king himself. Crossing the plain of the sea to Dalriada in Alba up in the north of Britain, he left behind him a girl most beloved—and half his belief in the justice of kings. And too he left behind the sword of his father, for in his hand it had slain a Gael in Eirrin. The sea had it, now.

How young he'd been then, this scarred, slit-eyed pirate of *Raven!*

In Dalriada, he sought obscurity and low employment. In the employ of peasants, he worked the land like a peasant for nigh onto a year. Close and silent he'd been, and unknown to any he had remained. Partha he'd called himself; Partha of Ulahd, a name he had used aforetime to cloak his own.

Yet Dalriada, founded long before by Gaels of Eirrin some called *Scoti*, was menaced ever by Picts from the Caledonian heather. Was not a place where a born fighter could remain forever obscure. Forever? In truth, that better part of a year was remarkably long. He toiled, and one day there came a Pictish attack on his master's lands. Heart and hand and weapon-man's training flashed awake in the peasant labourer. He did destruction on the shock-headed dark men with a reckless ferocity even they lacked power to match, and he emerged blooded but alive—perhaps because he hardly cared whether he died. The Pictish survivors fled, a thing seldom known. Picts were wont to slay to the last, or die in like fashion.

And so distinction in combat came again upon Cormac mac Art, now Partha mac Othna. Gol, King over Dalriada, had invited him into his service, and good service had the youth given . . .

Good, however brief. It happened that the king's own

daughter of Dalriada took undue interest in this Partha Pictslayer, mighty and envied weapon-man who had swiftly shown himself the best among her father's warriors. The king had eyes to see it. Now a king must and will protect his own and marry them well, and so it was arranged that Partha fell into the hands of the Picts.

For others this fate befell, the invariable result was death not long delayed. For this Partha Pictslayer—who had earned the name—the stocky, short men had plans more ornate.

They played with him right gently at first, whilst they argued the merits of all the contradictory, irreconcilable ends they wished to give him. Their prisoner even kept all limbs and members, so tender with him were his captors—though he was not left unmarked. At last they settled on slow starvation, with exposure and beatings at times.

They chose awrong. The lengthy process gave Cormac opportunity to escape. He was free again—and unwelcome in still another land. But there was the sea. From captive he became outlaw, nursed by bitterness. He gathered a band about him and took to the sea on a lifted curragh. And he came to know who had betrayed him into Pictish hands, and why.

On the wild coasts of Dalriada he left what had remained of his belief in kingly honour. His youth he left there as well, and him then not yet twenty. Nor did he meet with difficulty in making the men he led believe him older.

In vengeance and bitterness and hatred did the reiver Cormac savage the shores of Gol's kingdom. Mothers frightened miscreant youngsters with stories of Captain Partha, Captain Wolf, the scarred raider with eyes grey and cold and glittering as the metal of his sword. Cormac *an-Cliuin* he was: Cormac the Wolf.

Came the time when he must quit those waters, for they had grown too scalding even for him, and his crew was quivering on the edge of mutiny. Came then a long voyage down the coasts of Britain, and Gallia and Hispania. Those Gaelic reivers had reached even Africa, where they made themselves known too well to the Vandals. Yet return to the western isles he had, lest Gol forget the man on whom he'd done a king's treachery.

Time came when civil strife in Eirrin resulted in the sundering of Cormac's crew. Time came when he was captured again, and tossed into prison quarters colder and more filthy than even the Picts had given him. Here he awaited execution. Another prisoner in the same plight languished there, for company. Wulfhere Hausakliufr his name, and he admired the genius of the darker man who used their meagre victuals as food for the prison's rats, who provided nourishment for the two prisoners . . .

"Cormac."

The sound of his name returned him to the immediate now. She had been saying his name for some time, to no result; he'd been deep in the past, surrounded by this Eirrin-like land. Though he eased his abstracted walking, he did not turn to look at Clodia. She spoke his name again, on a falling note, and fell silent.

The young woman behind him bit her lip. By no means was it subtly that he conveyed to her that she was unwanted! Yet she durst not return to the ship and all those men. Not without Cormac. That fearful crew of fiery-headed pirates, and those genially brazen hands of Wulfhere who was big enow to wrestle bulls for pastime!

Clodia nerved herself. Whate'er it was gnawed within this reiver made this the wrong time entirely, and not being a fool the auburn-haired girl knew it. Yet there might not be other times. Besides, she felt a touch of

77

anger. With a ship and forty swords at his back, what had the great dark man to gloom so about?

That a ship and forty swords could be appallingly little on occasion, she did not consider.

"Cormac," Clodia said hesitantly. "What—what do you mean to do with me?" She bit her lip, swallowed, and then rushed on, finding that she feared an answer.

"This land is strange to me as to you. We have been friends, Cormac. That I'd have liked to be more in the old days, you know." Already they had become the old days to her, distant and dim. "That you ofttimes desired me, I know. Then what is it turns you so hard? You know how a woman fares with barbarian war-bands, an she lacks one single protector. Can you not bear the thought of being my protector, Cormac?" And then, her voice rising to shrillness, *"Look at me!"*

Cormac turned, and looked. Clodia's strong and high-breasted body was bared to him, her skirt and bodice a crumpled heap on the alien sand. Shame, desire and desperation commingled to heat the blood that darkened her face. He was astonished to see how far from the ship they had wandered along the strand, whilst thoughts had enveloped him to no purpose.

She came swaying, smiling, seducing . . .

Anger seethed in him, cold and sudden and inexplicable. The last simpering resort: her *body*. And see the tavern-girl trying to look the temptress! She reached him then, smiling—and of a sudden he caught her hard and clasped her hard.

Clodia yelped in shock. His arms tightened and the links of his mail pressed into her skin, hurting, marking her. She arched her back and set her palms in urgency against his steel-clad chest, pushing hard and then harder. Cormac lifted her off her feet, swung her around. Her struggles grew wilder. She cried out. Her lower body stretched out at right angles to his as he swung—

Cormac let her go.

There was a wild waving of white limbs in the morning sun, and a resounding splash that drowned a high-pitched squeal. Clodia was no swimmer, as her frantic paddlings testified. Nor did Cormac mean to drown her; the water was shallow, he saw, and the strand very near. When her feet touched bottom it would occur to the wench that she might stand and wade ashore.

Cormac left her to do so. He made his way back to *Raven. This is Galicia. This is now. Eirrin is the past. Eirrin is but a word. The past is dead as last year's leaves.*

"Now that was no long absence!" Wulfhere greeted him. "And where be the vine that clings to the wolf?"

"Swimming."

Laughter rose, but the Gael's tone and expression made short work of it. "Now tell me, what have we found?"

"We, do ye say?" Wulfhere lifted red thickets of brow. "Hmm. While yourself and the lassie strayed, Ivarr mounted yon rise for a vantage view. He has seen a great high tower that looks to be the source o' yester-night's beacon light."

"Does it so?" Cormac drummed fingers on the oar-loom before him, cogitating. "Sure and we can bear the risk of looking into that."

"So think I. It's certain we've naught better to do."

They were preparing to push off when Clodia appeared. She scrambled aboard with downcast eyes. Huddled as small as she could make herself, she spoke not a word.

Raven's crew rowed north again.

Cormac, rubbing a blackly stubbled chin that itched

79

him, was made mindful as the brilliantly blue sun-
flecked water slid by that he'd not shaved in well-nigh a
week. Though he was not wont to adorn himself, he was
of Eirrin: he was mindful of such matters as cleanliness
and his hair and aye, shaving—when circumstances
allowed. Indeed he kept a razor of finest eastern steel in
his belt-pouch rather than make do with a honed knife.
He was little twitted, though the Danes agreed that
never had they heard of a more amazing habit.

Nah, Wulfhere said; was only because the poor Gael
couldn't raise a beautiful *red* beard that he kept it
scraped . . .

Without benefit of oil or grease, he kept at the
miserable task. Lip and cheeks, jaw and chin and finally
throat he scraped clean. He rubbed with his fingertips to
ensure thoroughness. Well that his skin had weathered
hard over the years. As for the facial scars that lent him
a sinister aspect, he'd memorized them.

They had some time since left the tiny cove with its
point of land and the rise from which Ivarr had scanned
about. Now they came with abruptness to a triple bay,
miles across and miles deep. At its southwestern tip rose
the tower reported by the sharpest-eyed among them.
Now they saw it closer, and what lay beyond: the sun-
washed stones of a Roman city, falling into neglect and
abandon like many another in the west.

The men of *Raven* stared, cursed and invoked
supernatural protection, for Northerners were
superstitious about the engineering feats of Rome the
once-mighty.

" 'Tis the work of giants!" Knud the Swift declared.

"And I'm Idun," Cormac told him, "who has the
apples of immortality."

Back he tilted his dark head, and back, looking up.
He squinted. The great white tower soared forty men

high and more; there was no assessing. Its builders had reared it in several tiers, each smaller in crosswise measure than the one immediately below. The lowermost was shapen cuboid, the topmost a smooth cylindrical shaft against the pure Spanish sky. A sort of roofed cupola topped it off, around which ran a stone balcony.

"I should ha' known," Cormac said. "It's the Romans raised that lighthouse here. The greatest in the western world, I've heard say. It's the Pharos of Alexandria it had for a model. Yonder will be the harbour of Brigantium."

"And a fair harbour, too," Wulfhere said, with enthusiasm. "A fleet could lie here—nay, exercise here! Although there's little sea traffic it looks to receive nowadays. Who be manning the lighthouse, and why?"

Ivarr narrowed his keen eyes. "No one, Captain. From here it looks deserted. An it be not—why's nobody at the top, looking down upon us and giving alarums? Have we gone so harmless in appearance since yesterday?"

Cormac turned decisive. "It's finding out we'd best be," he said, staring at the immense tower as at some inscrutable foe. The Gael seemed to snuff the air like the wolf whose name he bore. "Do you see to the ship, Wulfhere. I'll be taking three men into yon lighthouse to see what I can find. Hrut Bear-slayer, come and climb stairs with me."

The enormous, brain-addled strong man had all but usurped the place of Cormac's shadow. His comrades had exerted their best ribald efforts to stay him from lumbering after Cormac and Clodia when they went off together. Mightily hurt he'd have been, had Cormac ignored him now.

"You too, Hrolf," the Gael went on, "aye, and

81

yourself, Knud. I'm thinking we can handle any bogies we may meet."

"Ha! Listen to him!" The protest was Wulfhere's, uttered loud. "And ye're not jesting so much as ye'd have us believe! I know ye, Cormac, and by the gods I know that look. Ye can sniff out battle and death and unholiness even as a ranging hound sniffs out boars in the brush, ye rangy hound of Eirrin!"

"Repetition. And over-stating of the truth, what's more. It's but that I was born suspicious and have since grown more so. We'll be after returning ere ye know we have gone."

"So ye will," the Dane agreed, stubborn as a rooted tree, "for the rest of us be coming along. Who commands here, I'm asking?"

"Lir and Manannan macLir!"

The oath aside, Cormac made no difficulty. When Wulfhere invoked his captaincy there was no budging him and mac Art did not fight stone walls. Thus all trooped ashore, save Clodia and those few men chosen to remain aboard ship as watch.

Slipping and sliding over weed-covered rocks, they reached the base of the lighthouse. Kittiwakes screamed at them, wheeling grey-cloaked and white-breasted about the tower. A huge bronze-bound door, closed and barred, greeted them blankly. Surely naught but a ram would be capable of gaining entry here—and handling one on the shore rocks was impossible. When Wulfhere looked of a mind to attack it with his ax, Cormac stayed him.

"I've a smoother way," he said. "Are ye after bringing the grapnel and line, Knud?"

"Aye."

The Gael took it, whirled it, and tossed the grapnel neatly through one of the slitted windows above their heads. The rope paid out, running up; the prongs caught and held.

"They designed their embrasures ill," was his comment. "It ought not be so simple. Tcha, well. It's not meant for a fortress this tower was."

Mac Art swarmed up the rope with a sailor's agility, mail, sword, and all; their weight was part of him, of long accustoming. A lithe bend and twist took him through the window.

Standing in a reeky dimness, he waited while his sight adapted. Little there was to see; stucco walls, rafters, a door leaning drunkenly from its hinges, and a deal of dust. Cormac frowned. The latter had been laid by a curious, bad-smelling dampness with no taint of age or mildew. *Recent for sure,* he mused. *A rainstorm in the past day or so?*

Yet never had rain combined with dust in an old house smelled quite this way. . . . Not even this near the sea. For a moment his teeth were in his lip, whilst he considered.

With a shrug he made his way down the angled flights of stairs and opened the door. Wulfhere Skull-splitter's armoured bulk filled the space instanter.

"You cannot come in," the Gael said sardonically. "The place is a mess."

Wulfhere disputed him. Cormac argued and cursed with the ability of long practice. At length he persuaded his blood-brother to remain outside, whiles he made search with the three men he had chosen. Not happily, Wulfhere made way for Knud and Hrolf and Hrut.

Ascending, the four found little that Cormac had not seen previously, save ruined furniture. The stench of brine and kelp pervaded, and was somehow *wrong*. Cormac saw Knud and Hrolf wrinkle their noses, though he made no comment.

They reached the topmost storey of the great edifice. Here was merely a hollow shaft of whitewashed brick, with a stair spiralling around it internally. They climbed, fighting dizziness.

"Mayhap those Romans sought to reach the sky, and gave up a ladder's length short," Knud suggested.

They reached the top. Pulleys and ropes were there, and a heavy capstan, for the raising of supplies; lamp-oil chiefly, Cormac hazarded. The big lamp the Romans had used was fifty years missing though, as were the mirrors employed to magnify its light and reflect it many miles seaward. Now there was a large iron brazier, and faggots of oil-soaked wood.

The tower's human occupants were present as well.

They numbered four, and all were dead.

"CORMA-A-A-AC!" Wulfhere's bellow.

Save the mark, Cormac thought. *Worse this is than being married.*

He trod to the circling balcony and leaned on the balustraded verge. "Damn your bull-roar mouth!" he shouted through cupped hands. "No danger is here, though something befell during the night. It's four corpses we're looking at."

"And them unmarked," Knud the Swift added; he was examining the bodies. "Save for old scars. These were weapon-men, or I know not the breed, and equipped for action. Now why should such be manning a lighthouse?"

"We be looking at another, down here!" Wulfhere thundered. "Found him tangled in kelp at the water's edge. Smashed out of shape till his mother couldn't know him. Hurled from the tower, he must have been. An he'd simply fallen, he'd be nearer the base."

"Or else he . . . jumped," Cormac muttered, half to himself.

Thoughtful, and thorough as always, he made examination of the beacon chamber. Lastly he looked at the corpses. Two gripped bare weapons with the tenacious rigor of death, yet they were unblooded.

Hrut Bear-slayer, huge, looming and rarely with a word to say, showed no comprehension of events. He waited, like an outsized hunting hound ready to track and slay on command. The blow that had left him with a grisly great dent in his forehead—and that by all reasonable chances should have left him stark dead—had rendered him ever silent and presumably thoughtless. His bulk and weapon-skills he had retained, however. Not even Wulfhere was stronger.

"Cormac," Hrolf Halfgarsson said. "This one clutches something."

The third corpse did. It was naught uncommon, save that they were a few hundred feet in the air; merely a length of dark brown seaweed. Its round, flexible stem sprouted long leaves like wrinkled streamers. These erupted bulges like air-bladders, or what appeared to be such. Each swelling was the size of a fat acorn.

Or grapes, Cormac mused, for they were tight-skinned as the latter in a vineyard of Gaul.

Interested, the Gael bent to touch the sea-plant.

With a coil and rustle it whipped about his forearm in serpentine constriction. Something round and sucking gripped the pale inner skin like a leech's mouth. Cormac, with a longtime horror of snakes or aught that resembled them, tore the thing away. He hurled it down and stamped upon it.

Two of the bladders burst like erupting seedpods—
—and spurted streamers of scarlet over the floor.

"Blood," Hrut said unbelievingly, and it was.

Comprehension of a sort came into that high chamber, and with it entered too the sombre spectre of the unnatural, the preternatural. The pervading odour of kelp, which had assaulted their nostrils all along, seemed to grow stronger. Now, in seconds, that smell had taken on sinister meaning.

The four men living looked at each other in silence. The four dead men stared on.

After a moment, a frowning Cormac thought to examine the beacon itself.

Its fire had been smothered out by what appeared to be a mass of kelp, though it was so completely charred to ash that he could not be certain. Buried beneath the ash was the beacon's legitimate fuel, choked and smothered by wet seaweed ere it could be consumed naturally. Yet he saw that first it had burned for some time. Now it was absolutely cold. He turned, still frowning in thought.

"This cannot be the fire we beheld on yester-night," Cormac said. "Else it were warm yet. That other fire burned too bright and it was too late; this was dead by then. *Seaweed* did this," and his voice indicated disbelief of his own words, gruesome and horrendous in their full implication. And—impossible.

With a jerk of his head as if to clear it of foreboding, he got on with what had to be said. "Some overwhelming mass of kelp with power of movement . . . and . . . hunger for *blood?* Aye. Be we mad, would ye be saying? *Kelp* smothered and soaked out the beacon-light. *Kelp* destroyed four strong men . . . by sucking . . . draining them pale and bloodless . . . and the fifth mindlessly sought escape by hurling himself from this window. And can any tell me how such things can be?"

They had no answers, but after a time Hrolf had another question.

"What was the luring fire we saw then?"

"I cannot say. Yet and well for us that we ignored it,

for it's not from this tower that light glowed!"

The four men of *Raven* stood suspended betwixt sky and sea, and with them lurked the glooming preternatural, and all was unreal.

CHAPTER FIVE: Irnic Break-ax

As the four men of *Raven* stood in that tower of the impossible and the unreal that was real, Knud broke the benumbed silence.

"Horsemen, Cormac! A goodly troop of them, leaving the city and coming down the quayside. Men of arms. They'll be here in a few minutes."

Cormac joined Knud at the tower's rim, looked, and saw that the Dane was correct. Too, he saw that his four were without hope of descending to the ground again ere the troop of horse-soldiers arrived. Be it so; they must meet the strangers openly, then. Cormac considered, he who'd earned a name for guile.

It did not follow that Wulfhere and all the crew must reveal themselves. Cormac liked having surprises in reserve when he dealt with strangers—particularly on their territory.

"WULFHERE!" he roared. The stentor voice he used had done credit to the Danish giant himself. "Riders will be upon us directly! They needn't know of all of us. Be getting half the men aboard *Raven,* sharp, ready to defend her or take to sea if need be. Do you and the others hide yourselves in yon patch of woodland! HIDE, I said! Be not *arguing,* man: *hurry!*"

And to those with him the Gael snapped, "Come."

While they made the swiftest descent they might, stamping and pounding down the tower's innumerable steps, Cormac mac Art was still thinking and inferring.

Predatory kelp that climbed a twice-lofty tower to take its human victims . . . that smothered out beacon-fires with great thoroughness *and then went away* . . . this argued intelligence to direct it. Its own? *Seaweed?* Was it belike a mindless vegetable mass in itself, whilst its master laired elsewhere, observing, directing—perhaps in the very city of Brigantium?

They reached the base of the tower and poured through the ironbound door.

Emerging from the tower of death, Cormac and his three faced a band of brightly-appareled Teutons who galloped down to the shore and hauled up with arrogantly superb horsemanship, to range themselves before the reivers. Staring. Waiting. Plainly these men were tense, and plainly it would take next to nothing to start them in to killing the strangers on their shore. As plainly, they were Sueves.

Moving toward them from the tower with deliberate slowness, Cormac studied the men of Galicia.

All were young, and warrior-nobles. Each bestrode a big Gothic destrier, dun or chestnut, whose harness flashed gems on leather well cared for by men in love with horses. A flame-red mantle was fastened upon their leader's thick, broad shoulder by a golden brooch large as his hand, jewelled with garnets like shining droplets of dried blood. The tunics of him and his followers were of various hues, all bright; short of sleeve they were and hardly descending to the wearers' bare knees. The borders of their green cloaks were crimson. Several wore shorter capes of wolf or fox fur as well. The sword each carried was a gift of his sovereign, mac Art knew, and could not be taken from these fiercely proud horse-warriors while they lived.

The hilts of those good swords thrust up from leather-covered wooden scabbards slung from baldrics and belted close on their hips; bright were those pommels, with decor of bronze and silver and gold. Sheathed at his belt each man wore a fighting knife as well; straight and heavy the vicious things were, and sharp enough along one edge for comfortable shaving. In the right hand every Sueve grasped an ax or nastily barbed spear. Shields with rims and bosses of gilded iron warded their left sides; these horses were trained to respond to voice and pressure of knee and heel.

Each man's brown or yellow hair was coiled atop his bare head in a thick figure-eight knot that Cormac noted made all appear even taller than they were—though probably no whit fiercer.

They stared at the strangers in *their* land, having come from *their* tower.

In the last possible instant ere the silence must have been destroyed violently, the leader spoke.

"Who are you? Whence come you, and what do you here, strangers?"

The language on his tongue was a German dialect. Cormac, fluent in one such and with experience of others, was able to make answer.

"Cormac mac Art of Eirrin. It's wind-driven I came here, in the ship you see yonder. As to what I do here—at present naught, save hope for a peaceful reception."

Had Cormac been a praying man, surely he'd have prayed then, for Wulfhere to remain hidden and not launch one of the howling shield-charges that were his favourite tactic on land. These riders bristled suspicion as they did weapons, but the Gael had them talking.

"Is it right I am in thinking this land must be Galicia?"

The noble who led the horse-warriors laughed, showing big square teeth framed by tawny moustaches. A weapon-man he was in truth; this, Cormac could see in confirmation of his instincts.

"Aye! Galicia is it, and you must surely be from far away. You talk to Irnic Break-ax, cousin to King Veremund. I lead his *comitatus*."

Cormac nodded. He was familiar with the word. A Latin borrowing, it was now common usage among the German nations, who applied it to an institution of their own; the king's band of sworn companions. They ate with him, hunted with him, rode to war with him, and if Fate so required, died with him. There could be no greater disgrace upon a *comes*-companion than to save his own life from the fight wherein his lord had fallen. In return they received rich gifts and honour and the chance of an unforgotten name.

Irnic Break-ax spoke more: "Yet when I put question, what do you here? I did mean *here*, before this tower. Strangers may come to Brigantium in ships and be welcome. Strangers poking about the lighthouse be another matter."

"Aye," growled one of the *comites*. "None would do that for any good purpose."

Others raised a mutter of agreement, and sounding through it came tones of unease and even fear.

Cormac asked bluntly, "Why?"

Irnic looked at him hard, obviously considering putting the sea-stained rogue in his place. Yet Cormac impressed as one who did not require to have this pointed out. Salt-crusted armour, faded nondescript cloak and all, he was a man who commanded other men. Irnic was such a man himself; he recognized the breed.

"Because," he said, "the tower has of late become haunted and accursed."

Cormac believed him.

"My lord Irnic, I never set eyes upon it erenow. Nor had I heard of it, save as a famous feat of building."

"Mayhap. We will make investigation of that. Gisivald, look after our guests and see they do not grow lonely. No harm is to befall them." Irnic's unspoken "yet" hung in the air like a hanged felon, and yielded about as much comfort. "They are not, though, to go aboard their ship, nor is the ship to leave."

Dismounting, he chose four men and led them into the tower of death. Cormac, Hrut, Hrolf and Knud stood well aside, in plain view of the score or so sea-fighters aboard *Raven*, the band of Suevic horsemen— and, so they judged and hoped, of Wulfhere and his small force within the nearby wood. The situation balanced on an ax-edge. Fortunate it was that all involved were used to such.

"Ahoy, Cormac!" Ivarr yelled from *Raven*'s low waist. "Ye bear weapons still, I see. Be ye needing help, or shall we bide as we are?"

The Danish words baffled Gisivald. "What said he?" the Sueve demanded.

"He's asking if need is with us for rescue. Shall I answer him?"

"Aye—carefully."

"Remain aboard, Ivarr! It's none so bad our chances are, of seeing out the day with our weapons dry." His words were uttered as much for Wulfhere as Ivarr of the sharp eyes. "It's king's men these be. I'm thinking when they leave we will have to go with them. Nor have I objection to that. Ah—should they be ordering ye to come ashore unweaponed, or to surrender *Raven*, ye know what answer to give, the very moment ye're able to stop laughing."

"That suffices," Gisivald said sharply. Too prolix an exchange in a language he could not understand was not to his liking, and his voice and tone showed it plain.

In time, Irnic Break-ax's head appeared over the tower's rim, tiny as a fly against the shining blue above him. After shouting intelligence that Cormac possessed already, the Sueve made descent and emerged. Question and answer were bandied.

"The same as before," Gisivald said at last, with moroseness.

"Aye. Men tracelessly slain—save that one is not there. Rechiaric."

"It's a broken body we're after finding among the rocks by the water's edge," Cormac offered. "Mayhap that's your missing man."

The Sueves went to the place along the quay on which stood the lighthouse, and examined the body.

"By his garb and accoutering, that's Rechiaric," Gisivald opined in a dull voice. "Eye of Wotan, little else is left to know him by!"

He lifted hard-clenched fists to the sky, and swore bitterly by other gods the Church dismissed as heathen devils. Cormac, impassively listening, took note with pleasure that any power the Dead God's priests might have among these men seemed scarcely to go deep. The Goths had imposed the Arian doctrine once, as a matter of form; however, naught Cormac heard had ever implied that forced acceptance had lasted long—or greatly impressed.

The man Rechiaric's shapeless corpse was wrapped in a mantle over-bright for a shroud. Scarlet and green, the Gael mused, were colours to be alive in. Five spare horses the Sueves had brought along, which now their comrades would never ride. The body went across the saddle of one, lashed in place. The others, cold in the high tower, could be fetched down later.

"Four horses, and four strangers to take before the

king," Irnic said. "It's an omen, clear as sunlight! Who says nay?"

He was asking his comrades. It was Cormac who made answer.

"We will accompany ye," he agreed. "Not as prisoners, though; we'll be retaining our arms. Else must ye take us along as ye take that one."

He jerked a thumb at the horribly shapeless package across the fifth spare horse.

"It's not impossible," Gisivald said.

"Not impossible, no." Irnic surveyed the four strangers. "Unnecessary is what I'd call it. There be twenty aboard yon dark ship, by my reckoning. Twenty of us remain here to watch them, leaving ten or a dozen to—escort our guests. Who have not the look of riders born."

Cormac disputed him not, and ignored Suevic chuckles. A good man, he thought, who'd observed his ship from the lofty window. Then a sudden thought and idea flashed upon the Gael. At first it seemed madness; yet it might work. There was none in this distant, largely isolated land able to prove it a lie . . . Clodia had nerve and ability to play the part . . . Surely the lass deserved a better time than she'd been having.

Besides, it might somehow be useful. Cormac turned.

"Ivarr, send *the Lady Clodia* ashore. We ride to audience with the king, and it's fain I am to present her. There be no reason why a *noblewoman* should kick her heels in the scuppers."

Ivarr, looking as if the world had turned upside down, nevertheless obeyed.

Clodia joined them in a seeming daze. At sight of her damp, sandy clothes, and the tangled mare's nest of her hair, Cormac was less sure she could carry it off; although the sea-crossing they had made would amply explain her appearance. He'd make assertion he had disguised her as a tavern bawd for some reason.

The story was thin, but it would do. Clodia—"the lady Clodia"—must convince by manner alone.

The Sueves were rocking with laughter at the three Danes' attempts to mount the tall Gothic war-horses. In their cold homeland was naught but ponies. Nor was the stirrup known among these men of the western world. The Persians had long used it, having borrowed the invention from the fierce Asian nomads they fought incessantly, but all of forty years would pass ere the great horse-general Belisarius would make it standard among the forces of the Empire. More decades would pass while the idea spread through the western kingdoms, until a simple iron device became the seed of the way of life that would replace Rome's. In the mean time Hrolf, Knud and big Hrut Bear-slayer provided the Sueves with a deal of merriment in their efforts to mount.

Their concealing mirth gave Cormac a moment to speak to Clodia. Few and imperative were the words he used.

"Carry this off, girl, and it's linen and unborn lamb's wool ye'll be walking in, belike. Fail, and it's tears of blood ye'll be weeping."

Clodia blinked. She'd spent the better part of a tormenting week on the sea. She'd grown to hate it. Too, there had been trying times both previously and after. Her head ached, and her stomach felt like a snail curled within her. The girl from Nantes was a far, far stretch from her best. Even so . . . he must be thinking her very slow. She forced thought from her exhausted brain.

"I'll carry it off," she whispered, with a coolness of voice and mien that indicated she was already entering her new role.

After a smile of grim approval, Cormac applied himself to getting a leg across a dun charger his clumsiness made restive. He performed better than any of the Danes for all that he was long years out of practice: Eirrin had tall splendid horses, and Cormac had ridden as a boy.

At last mounting in a bound, he clamped his right leg tightly while he lifted Clodia to perch before him. They set out, the Sueves matching their pace to the abilities of the strangers. They moved slowly. Within the narrow extended tongue of forest whose tip ended barely a stone's throw from the towering lighthouse, Wulfhere Hausakliufr watched them leave.

"Hel gnaw their bones!" he snarled. "The sows' abortions, the bow-legged sons of mares! That I let them ride away with my shipmates under guard! Nay, we can still make a raid to fetch them back, lads! This forest allows us cover even to the city wall. None knows we be here. With such advantage, can we not strike and win against ten times our number? What say ye?"

From his score of slayers came a fierce acceding rumble like a storm's first warning. Natheless, some shook their heads. Wulfhere glowered about, ice-eyed beneath thick brows like flame.

"Surt's burning sword! What ails you holdouts? D'ye fear Cormac will be slain and we make trouble? Small likelihood of that. He's not bound, nor even disarmed."

"And that's why, captain," Makki Grey-gull stuck out his lip gloomily. "They four went not like prisoners. Think ye *Cormac* had accompanied them with never a blow struck, an they had not spoken him fair? What's in his mind I cannot say. I'm just thinking we should wait and see."

Jostein the Grinner supported him. "He brought the wench ashore—*Lady* Clodia. He'd not have done that were he thinking of battle. He's some trick under his helm, sure. He shouted as much—at the top of his voice."

Wulfhere simmered with ire, and clutched his huge ax for self-control until his knuckles were as fleshless. And saw the force of their arguments.

"Well, this much is true," he grumbled without pleasure. "Can any man talk his way out of such a situation, the Wolf's he. Nor will we help his case do we rush in hewing."

"Aye!" Makki said eagerly. "An those horse-riders intend murder—" (this from a man with eight lives to answer for in the land of his birth) "—there's no preventing it now. But we can take such a vengeance that all the world will know of it, beginning with that lot." He gestured at the twenty Sueves between them and *Raven*. "With Ivarr and the lads aboard, we outnumber 'em twofold, and have 'em from two sides. We can crush them as grain milled in a quern. Or capture most living, to ransom Cormac and the rest, an that seems the better course. Those be their king's own hearth-companions, Wulfhere. It's good bargaining-counters they'd make."

Agreement was upon the others by this time. Wulfhere gnawed strands of his fiery beard, not liking to wait, and yet aware this was but his notorious lack of patience.

"Look you," he growled, "we will tarry till night falls or something else occurs. We will keep close watch on *Raven,* and these fools who think they be guarding her. Suppose dusk is here and no word has come; then we go aboard again, and should any try to prevent us, their women will bewail them. Although . . . I scarce think it will mean waiting so long as that. Even a city like Brigantium cannot be that deep asleep." He showed his men a piratical grin.

Jostein gave vent to a jaw-cracking yawn. "Talking of

sleep, let us wake in shifts of five, as when we stand night watches. I long to stretch out on soft leaves, and here we have 'em."

The others gave even more ready agreement to that. Wulfhere was astounded. His men must be growing soft. Granted, it had been a strenuous few days, but they had eaten and enjoyed a full night's sleep, and done naught since save row a mile or two, and talk much. Dane-mark was not breeding them as she once had.

CHAPTER SIX: The King of Galicia

Surrounded by watchful men whose hands rode their pommels as if casually, Cormac mac Art was escorted inland. Aye, there was old Brigantium harbour; another relic of Rome not yet moribund, and here the old city that was, Roman stone looking leprosy-afflicted, peopled by foreigners to these shores. Cormac passed through it without glancing to either side of the crumbling, pitted street. The Gael towered tall, and his helmet with its flowing crest added to his appearance of great height.

Dogs stared at him, quivering in limbs and nostrils, ears cocked forward, quietly rumbling without really growling. A little beast the hue of calf-excrement came on the run, yapping. The swipe of one soldier missed him; the spear-butt of another sent him tumbling while changing his yaps into squeals. The pup fled. Children, too, stared, and their mothers wound protective arms around them from behind—and stared.

I probably look Roman, Cormac mused without humour. *It's been a long time for these people.* And since he wore his weapons, the stranger couldn't be a captive —could he?

"Head straight; look ahead," the Gael muttered to

the woman before him on the plodding dun, and Clodia did. She also stayed very close. He was aware now that he'd taken out much frustration on her.

These were a mixed people, he saw, without distaste for hair of various hues and nigh as many dark eyes as blue and grey; those native to this land so long ago had married—and bred with, without marrying—the Roman conquerors. Now some had mingled their blood too with the Suevi that Constantius the Illyrian had driven into this northwest corner of Hispania. And they stared at the dark, scarred man with the grey eyes and the armour coat of linked chain. Only the burly smith did not stare; he was an ever busy man who but glanced, and went on pounding lest his sheet of yellow-glowing metal cool.

Hail Smith, Cormac thought, and the corners of his thin-lipped mouth twitched as if contemplating a smile. They discarded the notion.

The remnant of Rome ended. The former manse had been all but destroyed; King Veremund had his own keep.

Stony earth from a curving ditch ten or so feet deep was banked on its opposite side, and a single bridge of planking crossed the trench that would do no more than slow mounted attackers. Cormac glanced down at muck, and wrinkled his nose. He and Clodia and their escort crossed over to the sprawling grounds about the king's hall.

As the king was in truth little more than a tribal chieftain of what anciently had been a confederation rather than a distinct tribe or family group, his dwelling was no palace. Under its thatched roof it was but a large Germanic keep with gable-ends carved ornately into ghastly gryphons and corbels covered with a catenulate design. The fine great door of oak stood open. A weapon-man went forward to draw aside the hanging there: a door-sized sheet of fine softened narwhal. The heavy arras was stamped in an overall pattern with a seal or property mark consisting of three concentric circles centered with a horizontal oval that Cormac saw represented a watchful eye.

He continued with the Clodia masquerade, handing her down and astonishing the dirty rag-tag young woman by stepping aside in manner courtly. After giving him a look she thought austerely highborn, she went in. Cormac, stooping exaggeratedly low, passed into the hall of the king.

Now all must wait in an anteroom or defense-hall whilst Irnic in his scarlet Roman cloak went somewhere within. There were no sentries. Cormac stood easy. He knew that one must ever wait while the wearer of a diadem was apprised of one's presence. He also knew that a messenger had already galloped here on just that mission, and the Gael prepared himself to dislike the Suevic lord of Galicia.

Nor was there aught unusual in that; mac Art of Eirrin had had nothing good of kings but only treachery —and if there had been good of them too, he'd forgot it because he wanted to do.

The officer returned and Cormac was conducted into the presence of the king.

Others were there of course, the advisers and hangers-on called courtiers who ever clung about thrones. Cormac was careful not to notice them or even the young woman directly beside the high seat. He kept his dispassionate gaze fixed steadily on the man seated atop a two-step dais. He wore a robe dyed brightly in the vermilion hue of the *minium* brought up from the bed of the nearby River Mino, and its hem was purfled with cloth-of-gold.

He was tallish in the body and short in the leg, neither pale nor dark, neither handsome nor ill-favored. He'd a good brow and big hands. His twisted topknot, brown like his beard and droop-ended mustache, was worn over his right ear so as to accommodate his royal diadem. This was an inch-high band of gold sheet doubtless laid on over bronze plaques. The violet stones called almandines decorated it, with an interesting fleck of winking mica and two fair garnets, dull and lifeless amid the gleaming purple stones, which were convex. His swordbelt, mark of the military men of which he of course was supreme commander, was similarly decorated and the buckle appeared moulded of pure gold, in twisted bands like a fine torc.

Behind him hung a nicely woven tapestry, showing a battle or two and centering on the same eye-in-circles sigil that decorated the door-hanging. Cormac recognized a tall vase as Greek, stolen long and long ago.

Only another minor king, Cormac thought, remembering how Hengist had styled himself "king" in Kentish Britain when the Jutish pirate had but three hundred followers and perhaps a score of horses. The most notable aspect of this one was that he was little older than his visitor, and that he was making no effort to look ferocious. The Gael tried not to be impressed.

"Veremund, *Rex Suevorum!*" a voice announced from the king's left, without bothering to mention Galicia. Cormac didn't bother to glance at the annunciator.

"Who are you," King Veremund said, in a baritone that sounded more like a well-controlled tenor. "Why are you come here?"

Rather than answer, Cormac stepped aside and swung a courtly arm out to his companion of the torn skirt. "May I introduce to the lord King of the Sueves the Lady Clodia, of the Roman Kingdom of Soissons, and lately of Tours. Affianced through blackmail of her father to the hideous monster Sigebert One-ear, and now fleeing in quest of protection."

Ah, Sigebert mine deadly enemy—how ye'd be loving those words—dog!

The king leaned forward. "A Frankish noblewoman, here? Fleeing a legal betrothal arranged by your father, my lady?"

Bad cess, Cormac thought, and only just managed to seem unhasty in his reply: "A betrothal into which her most misfortunate father was scurrilously tricked and forced, my lord King. Indeed, her father is more than pleased that his lady daughter is after escaping the thrice-cruel Sigebert."

Clodia sopped that up like bread in the gravy, and essayed to appear the lady. *She succeeds,* Cormac thought, *about as well as I might.* Veremund gazed at her for a time, muttered "Lady Clodia" without further committing himself or his land, and leaned back. Again he looked upon mac Art.

"It's Cormac mac Art I am, a Gael of Eirrin—though not for these eight long years, lord King." And a little murmur rose in the great hall.

"Cormac, mac, Art," Veremund said, enunciating elaborately, and he smiled to let his visitor know he was known here. Fame—and infamy, Cormac thought—be damned. "The 'mac' is 'son of', is it not?"

"Aye, lord King."

"And the Lady Chlodia is not your woman." This time Veremund gave her name the Gothic rather than the Roman pronunciation, in the way that "Childeric" and "Hilderic" were the same name, depending upon who uttered it, and where.

"No, lord King! *Not* my woman," Cormac said as though shocked. "But under my protection."

Someone snorted. Cormac continued to gaze upon Veremund, who nodded and leaned a bit to one side, resting his arm and looking thoughtfully at the two strangers to his land. Now Cormac allowed his peripheral vision to take in the woman seated beside the king, on his left. Several years younger—indeed in her teens, surely—she was perhaps the queen, except that she bore strong resemblance to Veremund. Cormac wondered whether under his beard the king too had a strong chin, and dimpled.

The Gael was also sure that the young woman's pale blue eyes were regarding him appraisingly.

Veremund asked, "You bore my lady Clodia away from Tours?"

"From Nantes, my lord Veremund—a few spearlengths ahead of King Clovis's Loire fleet. We durst not venture south along the coast, as milord of Burdigala has a . . . quarrel with me and my comrades. It's the whole coast his ships are now patrolling, searching for our ship."

"*Raven.*"

Hardly out of touch, these folk whose shipping or shores I've never raided, Cormac noted, and said, "Aye, my lord. So . . . it's down to your shore we sailed, in hopes of finding a more friendly reception and fair trade for . . . a few items of trade that my lord Veremund, King, surely had more need of than the Visigoths for whom they were intended."

Someone among the nobles collected around the king chuckled appreciatively; a different voice laughed its scorn. Veremund again sat forward, having noted the visitor's first words more than his last.

"You crossed Treachery Bay?"*

---

* The Bay of Biscay. Its Roman names are Sinus Aquitanicus and Sinus Cantabricus, or Cantaber Oceanus, Cantanabria being Calicia's eastern neighbour, sprawled in a thin strip across most of the northern coast of Hispania. Only those who live far from it call that lovely body of water the Cantabrian Sea; to those who know it, it is ever the Bay of Treachery.

"Aye, my lord. And—"

"There has been a *storm! Storms.*"

Cormac nodded solemnly. "Aye, lord King, and storm and sea like to have swallowed us, I make admission without shame."

Now Cormac glanced significantly about him, for the first time noting the few men gathered here: Suevi under their tortured hair, darker Hispano-Romans though in the same short, decorated tunics, and a bald old man in a black-girt robe of aquamarine. Some looked most impressed and some were manifestly trying not to appear so; all stared at Cormac mac Art.

"A feat indeed, Cormac mac Art." Veremund glanced over his nobles. "And from stories that have reached these ears concerning yourself and the Dane Wulfhere, I am not disposed to disbelieve the unbelievable of you. Nor am I loath to welcome such intrepid sailors . . . who have brought such embarrassment to the Goths! And . . . why were you in Nantes, Cormac mac Art?"

"Seeking a market, lord King, for some items of trade."

"Items of trade."

"Aye. A Gothic merchant-ship's master is after seeing fit to bestow them on us a few days erenow . . . at the mouth of the Garonne."

"Even there!" one of the nobles exclaimed.

Cormac was in a king's presence; he did not respond to that, but kept his eyes fixed on Veremund. Veremund gestured for him to continue, and a little smile lifted the corners of the king's reddish-brown mustache.

"Aye my lord King of the Sueves, and it was right swiftly we coursed northward to Frankish shores. For my lord of Burdigala is after dispatching a pair of warships—and them crowded with snarly marines—to hurry us on our way. Though in truth is was to *slow* us those men sought, and that more than somewhat!"

Laughter ran through those others in the hall of the king, and Veremund smiled.

"Ye tell me that in the space of a se'en-day, Cormac mac Art of Hivernia, ye've raided the Gothic shores even at the mouth of the Garonne; succeeded both in plundering a merchanter and eluding warships; slipped into the Loire well north, stole this lady from her affianced—her wicked affianced—out-shipped my lord King Clovis's warships—which are huge and Romish—*And* crossed Treachery Bay to these shores."

"During a storm," Clodia reminded, and the hall exploded into laughter.

Cormac was nodding. "And, regrettably lord King, found evidence of murderous sorcery or worse in your own beacon-tower." Cormac paused while all laughter stilled and every face went sober, and then he added, "And so came willingly here with your men."

Veremund considered, gazing upon the tall and rangy pirate before him, and him darker of face than any present save the Hispano-Romans. The king turned his ring again and again with thumb and knuckle of the adjacent finger.

"It is in my mind that the waters you have been plying no longer hold much welcome for yourself, Cormac mac Art. Or prospect of continued health."

"Truth, lord King. But it's ever temporary such reverses are, and it's a large world we habit."

"Of a surety, and none will be crossing Treachery Bay after you! And . . . were Veremund of Galicia to tell you that ye be more than welcome here, and further that . . . he has offer of *employment* to ye, Cormac mac Art?"

"Despite my thirst and growing stiffness in my legs," Cormac said, for no son of Eirrin bent very low before kings, "it's listening I'd be, lord King. Methinks my lord of the Sueves would be borrowing from the wisdom of the Vandals, and seek to turn a landbound people into seafaring men?"

There had been a little murmur at Veremund's carefully phrased offer; another followed Cormac's straightforward words. Veremund's eyebrows lifted high and his eyes twinkled no less than the fleck of mica in his diadem.

"Ye be no fool, Cormac mac Art, as evidenced afore by your speaking plain truth to me. In this wise, too, ye be correct. You and the Dane ye've long sailed with are surely the very men to aid me in floating a fleet and training up men to ply it. How say you?"

Amid a murmur in the hall, Cormac shifted his weight from his left foot to his right. "Myself says I'd not be disagreeing, lord King. But it's Wulfhere Splitter of skulls who masters *Raven* our ship, and it's him I'd be counselling with."

"And where be Wulfhere the Dane?"

Smiling, Cormac said, *"About,* my lord . . . with others, watching those who watch our ship and doubtless waiting to learn if I require rescue."

There were gasps, but Veremund smiled as if in spite of himself. Then he chuckled. "Watching my watchers?"

"Oh my lord, your men at the shore outnumber him and his only by two to one, and that Captain Wulfhere does not consider even a fair match—for himself."

This time Veremund leaned back laughing. Others stared the while at mac Art and the king and the pretty girl who sat so near him in her white gown frosted with cloth-of-silver, and looking large-eyed on the Gael.

"Surely, brother," she said, in a quite high voice fresh with youth, "this is the boldest and most outspoken man ever to stand before you in this hall!"

Madb's breasts, Cormac thought, *his sister! Another damned unwed princess! The bane of my life!*

107

"Surely!" Veremund called, with his laughter slowly waning. And then he stopped it on a sudden, and looked full at her. "And one of the most dangerous, Eurica."

"Then why does he wear his weapons?"

"Because, my dear sister, it were *doubly* dangerous to seek to deprive a brave man of pride of his weapons," and Cormac knew this king was wise.

She gazed coolly upon Cormac. "Then might it not be wise to have him slain at once and scour our shores for his Danish comrade and others who may be hiding?"

Cormac mac Art kept his gaze on the king, and did not twitch his eyebrows. He looked cool, rather than dangerous—which assured observant men of wisdom that he was indeed a dangerous man.

"My sister is not known to be a fool, Cormac mac Art."

So it's to be a test, is it, and originating in this little girl all excited about the big pirate from the sea! "Indeed, lord King. The Lady Eurica may speak true, though detention were ever wiser than slaying out of hand—or attempting to do."

Someone laughed. Eurica stared angrily. Her brother now kept his eyebrows steady.

"It is true," Cormac added, "that though I pledge no acts against you or any of your people, kindness for kindness, neither Wulfhere nor I will vow fealty to yourself—or any other."

The small female voice piped, "Or to me, Cormac mac Art of Hivernia?"

Cormac ignored her, continuing to gaze at her brother. The girl stamped her foot.

"Ye make my lady sister no reply, Cormac mac Art?"

"Lord King. My business here is audience with the King of the Suevi, who would be building a navy—and who has another problem that comes not from this natural world, surely. I'm after standing before kings erenow, and know how to behave. It's fearful I am of doing insult on my lord by answering the queries of someone my lord King has not given permission to question me."

The thick silence that followed those words might have presented challenge to the well-sharpened blade of Cormac's dagger. Then the lady Princess Eurica rose with swift youthful sinuousness and a rustling of white skirts. Her sky-blue eyes flashed under darkened, down-drawn brows.

"As you said, lady sister, the boldest and most outspoken man to come before us. And . . . his point is well taken." Veremund looked mildly up at his sister, who, thoughtlessly, with her anger on her, now stood higher than a king.

"I'll not be chastised by a reaver from oversea and him with the stench of kelp about him!"

"Lord King," Cormac said quietly, "as it's naught but your good will I'm wishing, I make apology for bearing still the stench of that unholy stuff that slew your sea-tower watch . . . and I make apology too to your royal self for having angered your lady sister."

Standing close beside her seated brother, Eurica stamped her foot. "And still he speaks not to me, nor looks at *me!*"

The Gael pressed his lips together. With slow deliberation and as if stiff of neck, he turned his head just enough to look into the anger-bright blue eyes of the Lady Eurica, who appeared very young indeed. He studied her face for a space, then moved his gaze slowly down her slim, white-clad form to her very toes in their beaded felt slippers, and then back up again, as slowly, to her face. It flamed, now. She stared. Her mouth worked and silver flashed as her bosom heaved. Her hands formed knobby little fists.

With slow deliberation, Cormac gave his head the quarter-turn necessary to return his gaze to her brother.

Himself no fool, Veremund rose to end the tension. He made a snuffing sound in his throat. "We must needs bring Wulfhere Skull-splitter among us, Cormac the Bold."

"Cormac the Rude!"

"Unseemly, lady sister," Veremund said, without looking at her he now made seem small, by his standing beside her. He was the king; she was a girl in her mid-teens, unmarried because he was still pondering, Cormac was sure, the options open to form alliances.

Veremund descended the two steps of the little dais on which rested his throne of oak set with gold and coral, and rune-carved. Eurica need not be embarrassingly dismissed; the king, with the Gael, was leaving her presence. As Veremund walked to Cormac and bade him accompany him, only his topknot brought him an inch above the Gael's height of six feet.

"Ah—please have the Lady Clodia seen to, Zarabdas," the king said, and he and Cormac mac Art left the chamber and the hall.

The king and a little retinue of fighting men rode with Cormac, whose shout soon fetched up Wulfhere and the others. And still others, to the astonishment and consternation of the men set to watch *Raven*. Veremund ordered the setting up of two pavilions without the gates of the old city for the crew of *Raven*, and he turned to the Gael.

"Unless ye'll not be separated from your men, Cormac mac Art, you and Wulfhere will be quartered in my own hall."

Cormac bowed his head, and looked at the giant ambling toward them.

"The king would have converse with us, Wulfhere."

Wulfhere nodded, beaming, and shifted his grip on an ax whose weight should by now have stretched his right arm to his ankle. "Be there ale in Galicia?"

CHAPTER SEVEN: Bargain in Silver

There was ale in Galicia. Veremund and his people though, like the Romans, were drinkers of wine. Wulfhere downed a great mug of ale for his thirst before swiftly tucking away a flagon of wine to make his hosts happy. Then he was ready for ale again, and his hosts, seeing what sort of respect he had for their wine, did not say him nay.

In a low-beamed room whose walls were hung with draperies and tapestries that helped retain heat in winter and to ward it off in summer, they conferred: Veremund the King, and Cormac of Connacht in Eirrin, and Wulfhere of the land of the Danes—Dane-terre, Veremund's people called it, for all the folk of this continent were more Romanized than they knew.

With them were Veremund's tawny-moustached cousin and adviser, Irnic Break-ax; and the lean, bald, robed man of fifty or so years. Zarabdas of Palmyra his name, and him in a silver purfled, black-girt robe of aquamarine blue. From his belt hung an almoner of black leather. A ring gleamed with the dullness of gold on one knob-knuckled finger: a very old ring that seemed to consist of two twined serpents. A segmented sigil glinted on his breast, slung by a silver chain around his neck: a circle with wings. A winged sun, Cormac surmised, though it was no druidic emblem.

Zarabdas took ale but scant touched his lips to the glazed mug of vermilion pottery. Irnic had wine set before him in a goblet of beaten silver set with blue stones of some sort and what appeared, impressively, to be an emerald. He did not touch it. If a man of Irnic's height—which was far from great—should have weighed a hundred and seventy pounds, Irnic probably carried fifteen pounds more. Nor, Cormac thought, impressed with the gaunt-faced fellow's control and condition, could there be an ounce of fat on him. Irnic Break-ax was built for fighting.

The Gael had naturally been prepared to dislike the king, and instead liked him; the fellow wasn't a monarch, he was a man! As for a king's cousin made adviser—he should have been fat and impossible. The Lord Irnic was neither, and Cormac gave him respect.

As for the dusky man from the palmy deserts around ancient Palmyra, the fellow had the feel of sorcery about him, and only one sorcerer had Cormac mac Art ever trusted.

That man had been a druid, his name Sualtim Fodla. He was nearly nine years dead. He was long mentor to the boy Art's son of Connacht had been, and Cormac was long past those days. Indeed, it seemed a score of years agone when he'd been the more than promising young weapon man in Connacht, and then in Leinster, until the treachery of kings and his own momentary hot-headedness had resulted in his exile.

Zarabdas's twin beard was black as the wing of the raven, and Cormac had to wonder if the bald fellow weren't dyeing it. The five men sat, most privily, at table. Ere they could begin to discuss ships and shipbuilding, crew and payment, Cormac brought up

113

the matter of the vampire weed from the sea. When Zarabdas frowned, the Gael fixed him with a narrow-eyed look and recounted what he and his shipmates had discovered.

"This is the second time those managing the light-tower have fallen to such an attack," Irnic said, who was in general command of the horse-soldiers of little Galicia. "Though on the previous occasion," he said with teeth tightly set, "there were no signs of the killer of three men."

"None?"

"None, Cormac mac Art. For that reason I ordered the crew increased to five."

"And they died," Wulfhere said, "just as three did."

"The solution is not in numbers," Cormac said. He sat back, legs asprawl, and toyed with the mug he stared at. "My lord Irnic . . . it is in my mind—I cannot be sure, o'course—that . . . the deadly kelp we found is somehow *directed*. With intelligence behind it, I mean."

Mac Art gazed only at the mug, but saw nonetheless that Zarabdas frowned and seemed to arrange his features into a scoffing expression. Zarabdas appeared Irnic's opposite: he must have weighed ten or so pounds less than whatever was normal for his height and his weight. In consequence he looked taller than he was, and his face was wrinkled like that of an old hound of Britain.

Cormac said, "Else why did the vampire weed *withdraw* after it did death on those manning the tower, and leave no trace of its presence or nature?"

"Such things are not possible," Zarabdas said, in his voice that was dry as wind through the desert whence he came. "I would see such seaweed with these eyes."

"An I see the kelp again, it's calling ye I'll be. See ye bring a sharp blade."

114

Immediately Veremund snuffed, in his throat. "I am most pleased you are here, Wulfhere and mac Art. And I admit, Zarabdas, I am impressed with this canny Gael. His mind works logically even when it reaches an apparently illogical conclusion."

Wulfhere tipped more ale into his mug. "Oh, it does that, all right."

Cormac gave the king a little smile. A good man for avoiding trouble, this Veremund of the Suevi! "Myself has had thoughts on the matter. I'd be coming forward in an attempt to remove such a danger, an we're to be dealing otherwise with my lord king."

"Good!" Veremund and Irnic said, almost together, and they smiled each at the other then, so that Cormac knew they were friends.

"The weed," Cormac said, "fears me."

"*Fears* you?" Irnic echoed.

"And how is that?" Zarabdas asked, nor was his tone solely that of one seeking information.

Cormac tugged at the chain around his neck until he'd drawn up the Egyptian sigil from beneath his tunic. He displayed it with a dramatic air of significance.

In truth, the Gael had no notion of the thing's meaning, or if it had one . . . or indeed if it was aught other than jewellery, which he did not wear. As he had thought it wise to lie about Clodia's station, he was minded now to impress these people and create some mystery—and to test the Palmyran, who was bending forward to gaze upon the sigil. Zarabdas's mahogany eyes peered keenly, like those of a hunting hawk.

Cormac said, "It is not merely by armour and arms of good steel that I am protected, my lords."

Cormac was gambling. Superstition held power even over kings. For aught he knew it was a bit of jewellery, this odd sigil that hung glittering on his mailed chest. He knew of no magickal significance it held. Nor was he the sort to rely on such even when their repute as talismans was established. No, it was that he had need, though, to impress these people. Too, he wanted to test the king's mage, who had bent forward to stare closely at the golden serpent. Zarabdas's narrow right hand was crooked possessively around the solar disc on his own thin breast. Cormac had observed how the Palmyran fondled it constantly.

As for the king, he was gazing questioningly at mac Art.

"It's from slumbering Egypt this *bauble* comes, and men have killed each other for it. Excepting the most ignorant of them, that slaying was not merely for its value as precious metal." Cormac paused for effect. "I am content to test its powers in your deathly tower, lord King, in attempt to remove the danger. As I believe I can."

Veremund disrupted the silence so that Zarabdas jerked; the king brought a hand down on the table in a slap of decision.

"A noble offer," Veremund said, "to be treated nobly!" And he strode to the door, which he flung wide so that it banged echoically. He gave the ornate ring from his first finger to a guard in a leather war shirt studded with iron. "Take this for authority, and fetch me Motsognir's Chain from the treasure room."

Turning back swiftly, Veremund surprised gape-jawed looks of consternation on the faces of Irnic and Zarabdas. Their dismay did not escape Cormac, or Wulfhere either. While the reivers did not know what Motsognir's Chain might be, they grasped well that it was kept in the treasure room. They traded glances of bland meaning.

"My lord—" Zarabdas ventured.

"I know to the word what is on your tongue to say. Let it rest."

Zarabdas let it rest. Nobody said aught more. Mage and horse-soldier were clearly plagued by unease, while the king's guests were all waiting attention. Veremund himself did not seem disposed to talk until he had that which he'd sent for, and wise men obliged kings.

It came.

Three strong servitors were bent by the weight of the thing called Motsognir's Chain. The guard led them. Behind, the very mirror of grave dignity, came a Hispano-Roman in grey and tawny brown, with a ring of ornate keys stapled to his belt. Anthemius his name, they soon learned: he kept the king's monetary records and had responsibility for the royal strong room. Hair stuck out in grey and russet shingles from his oddly-shaped skull. His eyes blinked and watered much.

Him the two sea-rovers scarce gave a glance. The great chain was forged of nine times nine massy links and each was deeply incised with an ancient rune. Through the last—or first—link ran a large iron ring, a circle of smaller runes cut around it.

Every link was of shining silver.

"Aye, look well," Veremund bade his guests. "This thing came from the land of my fathers, long agone, when they saw rivers but never in all their lifetimes the sea. The dwarves made it. It bears the name of their king. Time out of mind has it been the chief treasure of the Suevic kings. Anthemius: how burn the trench-fires?"

"Low, lord King. However, we feasted late and the coals are hot still. I have had the great hall cleared and more fuel thrown on. None will be there to gawk."

"That's well. Wulfhere Hausakliufr, Cormac mac Art —what you see now you will long remember. It is my

117

desire that you speak no word of it in Brigantium. This chain has a special property, the which is hardly a secret, but . . . one does not make public display of such. Thus it is dismissed as rumour even ten leagues away, and thus there be fewer ambitious thieves to guard against."

Veremund led the way to his long dining-hall. His serving men laid the chain out straight on the floor's strewn rushes. Beside it, the long fire-trench breathed hard dry heat between its stone hearths. At the king's bidding, Wulfhere paced the chain, nor was Wulfhere loath to do so. Twelve strides took him from end to end of Motsognir's Chain—though his strides were a deal longer than most men's.

"Twelve," he rumbled.

Veremund gestured to his serving men. They lifted the chain and walked forward, the chain hanging down in curves between them like a mighty silver serpent. With a concerted lift and heave, they flung it into the fire. None need say aught; all watched. The silver chain curled and writhed in that heat like a thing alive, a bright segmented worm with a black head.

Is it to come alive, then? Cormac wondered, and his nape-hairs stirred. His swift-swerving eyes checked the positions of other men, lest he must fight; his was not an unsuspicious mind, ever.

Flames obscured the chain. Heat struck the reivers' eyeballs as they peered closer. Sight blurred in the smoke. They narrowed their lids.

"Cormac," Wulfhere muttered only half aloud, "an the thing be not *changing,* Fenris eat me!"

"Aye," and the Gael did not ask, *changing how?* He'd sight as keen as Wulfhere's, and he seldom put questions with small likelihood of useful answers. He watched. They all watched.

At last the chain went still. Veremund the king gave

orders. With a long-handled iron hook, his serving men fished it from the trench-fire. The hook was for hot cauldrons; the chain was hot, and they stretched it hearthside a second time so that it lay cooling.

"Captain Wulfhere: will you tell me its length now?" the king invited, smiling.

Wulfhere Skull-splitter looked at him, wondering if he were being made sport of. A pointless sort of joke . . . but he trod the measure again—and stopped in bewilderment ere he reached the chain's end.

"*Twelve!*" he announced, and paced on. "And . . . five more! Cormac! 'Tis nigh half as long again as it was!"

"Right you are, Captain," Veremund smiled. "Such is its property: the chain grows in fire. The longer since it was last so heated, the more it grows—whereby you will see there are limits to the wealth it can provide. A too-greedy man might even exhaust its powers."

"Like that yarn of the goose that laid golden eggs."

"Aye. One must be sparing, and cunning smiths and armourers such as I must have do not labour cheaply. Another reason why this curse on my harbour-tower is so dire. I have been seeking to increase Galicia's sea-trade, which has been worse than poor these last thirty years—and by Ertha!" The pagan oath slipped out unregarded. "Such as this business in the tower could ruin all!" Veremund grimaced, made his little throaty snuffing noise, and grew calm. "However, Motsognir's Chain is still a bauble worth the having. And settles, methinks, any doubt as to whether I can properly gift those who do me service."

"My lord King understates," Cormac said. "And impresses us much, as I daresay we show. Yet were it wise to show such treasure to outland pirates?"

He's spoken the very thought the king had warned Irnic and Zarabdas not to utter, and he knew it. Yet this ought to be said thus plainly at the outset, and answered in the same way.

The king spoke. *"Zarabdas."*

The mage's hand rose to the winged solar disk that hung pendent on his chest. The while he stared at Cormac mac Art, who met that gaze. Numbness and darkening entered into his mind. He felt a sense of heaviness; a great weight seemed to grow in him, as if Motsognir's chain had been looped about him invisibly, and that without pressing more on one part of his body than another. Like the chain, the sensation grew, a steady, increasing drag throughout his entire organism. Cormac's very bowels sagged in his belly. His bones went leaden. The blood ceased to flow in his hands, pooling heavily in hands he could scarce lift. His heart laboured. The thought came, and with it horror: *Any tyro sworder could take me now!* He sweated. He struggled to move. His very bones seemed to have gone heavier and were dragging at his muscles, down, heavy, heavier. . . . The inexorable weight rooted him to the floor and grew still stronger. The Gael gan tremble with the stark effort of merely standing upright.

"Cormac!" Wulfhere stormed. "What's wrong, man?" He rounded on Zarabdas. "Ye scrawny wizard! Whate'er it is ye're at, stop it *now*—else I'll see your head this chain's length apart from your body!"

Zarabdas did not look to his king for guidance. Closing his eyes, he lowered his hand from the winged symbol of Behl. A cool breath of air seemed to waft over Cormac then, and slowly natural feeling returned. It was accompanied by a tingling, as though circulation had been cut off in every part of his body. He staggered, forced to advance a foot to keep from falling.

"It's sentimental ye're after growing in your eld, Wulfhere," he said, striving not to gasp.

The giant Dane snorted and shot Zarabdas another look.

"Your query is answered, mac Art," King Veremund said. "Wulfhere Hausakliufr: I did not care overmuch for your way of speaking, a moment past. Let me hear no repetition of such threats against my honoured servant. Was I gave this command. Take the matter up with me, if you wish."

Wulfhere looked back at him truculently, and tension trembled on the air. "The mac Art is my comrade," he said, nor did he add "my lord."

"I do not ignore that; was why I spoke ye so gently, Captain. Now hear my word! Rid this coast of the sea-born death that haunts it, and that for me will amply prove your worth. Do you but agree, I'll make you immediate dower of this new growth of silver chain. Do you succeed, you shall have the weight of your own mighty ax and haft, Captain Wulfhere. Too, you'll not find me niggard later, an you twain decide to commence the training of seamen from among my people."

Wulfhere looked at Cormac, who said, "Fair enow." Wulfhere nodded, but a man must bargain for his own self-respect. "The weight of my ax, and Cormac's sword."

The king gestured. "Done. And here will ever be safe anchorage and guest-right for you and yours. Though the world and the gods be against you, I will be for you."

Cormac swallowed. *King,* he mused, *the praises and promises other kings have heaped on me ere this, ye'd not believe. And what they then did to me, ye'd all too readily believe.* He and Wulfhere exchanged a look, though, and nodded.

"Good!" Veremund said, and he chuckled. "I feared you might demand the impossible: your own weight in silver, Master of *Raven!* —Battle-girt."

The reivers laughed; the Dane's ax, buckler, helm, and coat of scale-mail ran close onto a hundred pounds. In them, Wulfhere's weight approached four hundred.

"And if I fasted a day before the weighing?" Wulfhere offered heroically.

Amid laughter, the king's offer was accepted, and hands were clasped on the bargain. "Now I have other duties, and do sore wish you could handle them for me," Veremund said. "Let us confer again at eventide; come sup with me. Anthemius, see this is known. By now a room has been prepared for you twain, here in my hall."

First the king took hammer and chisel and himself parted the new-grown length of chain from the original. This was an act forbidden on pain of slow death to any hands but the king's own—and with reason, as he explained. Were any link of the parent chain broken, its power would be lost. Anthemius blanched with horror at the notion. Two pirates quite shared his feelings.

Motsognir's Chain went back to the treasure room. The reivers made great gesture of good faith and sent their portion there also—as they had no safer place at present for its stowing. The five plotters parted company. A bright-eyed, most impressed lad had been delegated to serve the wants of the visitors, and he conducted them to the good clean room they would share. There Cormac and Wulfhere at last disencumbered themselves of their armour. Both sighed and Cormac remembered Clodia's comments on his armour and padded underjack. A man worked and fought and even slept in his battle-gear until he forgot he'd not been born in the stuff. It was when it came ringing and sliding ajingle off him that he noticed the difference.

They refused offers of royal servants; these two

professionals would inspect and clean their own weapons and mail. Good oil they requested, for leather, and rags. These they used methodically, along with fine sand, on Cormac's finely wrought chain and Wulfhere's scale sewn on leather.

The king's table for dinner, Cormac thought. *We be rising in the world!* And when asked what else he required, he named it: a bath. Mir, the boy loaned them as attendant, looked more than surprised. The Sueve were hardly so fond of bathing as were the Eirrin-born —as indeed were none on the ridge of the world save the Romans. They had left public baths of a sort in Brigantium, though the Roman plumbing had long since failed of its function. They were conducted thence, though the lad seemed ashamed, that such heroes might require that which was so effete—and that his friends might see him contributing to this Romish softness on the part of the king's guests.

Here water was heated in long open vats, not in the boilers of old. Steam was made by dashing water over glowing hot stones. Such an arrangement Wulfhere of course took for granted; it put him in mind of northern sweat-baths—though Galicia lacked snow to roll in after. Natheless, he admitted that it felt very good.

His disappointment in them and these wants did not make Mir careless.

While the sea-rovers turned crimson and sweated rivers that much darkened the water, he had their garments taken away to be washed by house-wenches. By the time his charges had scraped each other's hides clean of sweated dirt—with implements taken from slaves they had briskly sent away—and sloshed and wallowed to their full content in tepid water, Mir had returned with fresh linen and tunics. Now mac Art was at considerable pains with his hair, for he was of Eirrin, while Wulfhere concerned his huge self more with the cleansing of his fiery beard. It caught brine asea, and itched.

Cormac's new tunic fitted sufficiently well, and looked good on the sombre Gael besides. Plain black it was, bordered with gold.

"Wulfhere: realization is on ye of too much coincidence, isn't it?"

"What?"

"Consider. The availability of that merchant-ship. The proximity of ready, marine-manned warcraft. The raid on Balsus's: that mincing Sigebert was at pains to let us know he did not expect us, but why else had he such a herd of armed men posted outside? And then came *more* warcraft. Y'see? Someone set traps for us, Wulf, someone with power. Great pains were taken, all for us. Best we be staying well away from that coast. It's not unpleasant to be gaining useful employment that suits our talents . . . particularly in view of the extreme inhospitability of those waters!"

"Aye, and a good bed is a welcome prospect," Wulfhere said. He flashed the darker man a smile. "So is Veremund's silver, sorcerous or no!"

"Uh—I did take note of that chain when we left. Our links remained intact."

"Crafty Cormac, trusting no one! Well—I even like Veremund. As to that other business you mention—naturally I had thought on all that. Likely Caesar himself sent orders for the capture of such monsters as we!"

Cormac smiled. "More likely that old throat-slitter Guntram, with an ax over his head from Alaric. As for Veremund . . . aye. I like the man."

"You? Like a *king?"*

"Split a knuckle, Wulfhere."

The Dane laughed, then sobered. "And Irnic. Good

soldier. Arms like slabs of meat and hard as oak. Now then—am I pretty enough?"

Cormac looked at his comrade-in-arms. He grinned. The Suevi wore their tunics short, and no man among them stood even nigh so tall as Wulfhere Skull-splitter. On him, even the largest available Suevic tunic was nigh obscenely short.

"Hunch forward like a gnome and it's middling decent ye are," the Gael said, never cracking a smile. He went on gravely, "To be sure, it leaves ye as bare of arse as my father's prize boar. And whate'er befalls, be careful of keeping your leggings well pulled up, and don't be stretching. Ye'd vanish at once under a burial-mound of all the Roman ladies within seeing-range."

The Skull-splitter was not amused.

The well-born lad Mir, indeed impressed with their kemptness, suggested that mayhap a sewing-woman of the king's hall could add a border to Wulfhere's tunic. A deep one.

They left the Roman city then and returned to the king's dun, ambling on a lovely day that was well-warmed by a smiling sun and cheered by Hispanic birds. Attracted by the clamor, they found a score or so of the king's troopers at practice. Their target was a massive slab of seasoned oak, indeed a log split in two with its flat surface facing the throwers. Buried three feet in the ground and braced with great stones, the revealed target was tall as a man, and broader. Eyes, genitals, and internal organs had been crudely drawn on it.

At it the Sueves were hurling the Frankish assault-ax, of the sort that gave that fierce and treacherous tribe its name. The missiles hissed through the air, short-hafted, single-edged, and deadly sharp. Wicked weapons they were, though their main use was in hurled volleys immediately before a foot charge with swords or second axes.

Watching, noting the skill of these Suevi as well as their spirit and the manner of their training, Cormac held his gaze on them. He had become aware of himself being watched. That slim, richly-clad figure on the far side of the compound was past mistaking. Did Eurica stare at him in invitation, or malice, or foolish-innocent curiosity? She hadn't the wit to veil it, whichever. *At least I need not suspect her of cunning,* he thought, and affected not to notice her. Thus he missed Wulfhere's departure.

The Dane returned . . . carrying his horrid three-quarter-moon ax with its prodigiously heavy head. Oh, anyone could lift it; it was only Wulfhere could swing it for more than a few minutes. Only he could throw it at all. Swing it he did; when Wulfhere Splitter of skulls hurled himself into battle, bloodstained, beard like blood and fire bristling and those terrible blue eyes blazing, his great ax clotted with blood and brains, few dared face him.

The two reivers were a good twenty feet behind the line of Suevic *francisca*-hurlers, who were essaying thirty-foot throws and had not seen their observers. Some axes struck, bit, and dropped; a few slammed into the wood's painted targets and stood there amid the sound of cheers. Too many struck with the sound of wood against wood, or the chringing of steel against wood but not edge-first. These bounded away to either side of the target and littered the ground until all men had thrown, after which axes were collected for the next round. Trainers harangued in loud voices and praised not so loudly.

Wulfhere gauged, squinting, noting even the wind despite his ax's weight. He muttered and cocked his head and moved his fingers in laborious calculations. And he backed a half-pace.

"Cormac," he muttered as warning, and with a mighty heave and a grunt, he hurled that ghastly doer of death that was definitely not designed for throwing.

The ax flashed through the air, lofting high to arc well over the heads of the Suevic warriors. The seven-pound chunk of sharpened steel glinted and winked in the sun as it flew, turning slowly, and turning again . . .

With a frightful slamming crash like unto Loki bursting his chains, the Danish ax smashed into the target. At its mighty impact, a couple of feet above the ground, another ax fell. Obviously it had not been well imbedded; Wulfhere's ax clung and its haft stood forth like the ridgepole of a barn. The heavy timber slab vibrated from top to bottom and a brace-stone moved.

Bedlam came swooping down onto the practice field.

Amid the commotion Wulfhere muttered, "Shit. See how low I struck! Either I misgauged or I'm growing weak with my years."

Cormac said nothing. He was as impressed as the Galicians. Some embarrassment and laughter followed, for them; a young weapon-man ran, topknot bobbing, to pull the ax free of the target—and had to lay hold of the haft with both hands while setting a foot against the slabbish target. His comrades laughed, called comments and suggestions and turning, invited the huge man from the far north to join them.

A grinning Wulfhere did. He reached their line as the well-muscled lad, having at last succeeded in wrenching loose the prodigious ax, brought it back to him.

"Thanks, youngster," Wulfhere looked about at the others and grinned. "Mayhap ye should ha' left it for these big-mouths to try their strength also!"

The Suevic troopers laughed in the good humoured appreciation of weapon-men for a superb one, and excitedly babbled that he should join them now, and later at a beast fight at which some rowdy local wenches were meeting them. A grinning Wulfhere observed that they seemed to be planning his kind of afternoon.

Cormac shook his head. *We're here to see to the building of ships and the training of crew, and what does that man-mountain do? —starts in to make ax-throwers of them!* It was pleasant, though, to know that Wulfhere would not lack entertainment. He'd a way of finding drastic remedies for his own boredom. Once over in Britain he'd forced a bishop to marry a thieving smith to a heifer, and burned the church when he found the ceremony too tame.

The Gael turned smiling to enter the king's hall.

Acting on sudden thought, Cormac turned, knowing he'd find the heaven-blue eyes of Eurica king-sister watching the rugged wolfishness of his walk. He bowed to her as might a court-raised fop.

Then he turned again and passed through the dark oblong gape that was the hall's entry, seen from the sunlit outside. Wondering why she was watching, what she thought of him or might be planning, he strolled inside.

He stood in King Veremund's eating hall while his eyes accustomed themselves to the shade. The great hall formed two levels. The lower, with its long trench for fire and its double row of pillars, was public: the scene of feasts, weddings, and all noble gatherings. Above, upheld by the pillars of carven wood, a timbered gallery ran around three sides of the hall. Doors led off it to bedchambers. That one of those had been assigned to his and Wulfhere's use was a measure of the impression they had made here. True, the king's companions had quarters elsewhere, and lovers—and some of them of course had wives. But when they nighted in the great hall, they slept on benches.

Two pirates from oversea had been granted considerable honour, Cormac thought, as he ascended to their chamber.

Here was neither Rome nor Eirrin. The room was a rude wooden box with a door. Woven hangings softened the walls and two dyed sheepskin rugs lay amid the rushes on the floor. The great bed was piled with fur covers. It was most tempting, and Cormac wanted to fling himself down with sighs of content. No; with ingrained suspicion he first hurled off some of the covers and ran exploring hands over the rest. Beds could hide a number of nasty surprises, such as poisoned daggers fixed upright to the frame. Cormac checked. A king had no need of such subtleties, but others might; whether they worked or no, they could sow distrust betwixt the king and his outland guests. Was foregone and certain, aye and inevitable that there would be factions to contend with. In all the history of the world, Cormac knew, there had never existed a kingdom that lacked them.

Here, at least, were no bed-hidden traps.

Thoughts of Eurica slipped from his mind. He sprawled, with sinewy fingers unterlocked behind his black-shocked head, for a nap. His brain was aroused, he discovered, and without trying he cogitated on the menace to the tower—and to ships approaching this coast—and how best to attack the problem.

The door opened softly, and Cormac bethought him of his nearby sword.

The figure that entered presented no menace. She was clad as he had foretold. Her thick brown hair was brushed till it shone, all coiled on her head bedecked with combs of enamelled white bronze. Fit for a provincial Roman lady was her long gown, in colour a dark rich red-brown like her hair. Broidered gold stiffened its hem and a golden belt cinctured it. From her shoulders swept an enveloping sky-blue mantle or paludamen-

tum, its shimmering line the hue of fresh cream. The change in her was enough to take a man's breath.

"It's hardly yourself I might have expected," mac Art said.

"Why?" Clodia asked. She was not trembling; the firm-held tautness of her body within gown and mantle was that of tremors repressed. The one short word was all she trusted herself to utter steadily. Taxing had it been to play—to be—the noble lady in misfortune, befor the shrewd king. The tiring-wenches who bathed and dressed and coiffed her, with their chatter and questions and thinly-disguised malice, had been worse. She strove for controlled speech.

"Why did you do it?"

"What?"

"Cha, Cormac! Introduce me as a lady!"

He essayed a supine shrug. "Ye had no pleasant time aboard *Raven,* or ashore this morning either," he said, though he was stating fact, in no wise making apology.

She made a jerky shrug like a spasm. "You stood my friend when it mattered. It was . . . fortunate, that I did not have to say much."

"Sure and it's up to yourself what ye be doing with your new station now—my lady."

"I'll never make them believe it." She was starting to tremble.

Cormac said naught. He agreed.

"It was sweet of you, Cormac. You'd been treating me so—"

"Gods, woman! Your tongue! The gods themselves shudder at thought of a *sweet* Cormac!"

"Y-you—" She was trembling openly. "I see that you ha-andle compliments about as well as you would a di-distaff."

"Say no more, then. Be ye weary?"

"Terrified! Drained! I've been afraid so much as to speak—*Cormac, for God's love,* hold *me!*"

There was naught of the contrived about the way she toppled forward, else it had been more graceful. The impact of her was substantial and alive. Cormac grunted, and held. Sobs hit Clodia then with a rending power that twisted all her body, torn as with hooks from her lungs and very bowels. She wept for her father, perhaps, enduring torture for his avarice or dead and glad of it. For all her hanging on throughout the voyage here, and all the strain with king and the women who attired her as the noblewoman. For herself she wept, and even for Cormac, and the world of slaying and treachery that wrapped them both about.

Art's son of Connacht held her, the while she groaned and bleated; she was no silent griever, Clodia of Nantes.

Like the storms of Treachery Bay, it passed, to leave a great quiet and wreckage untidily adrift. A comb had come out of her hair and the other hung awry so that her brown locks were ravelling down onto Cormac's breast. She had made a swamp of his shoulder.

When she moved, he did not let her go.

She uttered a small sound, neither protest nor great encouragement. The sound of query was in it. Cormac made her definite answer. The girl from Nantes was drained and passive, but not completely, and Cormac postponed both planning and nap for a time, and slept the better.

CHAPTER EIGHT: A Bargain with Pirates

At dinner the two newcomers met more of the king's cronies and relatives—the *comites*—and them without helms and armour, now. Some were friendly and others disdainful of a pair of foreign pirates in borrowed tunics. All the others were better attired for dinner, though Cormac noted that some of the fancified leggings and decorated tunics or robes showed wear, and too he saw the marks of re-sewing; mending of hems and little snags. He had first frowned at the leggings provided him; they bore a yellow chain-design running up the outside of each leg. The fabric itself was slate in hue.

He and Wulfhere had too their first view of Queen Venhilda. Tall Veremund's wife was, and splendidly formed, so that she should have been a commanding presence. She was not. Her appearance was pale and haggard. She seemed unwell, with a deadly lassitude on her. This was made but the more noticeable by the richness of her garments. And too . . . her gaze was strange.

When Cormac was introduced to her, the large grey-blue eyes rested on his, and never blinked. Nor did she blink at any other time that he observed. Her shadowed lids seemed fixed, as with congealed wax, and never so much as flickered. Cormac at last felt a little chill and looked on Galicia's Queen no more.

Not so Clodia! Clodia was happily resplendent in a lovely gown of red vertically striped with beige. It had been provided by a lady of the court, of course, for the merchant's daughter introduced as Lady Clodia. She received more than a little attention, Clodia did. She was visibly delighted to be seated between Irnic Break-ax and a lean, broad-shouldered Hispano-Roman who obviously bore the blood of both peoples.

My Lady Clodia, Cormac mused. *She will never carry it off, not buxom Clodia; she must be hard put not to pick up a pitcher and serve wine!*

Each time he glanced at Princess Eurica, he caught her in the act of averting her eyes, so that he knew she'd been witching him. The mac Art tried to look elsewhere.

The princess's behaviour was true, too, of Zarabdas the mage. Cormac wore the Egyptian sigil within his Suevic tunic of brown-stitched blue, and forebore lifting a hand to the chain. Was that Zarabdas's interest? Why did the Palmyran watch him when Cormac's own gaze was elsewhere? Had Zarabdas another interest in the Gaelic pirate who had contracted with the Suevic king he served in Hispania as . . . adviser?—as mage?—seer?

And Eurica. Was she one more fascinated female like others Cormac had known, of varying ages and races. The wife of the lord Hermanric Marcellus right now, for instance, and her name a very Roman "Plotina." She favoured the Gael with her dark-eyed gaze, and did not look away when his eyes swept her. *Look away, milady,* Cormac mused; *mac Art has rules about women with husbands; 's called self defense!*

The queen was unusual enough among ruddy, healthy, buxom women. There was something else about her that caught Cormac's eye, with the fascinatingly fluid motions of her hands—one of her three rings. The band was plain enow, simply a little circle of gold. Atop it though, caged in two strips of gold wire, flashed a most extraordinary opal. So he supposed it to be; he had seen two others similar, though not so beautiful. A thousand tiny speckles of colour lay imbedded in the black stone, like the stars of night save that these were of yellow and red and blue and shades between. A gift of love, Cormac mused, and he'd lay wager.

Putting women and rings out of his mind, Cormac turned to the man beside him.

This minor lord of the Suevi seemed delighted to know him and Wulfhere. Some were, whatever their motives, and Cormac was accustomed to those who nigh fawned, fascinated with men of deeds striding the world ahead of a wake of blood. He asked Lord Rhodoghast about Zarabdas, and was bidden to call Rhodoghast by name alone.

"Zarabdas," Rhodoghast said, nodding. "To begin with, the man may or may not be a wizard!"

Realizing that the Palmyran's powers were not known to everyone, Cormac made no comment but affected to show the surprise expected of him.

"Aye! He came here two years agone, mysteriously methinks. Said he sought sanctuary in a land he knew had not *really* embraced the faith of Iesus Christus. He was a fugitive from the Visigothic lords, he claimed, having offended the emperer with an over-vociferous opposition to his religious policy."

Cormac nodded encouragingly. That policy was the making Christian of all "subject" lands. Or so the emperor said, living in the past of imperial glory and power. Stupid, Cormac thought. Emperors came and

134

went, as would surely this religion designed for slaves who needed something to look forward to—such as a slice of honeycake in the sky. How surprised the "Saints" or Christians must be to discover that what followed death was return to earth in a new form, as a helpless babe fated to begin all anew!

"Just over a month after the arrival of Zarabdas," Rhodoghast said, "Queen Venhilda fell ill—very ill indeed. Eventually the court physician Lucanor advised the king that she could not live. It was then that Zarabdas prevailed upon Veremund," Rhodoghast said, lowering his voice even more as he pronounced his king's name unadorned, "to allow him to attend our lady queen. Lucanor Antiochus had given up in defeat, and so there seemed little to lose. Whilst Veremund was considering, Lucanor sought to make a religious issue of it. The king was angered by that and the threat implied, and he bade Zarabdas do what he could for Venhilda."

"This Lucanor . . ."

Rhodoghast gave his head a jerk and made a swift gesture. "A Christian, of course. A . . . semi-sufferable cross-wearer from that far old place of Antioch. Not as dark as one would expect; he be Greek or has Greek blood."

Rhodoghast lifted his winecup, waited to catch the eye of a serving lad, and glowered at him. His and Cormac's cups were immediately filled. Cormac lifted it, looked over its rim to find the Lady Plotina Marcella gazing at him. Rather than look away she held his glance, and ran her tongue, slowly, all around her lips. Without acknowledgment Cormac returned his attention to Rhodoghast.

"Is't true you have sunk a score of ships?"

"It is not," Cormac said. "It's but two we're after sinking, and four others we've disabled. Nor have Wulfhere and I done death on so many as is said. And hear this Rhodoghast: neither of us has ever slain any man who did not have a weapon in his hand. Now what ye're after saying of the queen interests me, for she is thin and wan. Ye were going to tell me that Zarabdas cured her."

"How did ye know?"

"She be not dead."

"Ah. Aye, within two days it was obvious that she was recovering. Within four she was on her feet again, though weak. In less than a month she was fully recovered—or as ye see her now. In truth she's never been any sort of buxom woman, though. Since then Zarabdas had been naturally enough held in high esteem by the king and queen. Gradually he's grown strong in the king's counsel, as well. All know he is a most wise man and knowledgeable in physick. Many of course wonder if he be mage or no; he is a mystery among us who keeps much to himself and shares counsel only with Veremund and Venhilda. Some fear his influence; others are thankful for it. Some have naturally reminded that it was just after he arrived among us that my lady queen fell ill, and that it was most convenient for him to gain the king's favour."

That thought had occurred to Cormac, but he'd not indulge in gossip with such as Rhodoghast—or indeed anyone else. He asked, "And the Antiochite leech? Did he slink off to Gothish lands, or all the way back to Golden Antioch?"

"Oh no, neither. He is still here, though out of favour with those of us who count. Say something to me in Gaelic."

"Legach boina boinin," Cormac said, quoting a homile among those who'd been his people: "To every cow her calf."

"Hmm . . . what does that mean?"

"It means I am a vicious bloodthirsty pirate and am interested in Lucanor, not in language lessons. I will tell you this: the Gaels have no verb 'to have', but there are several ways of saying 'to do death on.' "

Rhodoghast chuckled, but the two sidewise looks he shot the "vicious bloodthirsty pirate" bespoke his nervousness. Cormac was careful not to smile.

"Lucanor remains here. He is leech for the weapon-men, and others. He stays very busy, though hardly as prosperous as beforetimes."

"Think you the lady queen is cured by sorcery?"

"Some do," Rhodoghast said, and grew most interested in the tumbler and female juggler who entered the king's dining hall then, bounding and jingling bells.

The entertainers were fair, Cormac thought, surreptitiously observing Zarabdas while he pretended interest in the leggy woman with her minimal juggling ability and less chest.

They departed amid applause, and the floor was clear. Veremund rose to announce that the Masters of *Raven* were here to serve the crown—and that mayhap the first act should be the creation of a new target for ax-practice. Amid general laughter, Wulfhere looked about, and grinned, beaming . . . and reddened.

"We would now take counsel with these twain," Veremund said, "on a matter of passing import to our realm, and our children. I would have Zarabdas and Commander Irnic join us, with Salvian."

All others were thus dismissed, as the king said naught about their continuing in the hall. The Lady Plotina—well overweight, Cormac noticed as she rose from board—sought to catch his eye, but he was careful not to see her. Or Eurica, though he made a head-bow to Venhilda, who despite her thinness and pallor, was a most handsome woman. Yet—gods, those eyes! He and

Wulfhere followed the king, his cousin Irnic, Zarabdas, and the Hispano-Roman secretary, Salvian. They entered the same small chamber in which they'd talked earlier in the day. This time bowls of wine and fresh melon, prepared in little balls, awaited them.

Soon Cormac was saying that the way to begin their task was to learn more about the mysterious beacon that appeared when the real one was extinguished. Irnic inquired as to whether he had a theory.

"One I like not, my lord."

"Call me Irnic, and say it out anyhow, Cormac."

Twice tonight had mac Art been invited to call nobles by name. While he had betrayed no reaction to Rhodoghast who sought to be friend of the exotic pirate, he smiled and nodded acknowledgment to Irnic. This fellow weapon-man, Cormac thought, just couldn't be bothered with the "lord" business.

"Suppose," Cormac said slowly, "that some . . . presence . . . *knows* when a ship approaches, and sends then the kelp to do death on those in the tower."

"Sends?" That from Zarabdas.

Veremund asked, "To what purpose?"

"To lead the ship astray," Wulfhere said, shrugging.

"To what purpose," Veremund repeated, and Cormac did not like the mind of one who knew causes from effects and motives from purposes.

The Gael was nevertheless forced to shake his head. "Who knows? Hopefully it's that we'll be ascertaining, among other things."

Veremund looked about. Irnic and Zarabdas were nodding. Salvian was making his notes. The king looked at Cormac, and nodded.

"It's my own self I propose to man this lighthouse, with a few men . . . and a large supply of quicklime."

Cormac gave the king a questioning look. "A large supply."

The king nodded. "Lime is plentiful here. I'll have the preparation of quicklime begun on the morrow, heat or no. At dawn."

"Just before sunset then, Wulfhere will take *Raven* well out, and sea-anchor. Then I and my troop, with the quicklime in quantity, will mount into the tower. Assuming that quicklime affects the vampirish kelp as it does other plants, it's we ourselves will be extinguishing the beacon in the tower. If the false one appears, Wulfhere will give chase—with all care, being forewarned."

Irnic's eyes were alight and he was smiling as he nodded repeatedly, a soldier hearing a bold tactic he more than approved. It was Zarabdas who spoke.

"There is the additional danger. . . . The wreckers, or whoever is responsible for the false beacon, may well have this dread seaweed with them. As . . . armour, and arms as well. It could surely swamp your ship, and drag the crew to the bottom."

"I will advise the men of that possibility," Wulfhere said in an equable tone, "and ask for volunteers only."

Veremund said frowning, "Great risks are being taken in this."

Wulfhere nodded, and with eyes full on the king he said, "Aye, and the most of it falls on me. Far be it from me to bargain like a Saxon, King Veremund, but my men will hereafter want and deserve wine, not ale, and . . . female companionship."

Irnic but smiled; when his royal cousin glanced at him, the Breaker of axes said in the same equable tone Wulfhere had used, "That is . . . within my powers."

"We will bid our Danes be discreet," Cormac said,

staring at Wulfhere, "and not flaunt their . . . receipt of
this largesse." He challenged Zarabdas with his gaze,
and then with words. "And would my lord Zarabdas
care to be joining us weapon-men in the accursed
tower?"

Was Veremund ended the ensuing moments of
tension, during which Zarabdas eyed Cormac coolly: "I
forbid it," the king said, and there was an end to that.
The five men looked about at each other, all knowing
they were pitted against the dangerous unknown. Only
Salvian's scratchings broke the silence. Veremund took
up his wine.

"To our mutual success," he said, and they drank,
with Irnic and Wulfhere first making sure to spill a bit of
wine. They parted, and only Zarabdas tarried a moment
with the reivers.

"Ye be brave men," he said, in his dry almost-
whisper. "Be ye well." And he and his robe ghosted
away into the dark deeps of the royal hall.

"Ah . . . wolf," Wulfhere said, laying a hand on his
comrade's shoulder. "I've ah, been invited to spend the
night elsewhere."

"Good," Cormac said. "Great pleasure will be on me,
not to be listening to the Thor's hammer of your
snoring! Do try to get some sleep, Wulfhere."

He was standing under a patriarchal chestnut when
his peripheral vision reported a swift movement but a
few yards away, at the hall. Automatically he eased into
the shadow of the tree. He was unpleasantly aware that
he wore no sword, for suspicion was on him; the exiled
Gael had achieved no renown for a trusting nature. Now
he saw a human figure well-muffled in a hooded cloak
that was so dark he could not distinguish its hue in the
night. It seemed to be a woman or girl, moving furtively.
Cormac watched, motionless.

The cloak had just left the hall, and took care now to skirt moonlit areas as it hurried from the courtyard. The cloak was voluminous, and so dark that it soon disappeared into the night.

Assignations, Cormac thought, relaxing. *Well, it's no need I have of such, thanks to Clodia's little visit to my room this afternoon!* And he returned through the cool, clear night to the kinghouse.

"Hivernian!"

The voice was female, and the single word was spoken scarcely above a whisper. It was the Roman name for his isle of Eirrin; Rome lingered on everywhere. Cormac turned warily to squint in the darkness. He was able to make out a smallish figure pressed against the hall's outer wall, on the lee side of the moon's light. Fabric rustled and a hand, pale and pale-sleeved, emerged from a long cloak. The hand beckoned.

It is a night for women to be abroad in hooded cloaks the colour of night, he thought with an inward smile. He had to assume, without enthusiasm, that it was the wife of Hermanric Marcellus who sought his company. "My . . . Lady Plotina?" he asked, as quietly as she had spoken.

Fabric rustled and a foot stamped. "No, damn ye for a rude foreigner."

"Oh." He glanced about, saw no one. "My lady," he said, and ambled over to Eurika.

Her tiny voice said, "Plotina, hmm?"

"It's both she and yourself stared at me whilst I ate. She, though, did not look away when our eyes met. I ignored her."

"Oh? Why? Be ye a vegetarian?"

"Because she is another man's wife," he said, content not to mention other reasons, including Plotina's meatiness.

"Ah. A pirate with morals."

Her voice was hardly friendly, but ere he could remind her of that and that he preferred sleep to slurs, the king's young sister said on.

"Do you despise me, mac Art?"

"My *gracious* lady . . . I do not."

She nodded shortly. "All my life have I dwelt here, Cormac mac Art. Never never have I been allowed beyond even the confines of my brother's personal demesne, and always with watchful eyes on me. I long to know of the world. You have seen it. Come with me and tell me of that great broad world out there beyond Treachery Bay, Cormac the Bold."

"Come with you where?"

"Why, to my chambers, where we'll not be interrupted."

"My lady, methinks that would be both unseemly and dangerous. It's happy I'll be to talk with ye on the morrow. In the sunlight."

"Hmp! Cormac the Bold becomes Cormac the Timid, is it?"

"Aye, lady Princess." Those words hurt or reduced him not at all; Art's son of Connacht had to respect a person before he paid heed to his opinion, or hers.

"Ye—ye say only 'aye' . . ." There was wonder in her voice. "Such an admission does not disturb ye in the least, does it? Ye be so sure of yourself?"

"Aye," he repeated, "lady Princess."

Eurica stared wonderingly with the moonlight sparkling on her large blue eyes, and she sighed, and looked pensively downward. Cormac said "My lady," and turned away to resume his way.

"I gave you no leave to go!"

He looked back at her without turning. "Then for your own pride, lady Princess, do so now, for it's to my bed I'm going."

And he did, and slept well, alone and with no snoring at hand, other than his own.

Nor, in the sunlight of the morrow, did Princess Eurica trouble herself to seek out the man from "Hivernia."

CHAPTER NINE: Zarabdas of Palmyra

Cormac could not believe it. He searched his room
again, both disturbed and greatly surprised. He was one
to sleep like a cat and awake at the sound of a busy
spider dropping to a ship's deck from a taut sail. Yet
while he had slept this first night in the hall of the King
of Galicia, someone had entered the room and taken the
Egyptian sigil on its chain!

He wore the linen under-leggings on which he'd laid
it, and was sure it had not been there. At last, convinced
that the medallion was indeed gone, he drew on his
leathern leggings and tunic. He stood thinking a
moment, narrow-eyed. And arranged his mailcoat on
the bed, and slipped into its jingling, heavy links.
Straightening, he buckled on weapons and pouch.

When he left the chamber, he took with him
everything that was his. Only the buckler he would not
carry, so as not to appear the prowling soldier and do
insult to Veremund's hospitality. Near the front door
was a place reserved for the shields of weapon-men
entering the hall; there Cormac left his own round
buckler, made of the yew of Britain and braced and

strengthened by bands of steel.

That day, when their paths happened to cross outside, he learned that Clodia had availed herself of her newfound nobility; she had nighted with none other than the king.

"Ye can hardly be continuing your masquerade of the highborn lady in his intimate company," Cormac pointed out.

"Oh . . . *he* knows," she said, and accompanied the words with an arch look. "Was you claimed I was a lady after all, not I. Once I knew he knew, I told him the truth."

"The truth?"

"Aye!" The look she gave him this time was appealing. "You'll not tell him different, will you, Cormac?"

"Different from what?"

"That I'm the daughter of a chieftain of the ancient Alani though I dare not name the specific house, for my father fell out with the Caesar before this one. I was raised by a rich merchant of Nantes."

Cormac shook his head, eyebrows up. "No, Clodia, it's no different tale I'll be telling the king. In truth, ye lie as well as I. Do let me know, though, an ye change that story." And he went on his way, his face looking strange wearing a whimsical little smile.

A mounted Irnic came upon him, and reined in. "Cormac! Why in full armour?"

Cormac looked mildly up at the Sueve. "It's a weapon-man I am, Irnic. This is the way I am comfortable. Relieve me of the weight of forty pounds of mail and another dozen of weapons and belt, and I might float!"

Laughing, Irnic rode on, and the story had spread through all the *comites* and half the soldiers by nightfall.

The peasants would have it by the morrow's night.

A short time later, Cormac first saw Lucanor of Antioch. The leech was a portly man in a wine-dark robe who wore his curly, grease-glossy black hair to his shoulders. A gold ring flashed in his left ear. An unhappy look shadowed the fellow's mouth and brow, which were separated by a thin nose with a bit of a crook. He was emerging from a noble house where he'd presumably been at the plying of his trade, and Cormac saw the gratitude on the face of the woman who saw the physician off.

He looked like the offspring of a Greek and an Armenian, Cormac thought, though in truth he'd never seen an Armenian.

It's prosperous enow the fellow looks, and Rhodoghast never said he wasn't competent. Just unhappy, for he's been the king's physician and is no longer. Well Lucanor, well . . . we all have our valleys and peaks and cliffs, in this life. Once I was a noble's son of Connacht in Eirrin, and later a hero of Leinster, and I've been lover to a princess and . . . something similar to another. Are you too an exile who dreams of your homeland, old hawk-faced grease-head?

He visited the heat-shimmering place wherein aproned men sweated and wore heavy gauntlets and boots of leather. There was one wall only. Five men laboured here. Three fed fuel constantly to keep their fire blazing high and hot. The others, with even more care, handled the lime from the Galician hills, calcining it into the more volatile quicklime. It seemed a simple enough process of heavy unpleasant labour, demanding constant exposure to the searing heat and the dangerous dust of the stinging lime, as well as poisonous fumes. Mac Art, who'd been feeling sorry for himself since his thoughts of Eirrin, decided he'd rather be in a battle against double odds than one of these sweating, miserable-looking men with their several lime-burns.

Later he had himself escorted to the coast. Wulfhere was already asea, with some of his crew along with Sueves: training. Cormac stood for a time, gazing across at the lonely, grim old tower. Restlessly the sea slapped at the jumble of rocks at its base, and Cormac wondered how long that salty assault had gone on.

The Romans built well, he mused, as he'd thought numerous times afore. And he was glad they had not builded and maintained their empire as well as they had their walls and forts and light-towers, their aqueducts and roads and superb bridges.

And now . . . who possessed this grim old pile of stone? Or—what?

He approached the cylindrical tower, accompanied by two nervous Suevi with their strange back-of-the-head hairknots. They walked all round about it, and once Cormac drew steel and prodded at lank runners of brown algae. The kelp acted like nothing but kelp. The three men ascended to the light-chamber. Here only rusty brown stains now gave evidence of the ugly occurrences here.

Eight men, he reflected, looking slit-eyed about, slain and sucked dry by . . . *seaweed?*

Was it possible?

Had it really happened, that viney thing locking onto his flesh and starting in at once to feed on his blood? Those dehiscent pods that had burst like pig's bladders to spurt blood over a foot across the floor? Could he really hold belief that the seaweed was sentient or nearly, that it had been sent and recalled once its ghastly murders were accomplished?

Cormac peered out on the sea, thinking, wondering at how much kelp the oceans held, thinking of masses of it crawling like worms in rich soil after a rain. And tiny cold feet seemd to walk up his spine, under mailcoat and padded jacket and tunic, and Cormac mac Art sweated. He turned to stare along the brooding, craggy coast backed by its dark trees.

"There is adequate fuel lying there, in the woods. I'll want some dry old rotted wood, and a fine supply of slim sticks, also dry."

"It will be done." Irnic had bade these men accept Cormac's suggestions as orders and carry out his instructions as if they were royal proclamations.

"Well. Let's be going down. It's naught there is to see now, and we do want that wood gathered."

"I don't envy you your vigil here, Captain Cormac," the Sueve said as they descended the narrow staircase of stone.

"Just Cormac will do, Eudo. I've not captained my own ship for some years now, and have little use for titles."

"Is't true you and the Dane have sent full a score of ships to the bottom, Cormac?"

Cormac sighed. "No, it is not true. We have sunk two. Nor have we ever done death on so many as one single man who did not have steel in his hand. Why, I've never even raped a woman!"

"Not *one?*" Eudo's companion said disbelievingly, and Eudo chuckled, "How about girls, then?"

"It's never been necessary," Cormac said, without thinking that he was not lessening his legend, but adding another line that would become paragraphs. "Ah, attend me, Eudo; I'm thinking of something else. See that a cauldron of grease is provided us here."

"Grease?"

"Animal, aye, and coagulated. I just want it after it's been boiled down, so that it will liquefy swiftly, rather than big chunks of fat."

"A cauldron."

They emerged into the sunlight. "Aye, and I'd not be minding in the least if the pot were *not* one of those monstrous heavy things. Bronze or iron; makes no difference. And it's welcome your lads are to carry up the grease in ewers or skinbags, and transfer it into the cauldron up in the light-chamber. I'm not bent on breaking backs!"

"Aye, Cormac. Very well. It will be done. And where will ye be?"

Cormac turned to look at the long-faced Sueve, and the Gael's face was open, almost ingenuous—if a visage so marked by experience was capable of anything approaching a boyish expression. "Why, right here, Eudo. It's only my life's at stake, man; I'll not be wandering off afishing while my little castle is being prepared to withstand siege!"

Eudo nodded with a chastened little smile, and he and his aide hurried away to see to the gathering of wood.

Cormac walked along the shore, ascending slowly. He knew would be no easy matter, muscling a huge iron vat of hardened grease up to the light-chamber of yon tower of death. Cauldrons were built to last, and they were not light. Nor was a solid mass of melted and resolidified animal fat. Too, Cormac had never seen a cauldron that was provided with more than two lugs, or handles.

Better that job than calcining lime, he thought, and tugged off his horsehair-crested helm. The salt-fresh air over the sea stirred but little this afternoon, but each little zephyr was most welcome. He whipped his head back and forth, shaking sweat and kinks from his black mass of hair.

He entered the woods that ended just above the bluff overlooking the sea, ascended, and emerged to sit in shade and gaze out on the water. From time to time he glanced at the beacon tower, or gazed speculatively at that enigmatic pile of brine-white stone. A sentry and a haven, turned into a trap of horror and a grave. How? By what?

As the afternoon wore on he twice rose and changed his position, seeking shade in the manner of a lounging dog. But Cormac mac Art was hardly at his ease. While his body rested his brain laboured and winged afar in both space and the misty past, planning, seeking clues to the root of this new menace that had fallen athwart his life-path.

He could think of no precedent, nothing similar in all his experience asea, and in Eirrin and Alba and Britain. He stared seaward, thinking, and from time to time Wulfhere went by . . .

The Dane was shouting and cursing. His flaming beard bristled as he turned face and supplicating hands up to Asgard. He had taken aboard *Raven* a score of his own Danish seamen, with half that number of Suevi, for training. Wulfhere had not the patience to train a genius to pick his nose, Cormac reflected, smiling. Back and forth the ship went, up and down the coast, back and forth . . . and all the while Wulfhere Skull-splitter railed at his tyroes.

He should have come in earlier. Toward sundown a wind rose up and whipped the sea into prancing choppy waves and breakers that crashed onto the rocks below Cormac's perch. *Wulfhere's trainees gain their seasoning now,* the Gael grinned, hearing the Dane's bellow even through the wind.

Raven plunged and beat up and down for a long hour ere the wind eased and they dared swing her swiftly in to gain shore. By then the sun had gone orange and was perching at the edge of the world.

Cormac rose and hurried down to meet the men from *Raven*.

Wulfhere snorted as he watched the half-score Suevi stagger and lurch ashore. Each quivered in every part and the skin of more than one showed a definite green tinge.

"Och, Cormac! We have a helpless task with these landbound plow-pushers! They'll never make sea-men!"

But Knud the Swift winked at Cormac, which told him the Sueves had done rather well.

"And what saw you, Wulf, on your little pleasure cruise?"

The Dane tried to fry Cormac with a look, then doffed his helm and slammed it at his comrade with a swift tensing thrust of both arms, from the chest. Cormac caught the iron pot in both his hands, and aye, mac Art rocked with the impact. He said nothing of the pain to the middle finger of his left hand, but did toss the helm aside for Wulfhere to pick up.

"Nothing!" the flame-haired giant said explosively. "We saw nothing! No sign of wrecked ships, not even a plank. And no slain men, sucked dry or otherwise."

Cormac made a sympathetic face and gave his head a jerk. "Will ye be ready to-morrow evening?"

"Aye," Wulfhere nodded. "To-morrow e'en. And . . . I'll not be sleeping in our chamber this night, again."

"My chamber," Cormac corrected. "Not a married lady, I hope."

"Frey's stones, *No!* Neither of them!"

As they were finishing dinner, Zarabdas quietly let Cormac know that he would have converse. The Gael was none loath and they went outside for a walk about the grounds of the king's hall. The sky was still a deep

151

slate colour, rather than black. They talked, but nothing was said.

"Was you suggested a talk," Cormac said at last, "but we talk not. It's but tentatively feinting each of us is, and almost desperately parrying. Methinks is because neither of us really wishes to tell the other aught of his knowledge and arcane powers." *Of which I have none,* Cormac added, but only in his own mind.

"Straightforward words. And true. Might one ask how came ye by the medallion ye showed us?"

Cormac but smiled, very slightly. He could be seen; it was answer enow.

"Well then . . . might I see it again, now we are sure we serve the same king?"

Cormac paused, turned to the other man, and stared.

Zarabdas at last frowned. "Ye seem to have suffered a seizure of the tongue, mac Art."

"What I have suffered, mage, is a seizure of the sigil! It vanished during the night just passed. Nor can I fathom how anyone entered my chamber without awaking me—unless by some sorcerous means. Too, Zarabdas, no one has been so interested as yourself, in that . . . bauble."

"Stolen!" Zarabdas hissed. "And I hear myself being accused without so many words . . . mac Art, I have it not. I do not steal. Nor do I believe that medallion to be other than a piece of Egyptian jewellery of no great age."

"Then why would someone in the hall of the king himself be going to such trouble to steal it? Surely no paupers sleep within the keep!"

"I cannot say," Zarabdas said, meeting Cormac's slitted eyes straight on; the two men stood still now, face to face. "Mayhap I am wrong about the medallion's meaning, and possible . . . use. And mayhap another *thought* it to be valuable, of thaumaturgic use. Hmm.

The thief woke neither you nor your bearish friend?"

"He . . . took his rest elsewhere."

"Ah. Rest, eh?" Almost, Zarabdas smiled. "Of course . . . Cormac mac Art: do you bolt your door this night."

"It had occurred to me," Cormac said with exaggerated dryness. "It's thinking too I've been of leaving it unlocked—and sleeping not, but waiting with sword in hand."

"Not unwise; save that when one sleeps in the hall of the mighty, one must be most cautious as to whom one attacks, in one's own chamber or no."

"I do not believe it's the king will be visiting me this night," Cormac said.

"I will think on this," Zarabdas said, and turned and returned to the hall while a surprised Cormac stood and watched.

Things were seldom what they seemed; Cormac mac Art had learned that, and too many times had he learned and re-learned the lesson to his anguish. Could Zarabdas be sincere, and guiltless, and without knowledge of the accursed sigil?

Mayhap I be well rid of the damned bauble! Well, I'll be going on in and—oh, blood of the gods! Trapped!

It was the Lody Plotina, wearing a darkish dress draped with care to disguise the fact that her belly extended considerably farther than her bosom, which was a considerable distance. Nothing sinister, at least, in that dissemblage—or in her brazen suggestion.

"My lady is a follower of the dead—of Our Lord the Nazarene?"

Frowning, Plotina asked, "Aye—and why do you ask? What has that to do with thee and me?"

"It means that you will understand my sad state, my gracious lady; I have taken a vow of chastity."

"Oh!"

She was most sorry, and departed with little grace,

though she tried. A grimly smiling mac Art reflected on his lie and was most happy that Behl and Crom of Eirrin were not like the Dead God of the Saints or Christians, threatening vengeance on those who professed a faith other than theirs.

He made a little bargain with a kitchen maid, who was not unhappy to be groped or to proffer a jug of wine and a cup on the king's guest. She asked twice, looking up from under long darkened lashes, if that were all "my lord Mackert" wanted of her. He assured her that it was, and was wondering at his own sanity by the time he was in his room and sitting back, sipping the best fate of Hispanic grapes. It was not the best wine he'd tasted—though it far exceeded in quality that stuff the Britons made from the wrinkly grapes their chill wet climate produced.

He filled a second cup, thinking, and was soon yawning—when there came a tap at his door. He set down the pottery mug, looked thoughtfully at his mailcoat and sword, and have his head a jerk. In the manner of a civilized man, he inquired who was there. It was Zarabdas. Cormac admitted him.

Zarabdas, whose pate was so clear of hair and yet whose beard was so dark, wore a different robe, light and ungirt. And he held a stemmed, round object with a piebald pattern on its knob, which was a bit larger than the Gael's fist. Merely a dried gourd, Cormac saw.

"A talisman?"

Zarabdas smiled, and shook the gourd. It rattled, dried with its seeds within. A nice children's toy; some folk hung them outside the door to rattle in the wind and frighten night-demons.

"No," the Palmyran said, "a doorstop."

Cormac blinked, then nodded his understanding. "Ah." He took the gourd, thanked the mage, and closed the door. He set the gourd carefully against its base.

And he retired, dagger close to hand and his sword standing in a corner on the other side of the bed. The wine soon enveloped him in sleep.

A strange sound aroused him. Cormac awoke as fully alert as any pirate, and but a moment passed before he realized that what he was hearing was a child's rattle-ball rolling along the floor. He had his dagger in his fist and was out of bed and several feet from it in an instant.

"It's in me hand my sword is, and if ye ope the door to depart ye'll become a sheath. Came ye to slay, or to steal more than ye did yester night?"

"Neither," a tiny female voice quavered. "I am come to return that which I . . . borrowed on yester even."

"Eurica?"

"Aye," she squeaked, and there was a pause while she swallowed and found her voice, which was very small even when she'd not been terrified. "And unarmed. Please don't hurt me—I am walking toward your voice. *I* bear no arms. Shall I stretch out my hands or put them behind my back?"

"Behind your back," he said, and stretched out his left hand. He heard the approach of her voice, but now she had fallen silent he heard not even the whisper of feet.

So! Who'd have guessed a girl who liked so to stamp her feet could be as silent as a cat walking on velvet! His armpits prickled, and he held forth his left hand, while his right held the dagger ready to strike upward. Then he heard a whisper of cloth, and knew she was close enough to touch, and damned himself mentally for a fool: she was short, and he was holding his hand too high. He lowered it—directly onto her head, and she made a frightened mouse sound.

"Hands at your sides. Be perfectly still. My blade is ready in my other hand."

He felt her, with his left. A long cloak, silk sewn to

155

wool. An empty hand; another. Aye, and within the cloak a slender chain. Tracing his hand down, he found two well-spaced little hills of flesh, almost hard in youthful firmness. Betwixt them was the winged medallion. And a low-necked shift of some gauzy stuff. Her under-dress, or perhaps a nightdress; he knew some wore such, even when the weather was far from wintry.

"Why took ye this?"

"I—came for an-another purpose," she said, and he both felt and heard that the girl trembled still. "I had not the—the courage, once I was within and found ye— s-s-sleeping. But—I took the sigil I knew you had worn. I . . . have liked having it between my breasts, this day."

"Ye've warmed it for me."

"Aye," she said, signally tiny of voice.

"And shall I be taking it now?"

In an even tinier voice: "Aye."

"Uh—oh, sorry. Hmmm." He groped under her hair, which was very soft. "Think ye I can be taking this from ye without your undressing?"

". . . no . . ."

Cormac heaved an elaborate sigh. "Ah, then I must be begging ye to hand it me on the morrow, lady Princess."

"Wh—wh—but—"

He leaned close, so that her hair brushed his lips. "It's not alone I am, here."

"But—the Dane is with—"

"It's not the Dane I speak of, lady Princess."

"Then you—*Oh!*"

"Shhhh—it's asleep she is, and we'd not want her awake and knowing the royal princess is here."

"oh!"

Cormac remained silent. *Go, damn ye girl, go—and all the gods save Art's poor dear boy of Connacht from still another princess—this is one king I'd rather not be falling out with!*

"I hadn't realized you . . ."

"Cormac the Bold; was yourself said it, lady Princess. It's flattered I am, and forever grateful. Have care that none sees ye now, returning to your own quarters."

Something jingle-clattered on the floor. "Take your damned bauble, pirate!"

The door opened and closed. Blowing out his lips, Cormac sighed again—this time genuinely, in relief. King's daughters were his bane, and would be his weird unless he protected himself. Aye, and king's sisters. Kings had a habit of thinking the royal women should leave alone un-royal males. Nor, an the ladies disagreed and took action elsewise, was it they on whom royal anger and punishment fell.

Yet he was not unaroused, and was long gaining his sleep that night. On the morrow he'd a few words with a lowborn and extraordinarily well-constructed wench, and she passed a few words back, and he and she exchanged a few more, and agreement was reached. He had his self defense, he thought, and besides, it was hardly meet for a man to have to lie to a princess more than once, that he was not alone!

CHAPTER TEN: Night of the Demon-Weed

The day came, and went again, and Cormac and Wulfhere went down to the sea.

Cormac chose his men and Wulfhere his. They disagreed only over Hugi the Nimble, whom they both wanted. With little grace Wulfhere agreed that orange-moustached Hugi was of more use to mac Art than to his shipmaster. The swift beardless Dane, rangy as Cormac though shorter by a hand's breadth, joined the Gael and those others he'd chosen to accompany him in this night's vigil and work.

"A fine afternoon for a little rowing!" a man called out.

Though negative sentiments and indeed thoughts were infrequent visitors to his mind, Wulfhere quoted Father Odin Himself: "Praise not the day till evening has come." He looked at Cormac. "Methinks it will storm."

Cormac glanced skyward. "The sky is clear enow."

Wulfhere rubbed his backside. "My butt says otherwise, and you know how dependable this old ham-wound is."

"Would ye be waiting for another night?"

"No." And with six-and-twenty men besides himself, the redbearded giant mounted into *Raven*. He stood dolorously studying the distant sky while his crew took twenty-foot oars from their holding forks and went to their seats. Ashore at the edge of the quay, Cormac watched while each stout wooden oar-blade was threaded into its narrow slot and dropped into the little oar-port.

Wulfhere turned, and he and Cormac stared at each other. Both men nodded. Then Wulfhere signalled, and oars dipped and pushed and lifted, and *Raven* began easing backward from shore. Her hawkbeak and gunwales rode high in the water, despite the sea-anchors: each rope-bound stone was of such size that two men had carried it aboard, with grunts and a smashed fingertip.

Cormac glanced up along the coast. There stood Zarabdas, in woollen tunic and leggings of plain mid-brown, buskins gaitered to the knees, and a cloak of dark blue. It hung still and straight and square-hemmed from the Roman clasp at his shoulder: no breeze stirred. To hand by him were two torches well-oiled, and flint and steel for their lighting. This night the Palmyran would see for himself what befell.

Cormac looked on his four companions.

Hugi the Nimble in his leathern jerkin sewn with armour bosses of whorl-dited bronze that did not quite touch each other, and armed with his short-hafted ax and the sword he had of a Roman cavalry officer who should have stayed ashore; Gudfred Hrut's son, who with his massy helmet, full beard, and sweeping mustachioes—and small nose—seemed little more than a pair of lake-grey eyes under a black helm and separated from his half-sleeved coat of overlapping steel

159

scales by his russet beard of a thousand curls; burly
Edric in his captured Roman helmet with visor all
esthetically tooled in blackened silver and the scalemail
coat his own mother had years agone enameled with
blue; was about half sky-blue and half steel-grey now,
from years of serving its purpose. And there was Hakon
Snorri's son, in steel-stripped coat of boiled black
leather and unadorned helmet of three steel bands
around a cap of leather lined with sponge. He'd a three-
inch scar down forehead and cheek, Hakon had, that
was white-pink and commemorated a sword-stroke that
had missed his eye by less than the breadth of his
smallest finger.

Each man bore a good round shield of linden-wood
rimmed and bossed with dark iron, arm- and hand-strap
within and chipped paint on its face. (Indeed on
Gudfred's shield only chips remained of the scarlet paint
that had once covered it, so that his buckler had a
blood-flecked look about it.)

Hugi alone wore sheathed sword; the others carried
the more common ax with two-pound head and haft just
over a foot's length. Each wore leathern leggings and
boots rather than gaiter-strapped buskins. At the hip of
each hung a broad-bladed long dagger; the hilts of three
curved into dragon-heads while Edric's was a large,
plain knob of night-blue iron. He and Hakon Shorri's
son bore another dagger in addition; Hakon could
throw a knife true as a sped arrow. Only Gudfred was
not red of hair, for at two-and-thirty he'd gone grey as
the cairnstones of his own Dane-mark. All were
cloaked, and two of those brooches were of solid gold
while the head of Hugi's brooch-pin was capped
with a rough-cut sapphire. Piracy were not all un-
pleasantry.

The four looked back at Cormac mac Art: tall and

rangy the Gael was, deceptively strong and beloved for his craftiness; steel-eyed and jet-haired, a man nigh as likely to use his sword daggerishly as to slash and cut. His mailcoat was in the style of Eirrin, not theirs; thousands of quintuply-linked circles of steel formed it and each was separately welded. He wore no decor; the Celtic torc about his strong neck and the bracer on his right wrist could not be considered such. Young was Cormac mac Art though old his eyes and scarred his face, which was darker than any Dane's and not with their ruddiness. He scraped his face daily, when not asea.

As Wulfhere was the bull capable of smashing through the side of a barn, Cormac was the wolf who craftily plotted and sought out the quieter, less dramatic entry.

Without a word, the wolf turned and walked along the stone-sided quay to the beacon-tower. Without a word, his pack followed.

Their spears they left at the tower's base, beside its heavy door. And they went in, and up, and up.

Cormac had deemed it wise to man the tower with but the five of them. More men might well hinder each other's movements. The light-chamber was hardly spacious. He and his companions were hemmed about by a goodly supply of prepared lime in sealskin bags, and two stacks of faggots soaked in animal grease, and the table with flint and steel and closed oil-lamp. And there was the beacon, and its platform against the niche of a window through which it shone.

Doffing their cloaks, five men piled them in a corner.

Peering out, Cormac saw Wulfhere standing out well offshore and his men still pulling their oars. Zarabdas was just visible, standing where on yesterday Cormac had sat. Though now their gazes met, he and the Gael exchanged no sign. Cormac turned back to his men. They went again through his plan, assuming that there would happen that which he expected.

They waited.

Well out on the water, *Raven* waited. A stout rope ran taut over either side to trail down into the dark water, bound to the huge stone serving as sea-anchor. They waited.

The sky went pink and lavender and grey. Orange suffused the horizon, and darkened. The sun crouched, was halved by world's edge, and sank from sight. They waited. A breeze stirred. Looking out and below, Cormac watched the formation of sea-clouds: creeping, shifting fog, white shading to pearly grey. It seemed to finger out from the shore, reaching for *Raven*. Gradually it enshrouded the base of the tower, though to no great height.

The sun was gone. Cormac and Hugi lit the beacon. And they waited.

"My eyes see only grey," Cormac said, turning from the beacon-window. His pupils were huge from his staring attempts to see aught amiss out there in the fog. "Hakon?"

Hakon took up the watch, and they waited.

"See ye nothing, Hakon?"

"The fog shifts and shifts, unfortunately. Only that. Stars twinkle. The moon comes." Hakon squeezed his eyes shut and knuckled them. "Ah that I had the eyes of Heimdallr!"

"Gudfred," Cormac said. "Your watch."

Gudfred took Hakon's place and they waited, and he watched, and heartbeats thumped away minute after minute.

"We should have brought a game-board," Edric said, in his voice that was so oddly high for all his burliness.

Outside, the breeze stiffened. It murmured, now. Far off, thunder sounded in a long rumble.

"Listen to Sleipnir gallop!" Edric said, and at the window Gudfred looked up as if to see Odin's eight-legged mount. Cormac remembered Wulfhere's boding ham.

"I am thinking of a thing," Hugi said, beginning a game, "and it is blue and grey."

"A gull," Hakon guessed.

"It comes," Gudfred said.

His voice quivered, and no man thought he meant a gull. The game was stillborn. Bored men came to life. They scrambled.

Like weird slender serpents rising from the sea, all twitching and dripping, that unnatural seaweed came. They saw it slither across the wet rocks in a way to make strong men shudder. Coming, coming to the attack. It appeared and disappeared amid tenuous wisps of fog that was never still. The door below was secured. They waited, while the unearthly kelp explored.

Then, like the natural process of climbing ivy or runner-beans, save that this climbing was incredibly swift, the seaweed came up the side of the tower. It was coming for them, and they crowded together to watch. It clung and ascended by means of its many sucking orifices, while they stood tight-jawed with prickling napes, and listened to its wet vinaceous rustle.

Up the wall came the vampire seaweed, unfazed by the wind that blew now harder.

"It is here," Cormac said, backing, and then all of them saw the first greenish-brown tendrils, waving at the windowsill like the antennae of some huge insect.

Hugi jerked open the door. Each man of them caught up a bag of quicklime and descended the steps at a trot. At the lower door Hugi set aside his sack and his Roman spatha slipped from its oiled sheath without a sound. Sword ready, he opened the door.

Like a sentry, a runner of finger-thick seaweed lay there on the great flat-cut stone. It reared as if to glare eyelessly at them, and started within.

Though his nostrils quivered and his hair prickled beneath his helm, Hugi pounced over it, curveting like a high-spirited horse. From behind thus, he hewed three feet of kelp from its main trunk. Only sap oozed. Hugi stood with sword ready to do battle for them while his four companions emerged with their burdens. They hurried around the tower to where the eerily mobile seaweed rose up from the ocean and slithered up the stones. Every man squinted against wind and sea-spray.

They poured quicklime all about the base of the tower and over the trembling plant runners there.

The wet kelp sizzled and twitched trembling, then trembled more violently as the quicklime burned, and burned. Fumes rose to ride the fog, and men back-paced. The plant withered, darkening, while Cormac and his men stood well back. They stared, forced to believe the unbelievable.

The kelp fell back from the tower, rustling, and sought refuge in its own habitat. Constantly burning, it plunged back into the water. The wind whistled. The sea lapped high against the rocks and was churned the more by the sorcerous algae, which lashed violently about like spitted serpents.

With ugly little smiles that stemmed from nothing humorous, Cormac and the four Danes re-entered the tower. Hugi paused to empty his bag of quicklime all over the flat stone that formed an outside threshold. Then he followed his companions inside. They closed the thick door of cross-braced oak, and barred it. Back up and up the steps they went, victors without laughter or cheering, though Hakon did bound as he led the way. Cormac made for the beacon and Hakon was there before him, peering forth into the night.

"Ah, surely this is the night of Loki the treacherous," Hakon said in a small voice. "Wolf: it comes again."

Cormac shouldered in while the others pressed close. They stared down, blinking and squinting, for the wind was well up and the sky rumbled so that Thor was surely abroad, exercising the brace of goats that drew his chariot.

The quicklime had been diluted and dissipated in the brine. Perhaps, too, algal reinforcements had been called up. The weed did indeed come again from the foaming sea.

This time Cormac waited until it was but an arm's length below before he opened a bag of quicklime. Squeezing shut both eyes whiles he held his breath, he dumped the bag out the window. He let it go when it was nigh empty, and swung from the window lest the wet wind blow the volatile stuff into his face. They heard only the banshee wind and the thunder, which was closer. The suffering algae did not scream as any natural foe would have done, assailed by searing quicklime.

When Edric looked, he reported that the weed had again withdrawn.

It came a third time. Again they dumped quicklime down upon it, with Cormac cursing the wind and high sea below that swept their volatile armament off the quay.

When the kelp tried to climb in at them for the fourth time, they used nearly the last of the quicklime.

It was then that they heard the terrible creaking and groaning of wood, and the wailing cry of tortured metal . . .

"*Hinges!* The door below!"

They whipped open the upper door to peer down the steps—just as the lower door, amid a terrible creaking and splintering, brast from its hinges. The demon-plant had crept under it, forced itself up into cracks that hardly existed, and crawled and grown, swelling. Malignant stems and runners had crushed and splintered the door as the roots of trees split stones—though in an uncanny speeding up of the time required for any such zoölogical feat.

A herbaceous slithering rustle ascended the stairs.

Cormac snatched up the last bag, only partially filled with quicklime, and flung it. The sack struck the stairwell wall and showered its contents over the enemy. It sizzled on the wet creepers and fumes rose in the narrow stairwell. The kelp lashed and churned so that some tendrils struck the stone walls with the sound of whip-cracks.

The men waited in chill dread, squinting, trying not to breathe because of the pungent, caustic fumes. The seaweed was no longer coming . . .

It came. In that narrow compass of the stairwell the thick relentless stalks pressing ever up from below forced its swift-slithering second wave past the destruction of the vanguard. Up came the preternatural kelp, for Cormac and his four.

The attack must be met in the doorway. Only two men dared hew in that narrow space, and Edric and Hugi leaped forward. Hugi wielded both sword and dagger. Edric soon saw the wisdom of that, for a buckler was of no avail against this sort of viney attack. That burly Dane shook off his shield and slung it behind him into the lightchamber. He fought then with short-ax and dagger against the ceaseless assault of a half-dozen snaking twitching vines at once.

A probing runner slithered between Hugi's feet and

started to arch up. Cormac sheared through it with his sword, dropped to one knee and sliced off another kelpy tendril that wound about Edric's ankle.

The assault thickened and more and more the two men struck sparks from the walls with their flailing blades. Indeed, they endangered one another.

"Gudfred—light torches from the beacon!" Cormac yelled, and used dagger and thumb to slice a tendril from around Hugi's ankle.

Grease-soaked brands leaped aflame; two, then three.

"Back," Cormac called. "Edric—JUMP back— disengage! Hugi—out of there!"

Hugi bent both knees, sliced away a serpent of horridly living plant, and pounced backward so that Hakon only just avoided being knocked down. Edric tried—and sprawled his length on his back. He'd been tripped up by the thallophytic serpent that whipped twice about his leg. Cormac's sword bit through the finger-thick algae stem inches from Edric's foot. He was forced to twist his sword to free it of the wooden flooring. Edric still had to sit up and slit the clinging bit of weed from his leg.

On one knee, Cormac twisted half around and seized a torch from Gudfred.

He swung back and hurled it down the steps in one motion. The brand never reached bottom; *Laminaria* clogged the stairwell now like the thick, impossibly living web of an enormous spider. Living plant crackled, for its wetness could not extinguish the burning grease any more than it had the quicklime.

It was even more sinister and eerie, their knowledge that something *living* and predatory was burning, alive —and without a sound. Only the constant rustle of its violent movements announced the vampire plant's reaction—awareness?—pain!—to its own burning.

167

The odour of the sea and its dread get pervaded the tower now. The mephitic vapours of sorcery could have been no more repugnant to the five besieged men. Faceless, eyeless, unseeing and unhearing, mouthless and yet provided with the most ghastly of mouths, the baleful algae came again.

Each man backed against a wall to diminish his danger from the efforts of his fellows. And in the beacon-chamber itself they battled the onslaught from the sea, with sharp steel and grease-soaked brands.

Leafy structures shook and rustled and through the doorway came the many-mouthed enemy, the thickness of its runners ranging from that of a brooch-pin to burly Edric's thumb—and behind them thrust algaeous branches thick as sword-hilts . . . and behind them?

The men fought in silence, resisting panic and heeding each the flailing arms of the others. Flames blazed high and yellow. Black smoke boiled so that they coughed. Their eyes streamed tears to mingle with their sweat and slice runnels down through the sooty deposit of smoke on their faces. This man and then that was grasped, so that another must tear and cut him free of the vampire kelp, and sear the base of that grasping runner. Each man fought with brand and dagger. Blood oozed from sucker-wounds. The pods for its storing popped under booted feet.

Cormac mac Art had reason to rue his wearing of mail, for twice seaweed snakes wriggled in betwixt rings and padded hauberk to begin a ghastly lacing of themselves to him.

First his own efforts and Hugi's, then his own and Edric's freed him. And then Edric was on one knee with a pommel-thick rope of living brown about his leg and another circling his left arm, and his companions sliced off his preternatural attackers in voiceless, grunting horror, and Gudfred was caught, and he had to be sliced

168

free, and in the doing of that Hakon cried out wordlessly as the runner that had snaked up his back slapped his throat and applied a sucker . . .

Gudfred's hand was burned. Hakon's neck bled. Cormac's cheek oozed red from a vampiric sucker he'd torn loose and crushed betwixt fingers and dagger-hilt. A swipe from Edric's dagger saved Hugi's leg and slit open his leather legging. Another time Hugi moved too swiftly and Hakon could not twist his blade aside, and now Hugi's wrist dripped blood from the little cut on its back.

Shuddering in primal horror, the men *heard* the kelp sucking up the blood from the floor . . .

Once the hem of Hakon's russet-hued tunic flamed up from his own brand, and he hurled the torch into the stairwell and slapped out the fire on his clothing himself. Up his boot as he did slithered a ghoulish little horror, so pretty in its brown pigment over green, and Cormac squatted and neatly sliced it away before applying his own torch to the thing's stem.

And still the rustling pseudopods of the awful weed came in unearthly onslaught.

Minutes had passed; an hour had passed; outside the wind shrieked in primal anger and none of those in the tower so much as heard. Grim death stalked them in awful silence and the wind had naught to do with it.

At last Cormac released a frustrated roar. Barely able to see amid the smoke and rustling lashing tendrils, he stabbed his torch into the cauldron. The great black pot was still partially full of grease. It spat and hissed, swiftly liquefying. Flame leaped up—and instantly melting fat extinguished the brand. Hugi thrust his in and sawed a kelpy serpent from his arm. Even as it died it snapped down and clung to his wrist, so that blood oozed when he tore it free.

Snatching up more brands, Cormac dumped them

into the cauldron. Flame leaped to darken the ceiling and plants withdrew from heat that was nigh unbearable to humans within helms, and their tunics, hauberks and mailcoats.

Cormac and thick-thighed Edric set each a foot against the big black pot, and exchanged a glance, and shoved.

The cauldron tumbled through the doorway, spewing hissing grease-fire. It bounded down the steps, clanging, throwing off blobs of unquenchable flame and blazing torches. It tore through the clogging plants it spattered with flaming grease. Resistless, the heavy hemisphere of iron fell and bounded and clanged, rebounding clangourously from stone walls as it came to curves. It smashed and rolled and bounced all the way to the bottom of the steps.

"Chop and chop and chop!" Cormac yelled, putting his strength against the door.

The others did, men with black faces and desperately staring eyes. They cleared the floor before the door. Cormac was able to slam it against a stairwell that was brightly aflicker with lurid flames.

With the cloak he'd taken off on entering this horror-besieged chamber, Gudfred drove the smoke out the beacon-window. Around him his companions crouched and knelt while they daggered serpentine runners of vampire seaweed ranging in size now up to one flopping monster thick as Hugi's wrist. It sprouted two foot-long fingers, and the men had to mince them to make the awful things cease their attack.

Swiftly as Cormac hurled a dagger-long piece out the window, a sucker fastened and drew blood as it was torn from the back of his hand.

The stairwell crackled with the burning of grease and dry wood and obscenely motile plants. There was no other sound from that quarter; the door was not assaulted.

Men with smoke-darkened faces stared at each other from pale eyes, and all were tinged with horror. They had existed and fought in a sort of mindless hysteria, disbelieving but saving themselves from the impossible. Panting, they leaned together, at once hanging onto one another's shoulders—and supporting each other. Their legs quivered. Blood dripped and now burns began to beat like little hearts of pain.

Staggering, streaming sweat through the greasy smoke that rendered his face unrecognizable, Cormac mac Art turned and extinguished the beacon.

"Wulfhere and the others!" Hugi gasped. "Tyr's beard—I'd forgot!"

Cormac had not, for the extinguishing of the beacon was another part of the plan he and Wulfhere had worked out. Outside, thunder stalked the sky like an enraged lion that frightened the wind into screams and howls the while it drove the ocean into restless dunes.

"It is no night for them to be out," Gudfred panted.

"It's as if . . . *they* knew," Hakon said, and all wondered who or what "they" might be.

Through set lips Cormac said, "Methinks those who sent the devil-kelp *do* know." He considered, frowning. "Now I but hope the unknown master of that killer weed will not think the ghastly attack has . . . succeeded, and show his . . . or its! . . . false beacon!"

"Aye," Hugi said, rubbing at a smoke-dark face with smoke-dark fingers so that he accomplished naught but the creation of a weird design. "Our comrades are better giving no chase on this sea!"

Cormac stepped past him, and after a pause during which each man sucked in a breath, he threw open the door. More smoke billowed up into the chamber, dark and greasy. Flames crackled, fitful and scattered. The cauldron had rolled over the smashed door, or through it, and though it was charred that great chunk of old oak did not burn. As for the plants; they were consumed, and none more came.

It was a time for the clarions and shouts of the victors, the prancing of steeds and the tossing of flowers 'neath glittering towers whose windows sprouted the smiling faces of children and desirous damsels.

Instead Cormac and his dirty, smudged little company sank weakly down to sit on the floor in exhaustion. Now they became aware of stinging pain from suckers torn from their flesh, and nicks from their own weapons, and two burns from brand or lashing, burning plant. Clothing was ruined and armour would require cleaning, and oiling. Yet their thoughts were as one: of their companions of *Raven*, asea in a night become a vast total blackness that was vassal to a howling roaring wind.

CHAPTER ELEVEN: The Sirens

The howling roaring wind drove the sea into foaming madness. Lightning slashed the sky like glittering daggers and thunder stalked on the feet of a thousand soldiers amarch to war. *Raven* rocked and was tossed. Rolling water slammed into her strakes like great fists and the foot-thick mast creaked and quivered as if become an aspen sapling. Her two sea-anchors were almost weightless in a sea gone insane and inimical.

In cap and oilskins, Wulfhere was able to stand at the bow because he clung tightly with gloved hands. He stared at nothing.

The tower was no longer visible though it was not so far as a hundred yards away. The tremulous yellow glow of its beacon had marked it; now that was extinguished. Morbid and horrific thoughts pulled at the mind of the Danish giant though he fought them. Was it Cormac who had extinguished the light, or . . .

An he and those with him are slain, I'll flood the sea with blood, he thought ferociously, and then realized that the Gael's little group had been attacked by bloodless algae, plants of the sea. Any blood he'd spill would be that of his former comrades.

He stared into the night of seagods' wrath, waiting for

another glow to tug at his peripheral vision. For Wulfhere would not take his gaze from where he'd last seen the tower's light, lest it be rekindled and mislead him. It was the false light he awaited; the wrecker's beacon.

His crew was silent. They huddled and clung while all about them chaos reigned and water came cascading over the 'midships gunwale to drench them. Beards were bespattered with briny foam like hoarfrost. They did nothing but wait because there was nothing else to do. The water drained sloshing into *Raven*'s bailing well, where its level rose slowly.

"Hrut!" their captain bawled. "Thorbrand! Blades ready!"

The two men rolled their eyes, but lurched each to an opposite side of the hull. With one hand they clung there, to slippery wood. The other was out for balance, and to draw steel at their leader's command. The wind dropped with the suddenness no man ever grew accustomed to. Eyes looked this way and that; wind-assaulted ears seemed suddenly to have become hyper-acute. Thunder grumbled like an old smith shackled to his forge.

Thorbrand and Hrut Bear-slayer drew swords because the pommels felt good in their hands. The two stood, well-braced on seasoned sea-legs, near the thick taut ropes that vanished over the sides.

"HA! See? See!"

Aye! they saw what Wulfhere descried through the troublous dark. A new glow. A light. A new beacon. It seemed to bob, as though someone with a lantern somehow ambled over the water. The decoy light! With the true beacon out in the old Roman tower, the wreckers had lit their own to entice *Raven* to her death.

"Oars! Half-sail! *Chop!*"

Men leaped to their feet and sprang to the oar-racks where their long poles rattled, stowed during the awful wind and plunging waves. Others hauled up the rope-bound yard. And as one man Hrut and Thorbrand chopped through the rope. The thick braided lengths vanished; below, huge boulders dragged them to the seabed. Oars dropped into their locks and stout arms manned the rudder.

"Pull!"

Raven spread her wings. *Raven* flew.

The wind returned, and men cursed and called on the gods.

"Aegir sleep well!" one said, hoping that underwater lord would not awake and come for them with his giant net.

"Nyrod . . . in the palm of your hands is *Raven* your servant!"

"Ran be kind to sons of the sea!"

But that man was stared at; none wished so much as to attract the attention of the goddess of the sea and drowner of those abroad on her bosom.

And Wulfhere muttered the names of Thor and the All-father and Frigg to please Odin, and Freya and her sunny brother and aye, those sea-deities too—and, just in case, he quietly mentioned that Mannanan macLir that Cormac was wont to call upon, for those of Eirrin did insist that it was he lorded it over the sea.

Again the wind whipped the water into white-topped, mobile mountains. They drove like gigantic fists against *Raven* and the ship rocked with their impact. Rocked, and sped forward. Wulfhere's commands were constant. Clinging to the side with one hand, the master of *Raven* made his way slowly, ever watchful, along the narrow planking that ran from bow to stern.

Raven raced through that howling inimical night of

dashing leaping waves, and all aboard knew they hurtled toward the doom that was planned for them. Wulfhere's sea-genius and their own strength could save them—and the gods.

Even as his ship wrestled the ocean and his ruddy face went scarfy with leaping brine, Wulfhere wondered. Did they but chase a phantom, a will-o'-the-wisp that would provide not even a decent battle for axes and swords . . . but might well give them watery death just the same?

Clinging, he glanced forward. The light loomed larger. When *Raven* climbed up from a trough to balance a moment on a ridge of water, the staring giant had a flashing glimpse of the wrecker's craft. Weirdly, he saw no sails and the other vessel looked white. Then his own straining ship plunged down a slope of rushing water and he saw only the walls forming the next trough.

Suddenly he gripped the rail with both hands and stared. "ROCKS!" he bellowed, and hurled himself aft along a foot-wide walkway, not even holding, defiant of the wind. "Steerboard oars up! Pull *hard* aport! Hard, boys, an ye'd ever be dry this side of Valhalla! Quarter sail to steerboard!"

Then the enormous strength of the Skull-splitter was added to that of Ordlaf. The steersman was a strong man, and muscular; Wulfhere's upper arms were big as his thighs. The sea tried to take the steering oar away from them. Even with so little sail on, the mast creaked and bowed. Ropes of walrus hide strained and seemed to grunt like men. *Raven* hurtled. Captain and helmsman bent their backs and the muscles of their calves bulged their leggings.

Wood creaked horribly, the ship fought, and turned, and of a sudden the sail flapped.

"Reef sail! Reef sail!"

"Hela's cold dugs—*look at those teeth!*"

"Hela indeed—the old bitch hungers for us and would have us join her in Elvidnit this night!"

This from those men aport who saw the awful rocks that had awaited them, wet jagged teeth that would have received *Raven* and turned her into driftwood in bare seconds. Only just had they saved themselves, by their captain's seamanship and main strength . . . and the strong backs of oarsmen who fought wind and leaping, dashing waters.

Even the wind eased, as if otherworld forces were reconsidering their attack.

Swift as a racing horse, *Raven* plunged past the rocks aport, showering them with a boiling white wake. The vessel shuddered as she slammed into a wall of water that drenched the crew anew. The world vanished; they were under water! No—they were plowing through that wet dune! Then they were out, through it, gasping, the decks streaming—only to glissade like an uncontrolled sled down a long mountainside of water.

"Up quarter sail! All oars—PULL!"

Water sloshed higher in the bailing well. Wulfhere glanced in. No; no men need yet be detailed to that churl's job.

Wind and wave struck. A man yelled and an arm was broken. Knocked onto her side, *Raven* dumped water as she rushed along showing her keel. The steer-oar waved ridiculously in air. Then the ship was up, shaking herself like a great wet dog. Her crew spewed water from noses and mouths and glanced around nervously. All were there; the faces of two writhed in pain and that Knud Left-hand's arm was broken was all too obvious.

"It's only the right," he said, and tried to wave, and passed out. Two of his fellow carles sprang to seize him and lash him down. *Raven*'s second Knud would not be holding shield or oar again, for a long while.

Mighty arms forced the tiller over and *Raven* bucked wind and sea. Somehow they dragged her about as a strong man drags a screaming stallion for the breaking. Wind and water buffeted her with a viciousness that seemed sentiently deliberate. Again the ship plunged for the light. It seemed to flee now, definitely amove on a swift-moving deck, its attempt to smash them on the rocks having failed. The wind glibbered obscenely and new thunder snarled with the voices of ten thousand rearing bears.

A bolt of lightning created noonday light, and Wulfhere stared at the craft of the wreckers. It was fleeing—and what a vessel was there!

He and his desperate men were far, far too busy to grapple the supernatural wreckers, for so Wulfhere at least now knew them to be. But he'd seen them, oh Odin's stones he'd *seen* them across those mountain ranges of water—ere they and their weird and shuddersome barge vanished away into the windswept night.

Aye, vanished, and the cursing crew of *Raven* set about getting her in.

Next day—late, after weary men woke on dry land beneath bright Hispanic sun—Wulfhere Skull-splitter told Cormac what he'd beheld, and the Gael stared at him. Already he'd seen what he did not want to believe and had been forced by menace to his very life; must there be more? Logic had become unreasonableness— but with reason that was unreasonable, Cormac mac Art resisted.

"Ye mean—*women?*"

"I swear," Wulfhere said, and drew himself up so that he was even more imposing; Wulfhere would have been imposing buried to the knees in mud. "I swear by the All-father's one entirely sufficient eye and by Thor's scarlet beard, aye and by the moustache of my dear father's woman Freydrid—I swear, Wolf: I *saw* them."

"Ran's . . ."

"Ran's daughters."

"Ran's daughters."

Wulfhere nodded.

"*Women?* Sirens?"

"Sirens? What's that?"

Cormac mac Art waved a hand. "A supposition of the Greeks. Comely women of the seas who entice seafaring men to—"

"Aye!" the Dane nodded emphatically. "Aye! Loki's eyes and Hela's dry gourds, Wolf of Eirrin—*believe!* They were the dread daughters of Ran sure, and afloat on a barge made all of bones."

"Bones."

"YES!"

"Bones, asea. In a storm."

"Bones, son of an Eirrish pig farmer! Nor had any or aught of them an oar in her dainty pale hands, nor was there aught of sail on that barge not of this Midgard!"

And the Splitter of skulls stamped, to assure them both that they still trod the land of mortal-kind. Galicians saw them there outside the king's hall, and stared, but went on their way. No man wanted aught to do with an argument between those two storied pirates.

"The sea was high, Wulfhere. It's black the night was as a bear's cave in winter. It's glad I am and no man lost asea, old battle-brother. But . . . how saw ye them in that darkness?"

"*Wolf.* Ye doubt me yet. Ah Cormac, Cormac—I *saw.* A fire burned on the deck of—"

"A fire! On the very deck! In the wind and a sea like mountains on the move!"

"YES, damn ye! A fire burned there on that otherworld barge. I SAW it! Without fuel and blazing high, within a sort of circle, a strange sort of circle that . . . well, it was all picked out in that . . . that Romish piece-rock. Ah—mosaic.''

Cormac stared at him, and he'd looked more believing.

Wulfhere stared at the Gael, the man he'd escaped gaol with, sailed and divagated with, these three years.

Cormac stared at the Dane, whose life he'd saved and who'd saved his; his battle-brother and respected companion.

The Dane said, ''Well?''

''I believe you, Wulfhere. If my battle-brother Wulfhere Skull-splitter says he saw it, it was there.''

''Aye! Of course it's impossible, blood-brother. And it was there. As the moving attacking kelp was. Aye, blood-brother, believe, as I believe all you tell me.''

And the two men gazed at each other in the sunlight of a quiet day the praises of which Galician birds trilled, and Wulfhere beamed and Cormac smiled. With his lips closed and his brows up.

''And you, blood-brother. Tell me what befell yourself and those four men with you in the tower.''

Cormac shrugged. ''Well, after Freya stopped in and we all supped on one of the cats who'd pulled her chariot, a hundred and thirty-seven Valkyries flew in, and all tall as yourself. And though 'twas boring and sore hard work, we were stout men and managed to serve them all. After that—''

Wulfhere went crimson and his face worked. With doubled fists, he wheeled and walked off. Stiff or no, the huge Dane would make the ax-target suffer this day.

Cormac stood reflecting for a time, and squatted and drew aimless designs in the grass and the dirt. At last he heaved a great sigh. Then he rose and set off after his battle-brother.

CHAPTER TWELVE: A Lovely Afternoon for a Murder

Ran was wife to Lord Aegir the Bountiful, and no kindly she-goddess was she. Any northborn seaman knew that she spread nets of disaster for ships, and delighted in dragging them and their crews down and down to her airless demesne. There she gave laughter whilst watching the pretty bubbles of those men's last breaths go dancing up to the sunlight. And, as the skalds were wont to refer to the sea as "the whale's road," so they called the rolling waves "Ran's daughters."

No skald was Wulfhere Skull-splitter. Like all seafaring men all over the world, he was certain that luring sea-women waited to drown good men in their white arms. And what had he seen? A barge made all of bones and women aboard—and there was no doubt of their enmity and destructive purpose. And . . . would not the very seaweed obey the daughters of Aegir and Ran?

"I *saw* them, Wolf!" the Dane insisted. "Eerie, blank-eyed bitches with long hair all pale with brine, and cold choking kisses on their lips for any man they can clasp in their arms, I warrant me! The very daughters of Ran, Cormac!"

And again Cormac mac Art turned away to let his brain wrestle with the ambiguous and the impossible . . . and seeming impossibilities.

The Daughters of Ran.

Very well. Gods existed of a surety, and their get; a fool and inexperienced was he who averred they did not. Sorcery existed too, as it had since the dim beginnings of humankind; ere Atlantis rose up from the greedy seas, much less sank again long later. Of a sudden mac Art *knew* that sorcery had existed in Commoria and Valusia and Aquilonia and Brythunia and in dark, jungle-shadowed Stygia, though in truth he was not sure how he knew so certainly. (What places were those?)

He stumbled, frowning. The very air had seemed to shimmer. No; a glance around showed him that all was normal in sunny Galicia.

Normal! Oh aye, normal . . . the Daughters of Ran— or the Sirens the Greeks spoke of still—had on their Cleopatran barge an unfueled fire that burned without consuming the craft. Cormac drew in his lips. He sighed. Very well. That seemed plainly impossible. And that meant it was totally inexplicable . . . by ordinary means.

There was no explanation for motile, seemingly sentient seaweed, or for the fire on that phantom craft.

No *natural* explanation.

Wandering, thinking, mulling, Cormac hardly took note of a happily chatting couple already causing talk: King Veremund, and Clodia of Nantes. Cormac would report to the king, sometime today; at present he needed to sort out his own thoughts a bit more. For another reason altogether, Veremund hardly seemed ready to discuss last night's events, either.

Without being fully aware of it, Cormac wandered back to the coast. There he stood gazing upon the endlessly lapping, glassy plain of the sea that was now emerald and now sapphire or lapis lazuli and now pure onyx crowned with ivory and behaving as if demon-ridden. The sea. Many men plied the sea, and some professed to love it. The sea loved no one. Nor, save now and again, did it seem to hate.

Standing over it, to Cormac's left reared that white pile of stone; the accursed tower the Romans had raised for the aid of ships at sea. It was sentry to the land, a brooding watchman over the water.

The sea. It had rolled on and on, Cormac mused, for untold ages, lapping timeless shores that changed only in name and in the peoples that claimed them. Surely the sea had been here forever . . .

No. Treachery Bay or the Cantanabrian Sea, he suddenly saw, would not be so in future, though his brain held no meaning for the strange word *Biscay*. And in past . . .

Again Cormac's world seemed to shimmer, to stumble.

The sea rolled out green. And grew greener, greener . . . And then it was gone even as he stared upon it.

Here sprawled rolling plains, and even as he stared, seeing not and yet seeing, he saw how the sun shimmered on burnished mail and silvered cuirasses and gilt-worked helmets. And mac Art was elsewhen; his *remembering* was upon him.

Horses pranced over grassland and their tails streamed out like fine cloaks. Their proud riders bore lances and swords that had oft dripped with red. Their feet were thrust into leathern boots whose variations of colour he knew derived from having waded rivers of blood like scarlet tides. For so was history made, and he knew then that he was watching history, on the land that had lain there ere the bay swallowed it.

In a neighing shouting jingling leather-creaking

squalling chaos that nevertheless bespoke the pride and
organization of civilization, steel-clad ranks of gleaming
mounted men galloped across that which in the long ago
had been well-grassed earth, not sea. And he was
looking upon the long, long ago. Guidons and bannerets
fluttered like bright butterflies above those mailed men
of old.

Before Cormac's eyes and yet behind them, history
rolled back. The intervening centuries were swept away
as the fog before the warm sun of morning; as had been
whole cities and civilizations swept away in the
relentlessness of uncaring time.

And he knew whereon he looked. Names came into
his mind, strange names in no language now known,
hoary with age and yet all glitteringly exotic.

Asgalun and Amalric and Arenjun, and Shadizar the
Wicked had existed, far over there to the east, and
Numelia of Nemedia, a place whose name toyed with
the tongue. Koth, and Vilayet—what names were these?
The bright Road of Kings had wound anciently across
this time-forgot land like a sleepy serpent testing the sun
of these dreaming kingdoms south of the Hyborian
demesnes. Plains rolled verdantly out to a placid river
whose name he knew—somehow—was Tybor. Along its
bank rose a city whose walls were etched by the sun in
fading gold. This was bastioned Shamar, and Cormac
knew, just as he knew that once he'd been there, once
he'd thefted there, and fought with sharp blade.

Aye, and once too he'd abode in the proud kingdom
that sprawled fertile and beautiful just northwest of
Shamar.

Aquilonia.

*Aye, Aquilonia, by Mitra! I know you well, Aquilonia,
lost in the grey clouds of time and space.*

*Aquilonia, far from sunburned old Turan . . . and I . . .
I came down from Cimmeria and was king in Aquilonia,*

once! Tarantis . . . be that a name? Aye: Tarantia. My name. No—my woman's? Perhaps one named Tarantia was queen to me, when I wore crown in Aquilonia so far from my native . . . not Eirrin for it did not exist . . . my native Cimmeria . . . But what is my name?

Amra? But no; *amra* was a Gaelic word, and how could a man be called by that word: "eulogy?"

The thoughts were swept away. Before mac Art the bodeful mists rolled, eddying, coiling, and history rushed along. The northern barbarians came down onto these plains, and met others, dark men, and the struggle raged . . . and then all was swept away like smoke before the winds of time.

Aquilonia vanished, with the plains of Poitain and the Tybor; drowned in a convulsion of the earth, and that cataclysm sent green-blue waves rolling in to swallow all those realms into that of Manannan macLir.

And history swept on, in a rush, where Aquilonia had basked had also stood a city of horror, a city haunted by a horrid ichthyosaurian shadow that was also somehow human . . . or almost . . . and now where Aquilonia had lain there rolled the Bay of Treachery, and the dark dense forests of Galicia blotted the sunlit green of the plains of ancient Poitain.

"Mac Art."

Cormac blinked and twitched his head. What—? What had happened? Was this a vision? Aquilonia and Poitain? What were those? *Blood of the gods! It's the . . . the* Remembering! *It's come on me again!*

"Mac Art?"

Aye, that was his name. Not—not whoever he'd been, in those ages tens of centuries agone, when the race of humankind had risen up only to fall . . . again. Once more Cormac mac Art jerked his head. He stared at the sparkling sea, he who had known from the time of his first Remembering at fourteen that once he'd been that fabled hero of Eirrin, Cuchulain of Muirthemne. And how many others? For he knew that Rome was not ancient. Rome was a child. Cormac mac Art was ancient; this life-force that had returned to tread this earth again and—

"Mac Art!"

Cormac whirled.

A few feet away stood Zarabdas, not robed but in a peasant's cowled tunic that was a bit longish for the Sueves, falling skirted over leggings and gaitered buskins. The bald old man with the raven's-wing beard was staring, and Cormac knew he'd been called more than once.

"Mac Art."

"Aye. Zarab . . . das. Aye. What do ye here, Zarabdas?"

"The king has asked for you, and I had observed your pensive walking. I thought you'd have come here, to contemplate that which happed out there last night." His nod compassed the sea and the tower standing over it. "But—I've called your name several times. You are all right?"

"I am all right, Zarabdas," Cormac said, hardly of a mind to tell this unknown quantity of an eastern mage of his Remembering. To avoid further queries and discussion, he said, "It's deep I was in thought, Zarabdas. Aye, deep in thought . . . what saw Zarabdas, the evening past?"

"I saw it, mac Art. I saw the kelp come from the sea like snakes, and I saw how it climbed, and was driven back. I heard your battle in the tower, and I saw the light die."

"Was I extinguished it, after we beat off that demon-stuff from the sea. Saw ye Wulfhere, or . . . what he saw?"

Zarabdas shook his head and his cowl slipped back; he stood in shade now, anyhow. "No. Only the dark, and the wind and the lightning, and crashing thunder. What did Wulfhere see?"

Cormac was still unsure as to whether to trust Zarabdas, but he told him. The Palmyran shook his head and looked grim.

"Manannan of the white steeds and sunlit waters is not the only god of the sea," Cormac said darkly, looking upon the waters with one brow cocked. "It's demons there are in the deep. Creatures that pull down sailors, good men and bad, down and down to their airless demesne . . . which men know by many names in many lands."

The Palmyran mage studied him, wearing a strange expression.

"Aye, though probably more exists than you know of, Cormac mac Art." Zarabdas seemed to stare at nothing and his sockets seemed nearly to swallow his dark eyes. "There are strange cults of Dagon hereabouts, spread about by Imperial legionaires in centures just past. And that dread belief and cult never dies, of the One who sleeps in sunken R'lyeh."

"Of Dagon I know. but . . . Releeyuh? That word I know not."

"R'lyeh. A most, most ancient cult—and foul. It's said the horrid demons emanated from off this plane, and were on the earth afore our own kind arose from the slime."

Cormac studied him, thinking. "Zarabdas . . . think ye any hereabouts yet practice the rites of this . . . R'lyeh . . ."

". . . no no, that is the *place*, a city or mighty palace . . ."

". . . who might be . . . calling up such . . . gods, or

demons, or creatures whatever they be? Living moving kelp, and maidens on a ship of bone?"

"I have no knowledge of it."

"Hmmm. Well . . . and the king is after asking for me, it's best I return to his hall. Suppose we both be telling him what we know, and ask him about cultists, hereabouts."

And so they did, met partway back to the old city by a mounted troop. The two men went to the king in his hall. There they gave him their knowledge and their surmises and their un-knowledge. And did the king know aught of any who practiced such dark cultism in his realm? Nay, but Veremund called in his Hispano-Roman advisor.

That hawk-beak, who bore the ancient name Vindex, came. With haughty Patrician distaste he did assurance on them that he knew of no such activity. Nor drew he too close to the Gaelic pirate. Vindex wore a lovely tunic of apple-green silk all broidered with goldwire thread. It was passing sweet, that garment, mac Art thought.

"Yet I'd not be wholly surprised at such a cult here," Vindex said austerely, wearing his eyebrows halfway up his forehead. "Most peasants here are still pagan in basic belief, though they do profess adherence to the One Church."

At this Veremund firmed his lip. Cormac held back his smile: he'd been apprised of the existence, in the king's own most private quarters, of a most private little Remembrance of the old goddess Ertha; and Irnic Break-ax flaunted the device on his shield: it was the horned head of Arawn, the Old God of the fair people of Germania and Gallia and Britannia.

"Shall I inquire?" Vindex asked.

Staring at the king, Cormac shook his head almost violently. Veremund saw, and said nay. He also advised

Vindex to keep silent on the matter altogether. The curly-haired man departed, tunic skirt swishing, eyebrows high, eyes just above the plane directly before them. Just the sort of fellow for whom being tripped would do a great deal of good, Cormac thought. *Ah Caius Julius who was surely nigh as great a king as my namesake, what have ye wrought, and to what have your followers come?*

"It is a matter to be investigated," Zarabdas said. "I shall be most discreet, lord King."

"So be it," Veremund said, "and be so. Cormac?"

The Gael shook his head. "We must try again, of course. It's several questions I have, King, but few answers. Methinks I'll do a bit more pacing and cudgelling of this poor brain of mine." *No help here*, he thought. *Sure it's long been said that Behl lends aid to him who aids himself!*

Zarabdas gave him a look askance, with an eyebrow raised, and Veremund smiled. This uncatchable reiver was hardly known for a "poor" brain!

And once again Cormac mac Art went awalking, to be alone with his thoughts. He and his companions had come close to death in that tower. There must be another way to deal with the demon-weed, even though the door was being replaced at this moment—with bronze.

He walked. He liked this land well enow, with its green and blue-misted hills and dark forests beyond which grasses waved on rolling land often wetted by rain; not all that different from green, wet, sea-ringed Eirrin, was Galicia of the Suevi. It was a lovely afternoon for a walk. Despite his cares he felt light and springy, unweighted by armour or helm and with his left arm free of his shield's fifteen pounds.

Meandering, he entered and paced through the dim

coolth of a smallish wood, mostly oak and the chestnuts beloved of Galician swine. He thought much, but decided nothing. Indeed he found it hard not to dwell on the strangeness of that past-vision that came on him from time to time. With his sword he sliced the green shoot of a branchlet, and chewed it as he walked, ambling. Many months had passed since he'd dared walk carelessly abroad; was good to be welcome, someplace.

The gentle tinkling of bells impinged on his outer awareness just enough to cause him to turn his steps along a side path. Soon he emerged onto a long broad stretch of meadow. Here was beauty, under the sun and misted by the air of this seaside land of much rainfall.

Like the plains of Poitain . . .

Mac Art shook off that thought. "Galicia," he muttered aloud, with firmness.

It was cattle he'd heard, he now saw, and belled; probably to prevent their calving in the woods and eluding their masters. Busy at the grass-pulling, these independent few; the rest of the herd lay about in that grove of piebald birch, chewing and belching and chewing.

It was a lovely afternoon.

Cormac ambled toward them, in the open now, and feeling ridiculous with his sword swinging at his hip in this pastoral setting. The farmers hardly wore swords! The farmers . . . peasants. . . . What shrine or cleared area like a druid's glade might lie hid in the deep darkness of that forest? He'd only just entered it, after all, traversing its bare edge. These peasants might well . . .

From the far side of the birch grove two horsemen appeared agallop, the one atop a bay, the other riding a garnet-hued animal. Both men wore leathern coats and carried spears and shields, and both booted their galloping steeds. They appeared not to be Suevi, though one could not be certain; both men were helmeted. The tunic of one was of cross-hatched double-stripes, green and red on bland white homespun, while the other wore a sleeveless tunic of plain blue under his long leather vest bossed with copper whorls. Though mounted, neither man wore leggings.

They were galloping his way. They swerved around the cows. Strange, armed and armoured men, here in the pasture—

They were galloping *at* him. They were attacking!

Though it was a peaceful country of late afternoon he was in, and among friendly peoples, mac Art was glad now that he had eschewed going about naked; sword and dagger hung at his hips. Of a sudden he was sorry that he wore neither helmet nor mailcoat, and carried no shield.

Yet that would have been ridiculous. Who'd have dreamed he would find himself about to be murdered in such a place on such a lovely day?

He was; the horsemen galloped at him, bending forward now, with lances poised to slay. Clumps of turf from a soil seldom dry flew from the pounding hooves of their mounts.

Though he was poised and full ready to draw steel, Cormac pretended to stare stupidly at them. Let them think he could not believe their mission, these silent racing assassins! They separated, with blue-kilt's bay digging up more grass and sod as he swerved to Cormac's right. The Gael decided; that man he watched, turning slowly. The fellow was a bit too distant to make a good unavoidable cast . . .

Cormac sprinted directly ahead, drawing steel and turning his face to the other man after he'd begun to run. He felt marvelously fleet, nigh sixty pounds the lighter without helmet, chaincoat, and buckler. Sword and dagger had long since become as part of him.

His timing had been so excellent it was as if Eirrin's ancient god Crom of Connacht had tugged him forward under Behl's shining sky-eye; with a whistling whizzing sound the lance of the man in the tartan kilt passed through the space wherein Cormac had just stood. That ironshod lance would have transpierced him from behind. As it was, the spear's head drove heavily into the earth, twenty paces away; thirty from where Cormac now stood.

So much, for a few seconds, for that attacker. Cormac swung his face back to the bay-mounted man.

That one had reined about and was charging in from the side, bent low with his eyes squinted against whipping mane. His spear was held on a downward angle. Cormac saw that he had no chance of running to the other lance, pulling it free, and wielding it in time to meet this attack. This idiot was gripping his mount with muscularly bulging calves and thighs, and obviously meant to skewer the unarmoured Gael. Surely the shock of impact would knock the fool off his mount . . .

That was hardly high among Cormac's concerns. The fellow obviously did mean to do it. Perhaps his horsemanship was that good and his legs that strong. It didn't matter; even if he did fly backward off his steed on impact, that same impact would drive the spear through Cormac's body. Here came death, at the gallop.

The horse plunged at him, seeming to grow bigger and bigger, its neck stretched forth and its teeth showing. Was it so ferocious? Almost in desperation, Cormac decided to find out. He bellowed out as loudly as ever he had in his life. At the same time he feinted left and dived rightward. He struck the ground to roll over and over, hanging onto his sword.

Without ever coming to a halt he hurled himself onto his feet and started a spring for the other lance, standing at an angle from the ground.

He never glanced back to see that the assailant on the dark horse had tried to follow the feint, missed, and was galloping on, rocking precariously in the saddle and using his shield-arm to tug his mount around. Mac Art was interested only in the imbedded lance—and the first horseman, the blue-kilted man on the wiry bay.

Their course was set to intersect. The man wanted his lance back, and could naturally snatch it from the ground as he raced by; these men were, after all, horse-soldiers. Not only did the Gael want that spear, he did not want its owner to retrieve it.

Cormac ran as fast as he could, yelling, brandishing his sword.

Neither of them got it. Cormac was on the horseman's right, and that hand was empty, set to grasp the spear. The attacker's shield was on his horse's other side. He could try yanking his mount about—and perhaps cause it to fall or, if he succeeded, get himself or his horse sword-slashed. Cursing, the fellow raced on, with a leftward swerve. The spear remained.

And Cormac heard hooves pounding behind him.

His own curses filled the air and he slashed wildly at the spear as he fled past. Pause to grasp it, he knew, and he'd be skewered from behind, or crushed beneath flailing forehooves. As it was, he too veered leftward, and his sword-blow, while it failed to slice through the spear's haft, did knock it flat to the ground. It wouldn't be easily regained from horseback, now.

Once again the Gael had little time for thinking or planning. On the run, he circled, and saw the garnet-coloured horse bearing down on him, seeming big as a ship with a strange horsehead prow. Desperately, he hurled his sword. A continuation of that all-body

193

movement sent him lurching leftward.

The horse snorted, then squealed almost humanly as only a horse can. The sword, turning in air, struck it crosswise just above the pale softness of its nose. The animal jerked up its head, trying to hurl itself aside. The thrown sword, without wounding, had served Cormac's purpose.

His attacker, rocking in the saddle, had to lever his right arm out for balance—and a ravening maniac, black hair flying and eyes burning like blue fire, pounced in to grasp the haft of his spear betwixt point and grip. And the horse lunged away leftward.

There was no brace for the rider's feet and thus no leverage for his body. Himself falling, Cormac pulled the tartan-kilted attacker off his own mount.

Both men struck the ground hard, with *whump* sounds and grunts. In a drier clime they might have broken bones. The assassin's impact was much greater than that of his intended victim, and he loosed his hold on his spear. Even so, as Cormac clung to the haft, it came treacherously up into its owner's armpit. His groan was loud, and pained.

That shoulder and arm would have given the would-be assassin a bad night and remained sore on the morrow as a family of boils, had not Cormac lunged to his feet and, twitching his hands into a new grip as he moved, driven the ironshod spear into its owner's guts. The man squealed with the sound of a gelded hog.

The Gael's biceps sprang up and under his tunic his pectorals leaped, as he gripped the spear with all his might and gave it a good twist while he drew it forth. Blood poured from the large wound. The man kicked weakly while with both hands he sought to stem the red tide from his stomach.

Cormac was already whirling, hardly winded, to brace

the other man with the dripping spear. He'd noted it was not barbed, as were those of the Sueves.

The other man was heeling his bay, racing in at his prey. Bent low, he swung the ax he'd pulled on its haft-thong from his saddle. Now he saw that he was alone, that his spear was irretrievable from horseback, and that his prey stood waiting—in a weapon-man's crouch, long spear ready for the skewering.

A dozen yards from the Gael, his attacker suffered an attack of wisdom. He leaned leftward while he changed the pressure of his heels against his mount's flanks. The horse swerved readily. Angrily Cormac ran after it as it galloped away. The Gael paused long enough to launch the spear—seemingly disarming himself in his zeal for vengeance.

The lance fell well short of the racing horse. Cormac's glance told him that now he was but four paces from the other spear, and he tried to look helpless, afoot and unarmed.

Blue-tunic gave himself no opportunity to fall into the trap. He went bucketing on without ever turning to glance back. Reins streaming, his partner's horse galloped in his wake.

Cursing fiercely and imaginatively enough to blue the air about him, the cheated Gael sought out and found his sword. He'd speared one man and driven off the other, and his blade wasn't even blooded. He returned to the man he'd unhorsed and speared. Feeling vengeful and robbed, mac Art would right happily tickle the bastard's stones with his sword point until the fellow told him a few things.

He found he'd been cheated twice.

The man's eyes were already filmed, and the merest glance from Cormac's experienced eyes told him his attacker had already poured out over half his blood.

He'd never suffer from the peritonitis a belly wound always brought, and he'd never be telling Art's son who he was or who'd sent him, either.

Cormac cursed sulphurously.

CHAPTER THIRTEEN: Lucanor of Antioch

Galicia of the ever-martial Sueves had become ever more martial in appearance. Extra guards had been posted, even at the perimeter of the farmlands whose habitants had been warned. Mounted men rode sentry. From the looks of those horse-soldiers, Cormac thought, they were akin to Wulfhere: they'd love nothing better than to meet more such as those who had attacked the mac Art.

No one could identify the corpse, and no one recognized his horse. The smith was summoned to examine arms and horseshoes. No; he knew them not. He also had work to do, and he returned to his hearth and anvil. (Cormac liked that. *A good man, Unscel the Smith,* he thought; *he has the way of Eirrin about him!*)

The dead man was not of the Suevi. Exchanging looks, men opined aloud. Perhaps the attackers were of Cantanabria, though thisun had died far from that neighbouring land of northwestern Hispania.

The horse now belonged to Cormac mac Art, as spoils of combat. No equestrian he, and he impressed all with supposed gallantry; he made Eurica king's-sister a gift of the animal. And whispered in her ear. And she made gift of it to the widow of one of those dead in the tower; the woman has hardly above a score of years in age, and had six children, all living. Nor did mac Art trouble to mention that he was no horse-lover and was no happy tenant of the backs of such beasts. Cormac far preferred the difficult footing of a rolling deck to the back of an animal to make him sore of rump and thighs.

"You have that of the statesman in you, mac Art," King Veremund said. They had retreated to the little room of the silver chain, to share a cup.

"Truth, lord King, I like not horses. And were I statesman, I'd not be asking ye again to show me the chain of silver."

Veremund gave him a look, but conducted him to the treasure room. Cormac was careful to be still, while Veremund showed the Gael the new chain. It had not shrunk.

"Beautiful as ever," Cormac said, with an affected sigh.

Veremund, wearing a tiny smile, stored away the chain. "You were in truth nervous that some sorcery had faded away the links you saw added."

"Lord King! How could a sea-pirate far from Eirrin question a king?"

"As easily as he could dissemble to him about a certain young Goth of Nantes," Veremund said, returning to resume his chair near Cormac's.

"Sorrow and grief are on me that I gave ye the lie as to Clodia, lord King."

"Never mind. I knew, in seconds—and have known that you knew I knew—ah, what foolish things come from our lips with this language! Ye but sought to help her. Poor girl, and her father dead or under torture. She's a pleasant companion. Few would believe how much talking we do."

True, Cormac thought, *for Clodia's hardly the sort one chooses for converse! It's not talking that men are minded of, when they look upon her. But then . . . I suppose Kit-cat's not the sort most would talk with so much as I do, either.*

The Gael said nothing. The king and his—conversations—were no business of his. Nor were the queen's, he added mentally; whatever that skinny woman did with herself whiles her lordly husband and Clodia . . . conversed. *But . . . be there no jealousy on the woman?*

"My lady queen has her amusements too," Veremund said. "We are . . . not such friends as formerly. Her illness changed her. Ye've been told that the lady queen came near to death?"

"Aye."

"Aye," Veremund said, echoing him. "I'd ha' thought ye'd know of that—and many other things as well, belike. Yet ye are silent, answering only when I make query. And then with but a laconic 'aye'."

After a time of examining his winecup—which was of silver, and misaffected the flavour of the wine—Cormac said, "I do not discuss queens with their lords, lord King. Nor the trysting of kings, with anyone."

"It seems very probable that you are a good man, mac Art of Eirrin."

"So thought I of your smith, King of the Galicians. He is most mindful of his own business."

The King of the Galicians chuckled, sipped. "Think you wine tastes better from crockery, mac Art?"

"Lord King, I do."

The two men looked at each other, and they laughed.

"Eirrin. What did you there?"

"Grew up."

"Oh come—a little more. Your father?"

"My father was the lord Art, commander of an outpost fortress for the King of Connacht. Rath

Glondarth, its name. Was my home until I was fourteen."

"Umm. And you fell into trouble, there?"

"Lord Art was murdered." Cormac shortened the story, then, just short of total veracity, which had never been a religion with him. "For me it was die or flee. I fled Eirrin."

He would not say that a nervous High-king feared him for his deeds and his name, which was that of a great High-king over Eirrin of centuries past—and which his father never should have given him. Surely his life had been different, and his father's longer, had Art called him Conn or Lugh or Conan or Midhir! Even "Niall mac Art" could not have put such nervousness on the High-king, unto treachery. Too, there had been that damned priest. And Bress of the Long Arm. The priest of Iosa Chriost that these called Yesu Christus was nicely dead. As for Bress . . .

Some day, Cormac thought. *Some day, treacherous Bress Cormac-hater!*

But had been eight years. Bress might by now be commander of all the armies of Leinster . . . or dead, morelike, the arrogant supercilious roughshodder!

Veremund was frowning, and Cormac realized from his words that the king was wondering if he'd uncovered cowardice in the pirate called Wolf: "And ye've never returned?"

"The slayer of my father was in the employ of the High-king," Cormac said shortly. "About that craft Wulfhere saw . . ."

"Think ye they were indeed sirens?"

Veremund had snuffed back in his throat just as he started to speak; he would allow change of subject. Veremund too, Cormac thought, was a good man. One of those precious few on all the ridge of the world who merited the sobriquet "noble," from the Latin *nobilitatas.*

"Lord King, I saw the impossible that night, and fought them. Belief's on me that Wulfhere saw *something* unnatural. Peradventure the Greeks' tale of the *Sirenes* is based in fact. Peradventure daughters of Ran do indeed lurk asea, luring good seamen. Be that as it may, Something is out there that likes not sea traffic —or rather does like it, as prey! It's minded I am to be offering them some. As bait."

"Umm. Aye, I see. Were best we—that is, yourself— risked not your good *Raven* to such purpose. What have ye in mind?"

"One of those *scaphae* I was seeing in your harbour."

"Umm. With a tiny crew, to attract the Sirens?"

"Aye, lord King, and weapons ready! My thinking goes thus. The kelp is ghastly, and to be dealt with. Ne'ertheless, it's surely but a tool it is. Sent by the . . . wreckers, sirens . . . sent to darken the true beacon, that they may display their own. It's the wreckers are the enemy, then. It's they I'd be going against, direct."

The king contemplated that for a space, nodding, and then showed his nod to Cormac. "In your hands, mac Art. And next time we'll have our wine from good fired mugs, umm?" He rose, and the Gael stood instantly. "Irnic awaits outside, I know—with some others. Time I returned to kinging it, whilst you do put a pirate's knowledge to work against an unnatural enemy!"

Outside the chamber, Veremund said a few words to Irnic Break-ax, and shortly that Roman-cloaked warrior and mac Art were on their way to the harbour. Irnic made the great concession of walking on his own feet.

At old Brigantium harbour, once handsomer and more bustling than now, they two chose a boat for Cormac's purpose. The *scapha* or coaster was a flat-bottomed skiff used for commerce, mainly in riverways and along coastal waters. Square and ugly was its stern and unusually large its sail.

"And the lighthouse?" Irnic asked, as he and the Gael paced the coaster they had chosen. Irnic had sent a rider for Wulfhere and Ordlaf.

"It's unmanned we'll be leaving that place," Cormac said, "with its beacon unlit. We'll want the tower close watched, though."

"My part," Irnic said and, when the Gael nodded, "I'll see to that."

"I'm wondering if there mayn't be a dark sail available . . ."

Wulfhere and the steersman arrived, along with Jostein, and the five men conferred aboard the scapha. The reivers detailed how it must be equipped and Irnic called over the burly man who was overseer of stevedores. He gave listen to plans for the skiff's modification, nor did he make mention that his men were hardly carpenters. Indeed he began issuing instructions for the work at once. He'd but few questions, and none regarding the purpose of Lord Irnic and the reivers from oversea. These harbour-men knew of the horror in the lighthouse, and its menace to them and their livelihood.

Still another good man, mac Art thought; *this is my day for dealing with such.* And he told Wulfhere a few little things, in private. Irnic was off to make a to-do of picking men for the lighthouse watch, and Ordlaf and Jostein would remain with the workers in their modification of the scapha.

Cormac asked his giant battle-brother if he'd been "having do with" Queen Venhilda.

"No!"

"Apology, Wulfhere. I assumed the answer, but

needed to clear my mind of the matter."

"What about yourself and that bottomy little princess?"

"Absolutely nothing, Wulf—it's off princesses I am for life! Note how discreet I am—ye know naught of me and the bosomy Marcovanda, eh?"

"The little one with—"

"The same."

Wulfhere chuckled. Abruptly he sobered, gave Cormac a keen look from eyes like nuggets of sky. "Ye asked because of Veremund, who's having so much 'to do' with Clodia."

"He says they *talk* a lot."

Wulfhere snorted. "So do I, to my sword. Well, I can tell ye this, Wolf. My, ahh, night-friends and I have twice seen her leave the royal hall by night, and head into the city furtive as a thief with a chill."

"Clodia?"

"No, dense son of a pig-farming Eirrisher! Ven—" Wulfhere lowered his voice—"hilda."

"Uh!" Cormac frowned, sighed. "Bad business. She must have a lover. Now her royal husband has. Bad business. We're after bringing him his consolation."

Cormac was sure now that it was Queen Venhilda he'd seen ghosting from the hall so clandestinely, that first night here. *Who out in Brigantium-town be admiring her leanness and that Starry Night of hers?* For he'd learned the queen's magnificent colour-splashed opal bore a name, as did some swords and other possessions. Starry Night, she called it.

That evening he was to see still another fascinating ring. Quite an interesting collection surrounded him; the Egyptian winged serpent he wore on its silver chain under his tunic and the winged sun-disk Zarabdas wore over his; Zarabdas's golden ring of twining serpents; the

queen's Starry Night . . . and now the Antiochite's
Aquarius.

Cormac was not alone that evening when a sentry
brought word that someone was without and would
have word with him. He donned tunic and went down
reluctantly, to find an oldish woman at the door,
straggly of thin grey hair and wrapped in a cloak of
plain dun hue, its scarlet bordering long since faded nigh
to invisibility. Someone, she advised, would have
converse with mac Art, elsewhere.

"Someone? Who?"

She would not say.

Cormac considered. "Do you wait then," he said
coldly, "whilst I arm and armour myself." And he
returned to his room without awaiting her reply.

"I will be back," he told the tousled head and pair of
bright—and disappointed—blue eyes peering at him
from the bed, while he pulled on leggings. "If I am not,
I'll ha' been slain. Sure and that's not likely. Sleep, lass."
He shrugged into a padded jack.

"Cor-macc . . ."

He said nothing, performing the hardly simple task of
getting forty pounds of linked mailcoat over his head.
With a jingly little rustle of chain, the armour settled
over him. He picked up the belt supporting his sword's
worn scabbard. He gave her a grin.

"I'll wake ye, Kit-cat," he said, and left his room.

In the corridor, the sentry stayed him long enough to
mutter, "Would ye be followed, mac Art?"

"No, and no. Yon hag hardly carries my death—and
if she has friends, I can handle myself." He showed the
man the steel under his cloak.

"Uh . . . pardon, mac Art, but . . . Marcovanda . . ."

Cormac flashed him a warning smile. "See ye stay

away from my chamber and Marcovanda Kit-cat,
Hermodh, or I'll be telling terrible things to your
Berilda. Carrying a boy, I'd make wager."

"One hopes," Hermodh said. "It's time. She's borne
two daughters, and she who lived is a joy. Still a man
wants—"

"Aye," Cormac said, and departed the hall.

Following the old woman in her much-worn cloak,
the Gael soon departed the king's grounds as well, and
entered into dark Brigantium. Oil and waxen candles
were dear, and he saw few lights. People who rose with
the sun were wont to lie down with its daily dying, and
so it was the world over. He noted how his guide clung
to outer streets, skirting the city rather than actually
entering it. Though Brigantium was Roman once, it was
no longer; they were untroubled by footpads. Over past
the city's edge they came to a smallish, darkened old
temple that was apparently no longer in use. Cormac
saw a cracked column and strewn bits of stone from the
interior of the portico's roof. Just beyond that grove
squatted a nice enough house, and it was to its door she
led him. She knocked twice, paused, knocked thrice.
And opened the door.

Inside was darkness deeper than that in which mac
Art stood, and he ignored her gesture that bade him
enter.

"Cormac mac Art," a voice said from within, "come
in." Just that, and Cormac knew this man's German was
as accented as his.

"Who asks?"

"Lucanor Antiochos."

"Ah. I enter then," Cormac said, and did, but cleared
his cloak of his right arm as he stepped into darkness.
"D'ye have Latin, Lucanor Antiochus?" he asked,
Latinizing the leech's sobriquet.

"Aye. In here." The leech who was formerly the royal leech lifted a hanging to reveal a yellow-lit room.

"After yourself, host," Cormac said, and after a moment the other man entered. Cormac followed.

An oil-lamp burned on a table in that chamber, and Cormac saw that it was of Grecian design. The room was cozy, carpeted and wall-hung and furnished with two Roman chairs and a couch Cormac thought came from the north of Africa. The room bore the aroma of herbs; Lucanor's stock-in-trade.

The Antiochite stood not tall. His crown rose little above Cormac's shoulder. There was a bit of curl to his long hair and short, kempt beard, and both looked greasy whether they were or not. Black was the hair and dark was Lucanor of Antioch to the east, darker than his visitor. He had, as Cormac had noted earlier from a distance, the look of a man whose veins bore both Greek and Hyrcanian blood. His excellent robe of silky-looking green fitted him so that Cormac reaffirmed that the man was well fed. His forehead was very high; Lucanor's hair, at about his age twoscore, was withdrawing as if in fright from eyes like two heated onyxes under thickets of brows just as black.

"Will you join me in—ah! I see you've come armed!"

"So I have. And mailed. When I'm called from my bed by one who will not tell me who desires my company, suspicion thins my blood."

"My housekeeper is unnecessarily mysterious. She thinks I am the equal of kings and is high-handed. She—"

"Does Lucanor think so?"

Lucanor waved a hand on which a single ring flashed. "The question need not be answered. I am but a tender to the sick and injured. I was about to offer wine."

"Do you pour for yourself only, Lucanor; I'll have none."

206

The physician nodded, gestured to a chair, and himself took the couch. Splashed with yellow and made to glitter by the lamp-light, black eyes gazed on mac Art.

"Your housekeeper," the Gael said. "Have you a wife as well, Lucanor?"

"None. Not ever."

"And no . . . friend, from among the distaff?"

Lucanor shrugged. "None that lives here."

"One awaits me," Cormac said. "Speak our business."

"Very well."

The Antiochite leaned forward a bit and his hand stretched out to lie on the table. Now Cormac could see the ring it bore: the stone was milky, though no pearl, and was incused with a sign Cormac recognized. Again he looked on the mix of Persia and Greece: the figure on Lucanor's ring was of Aquarius, bearer of water. In white opal, perhaps.

"Mac Art: I would tell you something for the good of yourself and all the Suevi of Galicia."

And not the Antiochite of Galicia, eh? Cormac was silent and showed nothing. He'd been told this and that "for his own good" rather more than once. The phrase usually prefaced someone's advising him against doing something, and that someone usually had a personal reason. He was about to be warned off something, he mused, and composed himself to show no reaction.

"Sure and a man ever appreciates being told that which is for his own good."

"I beg you give up this quest for the so-called Sirens of this coast, mac Art of Eirrin. The danger is enormous, beyond your ken. The consequences of interference will be dire for all the Suevi of Galicia."

"And the Antiochite, and the Gael, and the few Danes?" Cormac asked. Surprised, he essayed not to show it. "Ummm. It's 'so-called Sirens' ye said. Ye have knowledge on ye of the creatures, Lucanor? Of what they be?"

"I will say only that I know them to be terrible enemies when they are thwarted or endangered, or threatened."

"Ah, they and I have that in common, then." Cormac spoke in a light tone, with his gaze level on the other man's eyes. "Little else, I'm thinking. Is it their ally ye be, Lucanor Antiochus, or merely one who does only good and would warn and protect those of us not so wise?"

"You are bent on being hostile," Lucanor said. And he spoke on, but again he gave no direct answer. Instead he talked here and there and around, dropping dark hints unpurfled by specifics. The gist was that he knew much, and there were more things and forces than Cormac or Veremund knew of; Cormac had better cancel his plans and desist, for the royal house and the people of this land would suffer else.

"Royal House?" again Cormac sought to hear a threat, rather than carefully worded warnings.

Lucanor nodded and his butter-soft, middle range voice only reiterated the words. Yet again he refused to be direct, but must mitigate by adding, "and all the people of this land."

"And myself?"

Lucanor met his eyes directly, and spoke without change in expression or tone: "Go asea against the unknown and unknowable, mac Art, and it is your death, sure."

"Umm. I am warned from inimical water-creatures by one who wears a ring of the water-carrier. With nervousness one hopes Lucanor Antiochus is not a carrier to the shores of water and its . . . unknown and unknowable creatures."

Cormac had seen his host's hand tense as he started automatically to withdraw it and the ring from sight. Lucanor was bolder than that, though, and on thinking he left it where it was, closely lit by the lamp. He who had been physician to the royal house said nothing. He stared hard.

"It's said, then? All ye had to tell me—and ye *will* tell me?"

"You are determined to pay no heed and accept no counsel. I am not in love with words."

"Hm—it did seem otherwise to me, when ye were speaking around and around the answers to the questions I posed!" Cormac rose in a rustle of linked rings of steel and stood over the other man, tall, mailed, sword-armed. "Lucanor . . . if it's yourself the queen is coming to meet so many nights, ye'd best end it, man. For it's yourself is endangered thereby, not the house of Veremund or his people."

Lucanor stared, face working. Then he rose with the sinuous grace of a panther, and he smiled satirically at the taller man. "Ah, mac Art! The queen, coming to see *me?* Go to; it's the Greek ways I learned whilst I grew up, and studied so far from here, and I assure you the queen is not coming to see *me!*"

Cormac returned most thoughtfully to the hall of the king and to the young woman he called Kit-cat, who loved to hear piratical tales that fired her blood and who soon put brooding thoughts from his head.

Rain fell next day, in a blue-grey curtain that created mud everywhere while reducing visibility to little more than the length of a man's arm held before him. Work on the scapha was delayed. The excursion asea must be postponed until the morrow.

Cormac conferred with Wulfhere on the matter of

209

their new craft and very secret plans for the move against . . . "Ran's Daughters". Then the Gael gained privacy with Irnic Break-ax. To that respected fellow man of weapons Cormac strongly suggested that spies be set to watch Lucanor of Antioch.

"It's something dark is afoot within this realm, Irnic, and he's connected or I'll eat grass. Best he be watched, and closely, but with great care that he knows it not."

"I will use several, then," Irnic said, "that Lucanor may not grow accustomed to the same person about all the time. Aye, person, for there is this and that woman who acts for me, in Galicia."

"Good that you love Veremund," Cormac said, with a smile that was like a brief flash of light. Then, "And . . . Irnic . . . best too that this be secret for the present from all save yourself and me and your spies."

Irnic lifted a brow. "All, Cormac?"

"Aye, Irnic. Even the king and queen. Will ye agree to that?"

"This . . . bodes naught sinister for them?"

"Irnic! Your spies at watch over Lucanor will not be bringing harm to your cousin and his wife!"

"I will agree; they need hardly be bothered with every detail of what goes on in this realm. Will you explain, Cormac?"

"Soon, aye. Will ye be humouring me, Irnic, and let explanations come after? And, commander: the leech from Antioch is to be watched *night and day*."

Irnic nodded, and made as if to speak, and reconsidered, looking into Cormac's eyes while he held thought himself. Then Irnic went to see to it, without a word more. And another day passed, a grey-grim and ugly day of rain and mud, while a son of Eirrin fretted and fidgeted and aye, fell out too with his Kit-cat. And on the morrow Irnic had words for him, and that report was none too cheering.

"You saw the old temple, Cormac, there near Lucanor's house."

Cormac nodded.

"Was to the Old Gods of the Suevi that temple was raised, the gods my people held to when they abode back in Germania. It is long unused. That is, so we thought; it is officially unused. Now . . . I know not what transpires there now, but it was therein Lucanor went, on last evening. Nor was he open about it, but waited until darkness had closed and wore a robe my man had not seen on him afore, and too he took a circuitous route, all cloak-wrapped and hood-muffled— though this was after the rain had stopped and was not that cold. He walked many minutes and came in by the grove alongside the temple, and—well, my man described it thus: Lucanor scuttled within. This, when his home is practically next door. My man continued his watch from outside, concealed, and watched a half-score others enter that temple, and not a one with a torch or without furtive behaviour. They were as clandestine much later when they left, so that my men—there were two, now, a relief having come and the first having decided to remain during this *strangeness*—my men identified but two of them. And . . . one more joined them, in that old temple."

"Ah," Cormac said. "Twelve, then. The old magic number. The zodiacal total of Lucanor's eastern haunts . . . and him with a zodiac sign on his finger." Then he realized that the Sueve had spoken portentously, and wanted to be asked: "One more. Who, Irnic?"

"The queen."

"So. Now it's knowledge we have of her nocturnal trystings, is it!"

"My lady Queen Venhilda," Irnic said, nodding and looking not happy. "She was well and fully muffled, in a hooded cloak not of fine weave, an old green and red

211

one. A double disguise, then. And . . . I admit with some shame that I have checked. Such a cloak was indeed in the queen's chamber this morning. With much mud on its skirts."

Cormac clamped his lips and gave his head a sad shake. "So. Queen Venhilda. It's not to some nightly lover she goes, but to some damned rite in that abandoned temple! And presided over, I've no doubt, by that scowly eastern shaman. And him once unable to save her life! Hmm . . . mayhap he gained some hold over her then, while she lay so near death—how then was she recognized?"

Irnic smiled, though thinly. "A normal little error. She forgot to remove her ring until just before she was about to enter. By that time the moon was out, and my man saw it clear. What boots it how much care one has for disguise, when one wears the most distinctive ring in the realm?"

"Ah," Cormac said, and loosed a long pensive sigh. "That ring—Starry Night—a gift of her husband?"

Irnic snorted. "Hardly! Of Lucanor! Once he left her, and Zarabdas effected her cure, she could not remove it. I remember that the king wanted it off. She proved to him that could not be done, and would not allow it to be cut away—as it's of gold, a good knife would do it, in time."

"*Lucanor!* Rue will be worked by this man, Irnic—is being worked."

"I know," the king's cousin said, very quietly and with dolor, and for a time the two men were silent.

"Well," the Gael said at last, "to business. Irnic: Tonight we'll be going in quest of the sirens, or whatever lurks out there, directing kelp to prey on men and the beacon. A chancy business, this invasion of another's demesne, and worse when it is water and him at home in it. Worse still when the enemy appears . . . unnatural. Now additional nervousness is on me, Irnic."

With lips held very tightly, Irnic said, "You think the —the business in the temple may have something to do with the kelp and—Wulfhere's Ran's daughters."

"I think it may."

"I am personally involved, Cormac. A woman of the cult is married to my cousin," Irnic said, as if he were not talking about the wife of the King of Galicia. "Take command—my thinking cannot be clear in this."

"And you are too good a soldier to try. Irnic, Irnic— what a man you are! What great good fortune is on Veremund to have you by him! But I cannot take command—I shall be asea. Or rather hugging the coast in that merchanter coaster, looking for the false beacon."

"No, I mean—tell me what should be done by my men."

Again they looked at each other, the tall and dark Gael and the powerfully built Sueve with his auburn hair coiled into a tortured Arabic eight on his head. And Cormac nodded, and spoke.

"On the responsibility of mac Art: Lucanor and all those with him on this night, are to be arrested. All of them. As quietly as possible. Peradventure they could be held there, or near there."

Irnic, whose face looked as if he'd just bitten into a very green apple, was nodding. "Aye. And . . . Cormac . . ."

Cormac turned away from Irnic's face and put a hand on his shoulder while he stood by his side. He knew the man was in agony over his queen—moreso that her husband was Irnic's cousin.

"Her too, Irnic, an she be there. Ye knew ye must, man. Bring her away from the others. Mayhap she'll not be going, this time. As it's so muffled in the peasantish cloak she goes, mayhap she is unknown to the other . . . adherents, acolytes . . . whatever be their purpose."

"Aye," Irnic said, very low, and Cormac knew what he was thinking: *not likely none would know the queen herself was among them!*

"Though there is no doubt she be known to Lucanor."

"Aye." Terribly quietly. "And him? What of that damned Syrian himself?"

"He must be taken and kept closely mured up, Irnic. An he has powers, he must be given no opportunity to use them. And be ye mindful that the fellow may have to be made *ever* silent. An it chance possible to draw a cloak of silence about the queen's involvement . . . would that not be the better for all?"

"Were likely necessary all eleven must die. I'd do it, for Veremund."

"And meanwhile . . ."

"You suggest that we do not tell the king."

"That is my meaning. If it is possible, Irnic. I am no Sueve."

"How well I know, and that I am!" And King Veremund's military commander nodded, looked gloomy as a priest of the Dead God, and sighed, and departed.

My lady queen, Cormac mac Art thought, *remain this night within these walls!*

And he went then seeking Clódia, to gain her agreement to suffer a headache and her courses and chilblains as well this night, if necessary, to keep her and the king apart. Mayhap then he and his wife would seek each the companionship of the other; unhappy couple!

CHAPTER FOURTEEN:

The sea-spawn

The sky hung low in a veiling threat that glowered on the little band of Danes and Sueves. Not even the setting sun was visible. Armoured and well-armed, the silent men accompanied their dark leader onto the dock and aboard the scapha modified to conceal them. Well equipped with grapnels on stout cords the coaster was, as tough to be turned from merchantish pursuits into piratical ones. Spears, too, had been laid aboard, and the sail was of deepest blue.

Though he claimed that no superstition interfered with his excellent mental processes, their Eirrin-born leader had caused the flat-bottomed skiff to be given a name. It had been painted along her hull in green: Sword of Lir. *Scapha* had become *spatha*.

The sun that was only a cloud-fronted glow was setting when they eased the square-sterned boat out of Brigantium Harbour and set her big dark sail. At the steering oar was Ivarr of the keen eyes, not he who was surely the best steersman on all the ridge of the world, Ordlaf son of Skel of Dane-mark. Ivarr ruddered the ship out past the lighthouse, then back in shoreward.

The tower was unmanned, and its beacon dark.

An the volunteers aboard *Sword of Lir* saw aught of beacon-light this night, they would know at once that it emanated from their unknown and surely unworldly foe, whether wreckers or sirens or . . . Ran's Daughters.

The glow of Behl's Eye left the sky. Unusually subdued men exchanged looks and glanced this way and that, though from their concealment it was precious little they could see. The world about them went the colour of slate, and then darker still. Their coaster rocked gently amid waters that made lapping, slurping sounds. The men were silent. All knew their vulnerability. The inexperienced Sueves, hardly accustomed to the sea, felt it more than their Danish shipmates. All knew that in full armour as they were, any man who went overboard would sink like a stone and not return in this life.

The sky went indigo-and-black, shot through with streaks of azure and jet and grey-bellied clouds. The sail was hardly lively, in a breeze no more than a zephyr. Seagoing pirates and land-loving horse soldiers alike, the crew breathed deeply of salt-scented air. Crew? Nay; concealed war-men they were; marines.

Cormac stood forward, gazing steadily, moving his head back and forth, back and forth. Beside his left foot lay his helmet, upside down. His deepset eyes moved always, in a roving questing gaze. He strove not to strain his eyes to pierce the dark; any light would be easily seen, this night. *Sword of Lir* hardly more than drifted along. Across the water came the sounds of insects amid the woods ashore. A frog that must have been fist-sized glugged in a voice deep as the sea.

Behind mac Art men waited, concealed by the new additions to *Sword of Lir's* simple construction. Hardly normal soldiers these, in their byrnies of steel or metal-studded leather; with their heavy round shields of good linden rimmed with iron; their vicious, newly-sharpened axes and long swords slung from baldric or waistbelt. Each man's sponge-lined steel pot or iron-covered leathern cap lay close at hand.

They waited, looking up at their foreign leader's back and at the dark, unconcerned sky. Only four men were visible along with mac Art; unhelmeted men. They knew their duties. Insofar as words could tell, they knew what to expect. They too watched, and waited. The breeze drifted gently, riffling their hair and only stirring the sail. The Gael's black mop stirred and he jerked his head when a lock tickled his cheek.

A light appeared. A light flashed, a spot of citrine in the night.

"Cormac!"

"I see it. It's the beacon, lads—the false one, low to the water. Stand ye by for the fearful, and see ye're not affected as they expect. Ivarr—we're being seduced. Gudfred, Hermanric—they wish to lure us from the shore. Let us be succumbing."

They succumbed. The flat-bottomed boat was lured willingly away by the rocking yellow glow. The scapha, nigh immune to rocks no matter how close they rose to the surface of the water, closed as if naively on that beacon of treachery. Adam's apples bobbed as men swallowed. Darkness ensorcelled the world in a night haunted by the unknown. They knew death lurked in strange form, awaiting them.

The coaster slid over the gently tossing bracken sea toward whatever inexorable end the Fates held in store for her and her crew. Mac Art stared ahead, a dark-visaged statue wrapped in sombre anticipation. The spot of yellow grew, and now he could see that it was a dancing yellow flame.

217

"Closer," he reported. Behind him there were rustles and clinks as grim-faced men removed baldrics and belts and held steel naked in their hands. An they went into the sea, they'd be encumbered at least by no leathern straps.

"Ah, gods of my fathers, Wulfhere spoke true," their commander reported. "A barge, lads, broad and flat as this save with no hold or shelter—but a deck just above the water. Aye, 'tis plain now—constructed all of dead white bone yon craft is!"

"And—women?"

Cormac stared. "Something disports itself in the water about the barge. Many of them. Large, methinks —Crom's beard, those heads—their faces are men and fishes all at once, lads! It's some creatures called up from some damned kingdom 'neath the sea we'll be facing, and do ye remember who has weapons and who —or what—has none!"

The Gael continued to stare ahead while his unlikely craft closed on the unnatural one. Aye, he saw them now . . . women, or something like, of womanly form. The hair at the back of his neck stirred as though someone stood close and puffed air on it. Eerily phosphorescent were those beasties sporting about the bone-ship, and huge and round and without colour their eyes, save for the spots of black that were their pupils.

The unnatural fire did indeed burn on that dead white deck, and around it, close as though they were freezing or it a flame of cold fire, lounged . . . crew? Passengers? Mac Art did not know. Strange unearthly women these were, with large eyes that glowed like twinned lamps in every face . . . and those colourless eyes were blank, inhuman, fishlike, noctiluminescent glims staring and expressionless as death itself. Robed all in greenish-bluish-greyish sea mist these feminine creatures were, all

218

slim and sylphlike and gleaming. Peradventure that raiment, mac Art thought, protected the unworldly creatures from the heat and dancing flames of their deck-burning beacon. If flames those were.

Lounging, they stared unblinking at the approaching scapha.

Slim, and lifeless and unblinking . . . like . . .

Like my lady Queen Venhilda, Cormac thought, staring back. From time to time he lifted his voice in command to his four men on deck. He saw arms draped impossibly in sea mist lift, stretch toward him all aglisten; saw the loveliness of parting lips in piquant, point-chinned faces; saw the misted outline and swell of tiny, dainty girlish breasts that called to a man and sought to kindle his rut with visions of nubile youth.

He spoke low. "Now lads, remember. These . . . women expect the bemazement of their very appearance to draw us in . . . the horror of those eyes to ensorcel and panic us so that we may be capsized and drowned with ease. Such must be their way and their experience. Only Lir's son is after knowing how many they've thus murdered. Be ye prepared. Flinch not, but remember that it's deadly enemy they be—and that things be not always as they seem. Surprise is with *us,* this time. For we expected them . . . and it's hardly the ordinary sailors *they* expect we are!" And he added, "Trim sail. Rudder aport."

And his men obeyed.

And steadily, whilst fish-things cavorted in the water and made strange croaking sounds that rode the night air with ugglesome eeriness to prickle a man's nape, the ungainly craft yclept *Sword of Lir* slid toward the barge of bones.

The cold dead colourless eyes of those . . . *sirens* seemed to brighten with anticipation. The sea-creatures about their barge slowed their activities, staring. Waiting for the scapha's approach.

Then Cormac seemed to go mad.

He shouted, and his voice lofted high. "Five more on deck! Run about as if moon-struck, lads! AH, GODS AND BLOOD OF THE GODS! Aegir and Mamannan aid us! *Wulfhere*—all sail, all sail! Hard by steerboard!"

But Wulfhere was not aboard, and at the steering-oar Ivarr knew better than to obey: the calling of the absent captain's name was the signal they'd agreed upon hours agone. And Ivarr seemed too to go mad, even while five men sprang up from below. Unhelmeted they came, and bearing no shields. Given the order to swing hard aright, Ivarr ruddered leftward as if in panicky confusion.

With men running screaming and arm-waving about her deck, the scapha rolled in toward the unearthly craft.

Ever closer they manoeuvered, and each time Cormac called out Wulfhere's name before his command, that order was carried out in reverse. And the women aboard the bone-ship smiled, smiled and seemed to yearn toward *Sword of Lir* . . .

"Close enow!" Cormac bawled. "Grapple fast and haul us in to her, lads! Helmets and shields and fistful of steel! And by the blood of all the very gods, remember how many good men these creatures have done to death!"

Grapnels flew like steel claws from the hands of men whose sanity had been regained on the instant. Inexperienced Hermanric, unsteady on his feet on the bobbing craft, overthrew. A hideous shriek rent the air as one clawing fluke of his grapnel tore down the arm of one of the women on the bone-barge, and another sank to its back-hook in her shining white thigh.

Blood's red enough, Cormac thought, and gave no

thought to his own callousness.

Now the two craft were made fast, and up from the sea came horror.

Surely horror was the very name of these sea-spawned monsters of glistening, dripping, greyish-green. Scales plated their backs and shoulders like the hides of fishes. As fish-like were the enormous unblinking eyes that bulged from ugly piscine heads. Gills moved restlessly on either side their necks, sucking and palpitating.

When they rose up from the night-dark water to invade the scapha, their bellies were the dead pasty white of fish.

Hideous scaly beasts they were, with the thick-lipped, wide mouths of fish and yet a simultaneous resemblance to frogs. At the same time, their bodies were anthopomorphic, with the two-armed, two-legged bodies and chests of humankind. Rows of gleaming pointed teeth lined open mouths. All was as though man and shark had come somehow together in obscene mating and these monstrosities were their get.

It's nests of these things there are all over the ridge of the world, Cormac mac Art thought, and knew not how such knowledge was on him. Nor knew he how he was sure these creatures had existed before ever humankind had walked this earth. *Everything came once from the water, the seas, all and all of us; and it's but little change we need to return to our ancient demesne.* And he shivered.

Yet were these batrachian fish on their way to becoming human, or men somehow returning to that ancient home in the sea?

Up they came, dripping and shiny-slimy save for the scales on their backs. Huge pallid eyes stared from piscine faces above jaws like ragged bone shears. Like marbles were those eyes, with great black spots set in

221

pearl-white sclera without other colour. And where their fingered paws gripped the deck to pull themselves aboard the coaster, horny claws left deep rents in the wood.

They came, and gasps mingled with the oaths streaming from the lips of frightened men.

Yet these were fighting men, and fearfulness was but a cloak to be hurled from them. Swords and axes moved in stout hands, and swung high. Their steel flashed in the light from the fire on the bone-ship's deck. Danes and Sueves attacked in their numbers, for such abominations begged to be hacked and slain that men might feel they were indeed men, and clean.

The eyes of the attacking creatures, Cormac noted, never closed, not for so much as a single blink.

Swords and axes whined in the air. Sharp-edged steel struck with shattering impact on creatures spawned in brackish deeps. Demons vomited up by the sea were met by men become blood-mad demons themselves. Fishy skulls shattered and the blood that spurted was red enow. Fish-like heads flew on wakes of scarlet for men ever loved the satisfaction of the broad beheading stroke. Arms, man-like and yet clawed and scaled above, sought to grapple and were chopped away.

A Sueve whose name Cormac could not call chopped deep into the side of a slime-sheened creature, even as its arms enfolded him and vised tight. Man and monster toppled overboard, nor was either seen again.

"It's not here they want to fight us!" Cormac bawled, stabbing. "They be wanting to grapple us and leap into their own demesne, lads! Strike, and strike!"

Men struck and struck. Creatures at once batrachian and piscine and anthropomorphic died and died. Again and again had surprise and horror won for them, so that their leprous home below must be floored with human bones. These men knew horror too—but little surprise. Nor were they taken unarmed and without armour. No bigger than men, the sea-spawn had neither mail nor weapons save claws and teeth and strength beyond the human.

Those who had so long and horribly preyed on men became the prey of men.

A gape-eyed *thing* reached for Cormac mac Art. So strongly did he hew in his horror that his sword sheared off an arm and was hardly slowed, the way that it cut the other arm to the bone. Baying, the creature came on. The Gael smashed its awful face with his shield. And all about, men cursed and chopped, grunted and hewed.

The sea-get were maimed, disjointed, unlimbed, beheaded. They died and died. Most of the blood that spattered the deck was theirs; the blood that splashed human faces and weapons and mailclad men came not from men. Cormac and his band did slaughter, and right happily. They slew inhuman foe that would have been less repugnant had they been less human.

The coaster bobbed on the waters of night, and the reek of fresh-spilt blood vied with the tang of brine and the stench of unnatural fish-things.

A hand was scratched. A face was raked open by whipping claws. An ax was torn from an arm that had swung not hard enough and a woman was widowed as monster and yelling Sueve plunged into the sea. Horny claws tore the cheek of another, but slipped and skidded over boiled leather bossed with bronze.

Mac Art bore a shield he hardly needed for defense. He used it offensively even more than was his wont, smashing scaly arms and flat ichthyoid faces. He cried out and tried to get to them, but two creatures bore Hugi the Nimble into the sea and they clawed and chewed him even as they bore him down. They returned in scant minutes, and the Gael derived an almost berserker pleasure in chopping away the head of one and the forearms of the other as they sought to remount the skiff.

Three men had met their weirds, the while more than a score of their attackers died or were so sorely maimed that death was inevitable. The kelp had been worse menace than these creatures that defied nature—yet to sailors unready, these had been death, sure as the jaws and talons of tigers. Here and now, the sea-spawn came on and on, and died and died, and fell hideously maimed back into the sea amid the bedlam of shouting men and hacking blades and stamping feet.

Shrieks rent the salty night air. On the barge, the "sirens" danced in rage and hurled curses in a name Cormac did not know; it was k'Tooloo or something like. What man could know the meaning of such cries as *"k'Tooloo fhtagn?"*

While their beastly killers were defeated and annihilated, the mist-clad mistresses of dying demons bethought them to flee. They began striving to dislodge the grapnels binding them to the scapha. Three of four they had cast off ere a Dane noticed; so blood-spattered and a-drip was he as to be unrecognizable. Yet no wound was on him.

It was he who shouted and pointed, with dripping sword. He yelled orders without pausing to consider his right to command.

The last four fish-things were being chopped into bits by men on whom the blood-madness still lay, the way that panting men were left foeless on a deck gone slippery with blood. Others were booting hideous corpses back into the sea that had birthed them. Those bloodied men snatched up grapnels. The hooks flashed over, trailing walrus-hide ropes, and the two craft were linked anew.

Barge and skiff wallowed in the swell, six times linked, side by side.

Now was not curses the women yowled down on their attackers, but shrieks for succor in the name of the monster they served. Cthulhu, those lure-sylphs called desperately. Cthulhu! Save your servants who have sacrificed to you for centuries uncounted!

Asleep in R'lyeh, he whom the Philistines knew as Dagon and others called Aegir—without knowing his true nature—stirred not.

And Cormac mac Art bounded onto the white-gleaming barge. His sword stood out before his white-knuckled fist, and it slew even as his boots struck that rocking deck of bone.

Was then ended the illusion of fair, beckoning women like naiads.

A daughter of Ran she was not. No one of the *Sirenes* of the Hellenes was she either—unless those Greeks of old had never thrust steel into one and seen her change from a willowy beautiful lure-woman to . . . a horrid amphibious servant of the monster-god Cthulhu who slept in drowned R'lyeh.

Completely loathsome was the thing that slid off Cormac's spitting sword, part fish and part frog and aye; obscenely, revoltingly: part human as well.

Again, sickened seamen stared. Again they recognized their relationship to such a beast, and were revolted and as if tainted by that knowledge. None could know how old these creatures were, for none of the toad-looking fish-people *things* died, ever, save by violence. Were they, like some werewolves, born with the amphibian taint that later led to the horrid changelings? Or had they ever been human at all? Or, still yet again, might these barge-creatures include both those groups, as well as some that were victims of curse or spell of ancient origin?

Or, Cormac mac Art wondered, *changed and summoned by chants in an old temple to Dagon?*

And even then he noted that the false beacon fire on the barge's deck gave off no heat. . . . *O'course not. It's a fire of sorcery this be, for cold-blooded creatures from the sea could not otherwise tolerate such a fire so close!*

"It's no lovelies these be, lads," he called. "See what 'tis I'm after slaying! Come aboard—be ye fighting men or children to stand agape and tremblous?"

And the other women rose up then, to come for Cormac mac Art, and a Sueve from the coaster leaped across to stand at Cormac's left. And others came. At their leader's feet lay, twitching, a scaled thing of nightmare. Finned and gilled it was; web-footed and web-fingered it was, razor-toothed and claw-fingered . . . as the other "lovely women" now became!

As they commenced a hissing, croaking advance, out of the night came bellowing a mighty stentorian voice that might have been Father Odin, save for the words it shouted.

"Look to yourself, ye son of a Gaelic pig-farmer, and drag your hide off that accursed floating boneyard!"

Every man saw the appearance of *Raven,* drawn by the witchfire on the barge of horror and death. Plowing through the darkness came the ship, as Cormac and Wulfhere had planned—and told no one at all lest the Power behind the false beacon and these "sirens" learn of it. Impelled by all oars good speedy *Raven* came hurtling, and a great furl of foam billowed back on either side of the pirate vessel's bow. She plunged through the water toward the barge like an attacking shark, and it starving.

"Back! Back on our scapha, and chop free the grapnel ropes!" Cormac yelled, while *Raven* bore down on the barge he now knew was builded of human bones and the cement of sea-snails.

He pounced backward from attackers and made of his sword a silvery blur before him, and he saw his men off the bone-barge. One of the nightmarish sea-get pounced. Cormac managed to catch its claws in his buckler even as he chopped into the thing's neck. Then he had to lop off the arm of that dying obscenity, to free his shield-arm of its hampering weight. So deeply were steely claws imbedded in the painted, steel-braced yew wood. Another dived in low at him. Cormac struck like a madman, missing his own toes by the breadth of but a finger or two. That monster croak-screamed, its paws gone amid gouting blood . . . and wallowing handless, it strove to get at his booted leg with its teeth. The while, on the scapha, axes fell on walrus-hide ropes.

Cormac wheeled, ran three strides, and leaped out over the widening gap betwixt barge and scapha.

He came down flat-footed on the coaster's deck, squatting to absorb the fall until his hinderparts nigh touched the planking.

For an instant his balance was in question on the blood-slick deck. Then he was up like a catapult and spinning to hack through the rope holding the last grapnel. The vessel of men and that of monsters were no longer linked.

Hideous baying croaking fouled the air as the servants of the human-hating god saw *Raven* bearing down on them with the swiftness of a falling meteor.

Raven's copper-sheathed prow slammed highspeed into the barge of horror.

"UP OARS AND HOLD 'EM HIGH! Brace your-sel—"

The booming shout of Wulfhere Skull-splitter was

broken off by impact. With a great snapping splintering of bone cemented by sea-snail, amid stricken croaking, the hell-sent barge was smashed to white splinters. The coaster so nearby was rocked violently and it fell out that a Sueve saved a Dane from going overboard. A flying chunk of splintered white bone, three forearms neatly joined lengthwise, came end-over-ending through the air so that Cormac ducked to save his head. Catapulted, one of the sea-creatures flopped squashily athwart the skiff's gunwale. Another shard of flying bone brought a yelp from a seasoned pirate of Dane-mark. Slowed but not halted by the tremendous impact, *Raven* crunched on, cutting the bone-barge into halves and more. Two flopping helpless sea-spawn tumbled to her decks, and with great joy Wulfhere and Gudfred Hrut's son chopped them to pieces.

In fragments, the barge sank as though those bones of murdered men were filled with lead.

Dark waters rose over the deck-fire that had lured so many men to their doom. Once again the hair of Sueves and Danes and aye, one Gael among them, stood on end; for the fire remained eerily ablaze for many fathoms as it sank, until the darkness of the nighted water blotted it from ken.

One of the awful amphibians clung to *Raven*'s dragon-head. A savagely laughing Wulfhere clove it in twain with an incredible sweep of his ax that splashed blood over ten men—who promptly cursed their captain, that now they must clean their armour.

The scapha was wallowing the way that those aboard must brace their legs and set them well apart. Nevertheless Cormac was glaring at the last of the monsters when it turned in the sea to utter a hissing, croaking malediction. With disgust on him rather than fear, Cormac mac Art snatched up a spear and hurled it.

So had the men of Eirrin long fought, and the long steel-tipped stave rushed straight to its mark. Cthulhu's creature and spear vanished together; no man could be certain whether Cormac had struck it well. As for the Gael, he could only hope with fervor that Crom of Eirrin had guided his powerful throw.

The scapha tilted now, and men fell. The craft had suffered some little damage of the creatures, and more of the ramming that had slammed a large section of the barge into its squared stern. Too, a great chunk of bone splintered from the other craft stood forth from the skiff's hull, just at the waterline. Cormac's *Sword of Lir* was dying under his feet, and he wished he'd named it else.

Silent, grim-faced men on *Raven* aided silent, blood-splashed men from the coaster in transferring to the ship. Her bow plated for ramming, the Dane-built pirate craft was unharmed. Swung upward in instant response to her master's command, not one of her oars was damaged.

Pirates and Suevic Galicians, almost in silence, swung the ship out and rowed toward the harbour. Behind, the ungainly scapha floundered amid lapping wavelets, a floating marker to the graves of three men, and the monsters of Treachery Bay.

CHAPTER FIFTEEN: The Last Monster

Irnic waited on the dock at Brigantium Harbour, with Zarabdas. The two stood at sea's edge with cloaks blowing in the salt breeze. They watched while *Raven* came in. Well behind the king's cousin and his mage-adviser stood two others, companions or bodyguards of Irnic Break-ax. They held torches whose yellow flames leaned far and danced in the breeze.

The men of *Raven* came ashore, and none could hurry too much to get to ale and wine. Irnic said naught, but his eyes questioned.

"Done," Cormac mac Art said. "And your mission?"

"Done," Irnic said, and they betook themselves in silence from the harbour.

The triumphant seamen, Danes and Suevi as one, entered the encampment set up for Raven's crew. Waiting women there were, and wine and ale both to quaff, and a story to talk on for hours.

Cormac and Wulfhere, with Irnic and Zarabdas, must confer. Ugly or no, dangerous or no, there were matters of which they still did not wish to apprise Veremund. Therefore they must conceal this conference. This Irnic and the Palmyran had already discussed. They guided their piratical allies to Zarabdas's spacious and cozy home, which Veremund the King had caused to be raised close by his own keep.

Cormac was surprised to see no old servant tenanting this tapestried, carpeted home of the eastborn mage. No; the servants of the dark and bald men who was so serious of mind and purpose and who advised a king were . . . most attractive, and far from old. Perhaps five-and-twenty was the sleek-hipped woman whose hair was almost black and whose eyes were kohled, and the blond, milk-skinned lass with the swollen hips and bust must be no older than in her middle teens. Both were passing well-favoured of face and figure, and quiet. They looked adoringly on their black-bearded lord.

An amazing man, this Zarabdas of Palmyra of the sands! Full and full of surprises had he proven, this man Cormac was now sure was far from the plotting inimical magicker he'd at first thought.

Wine was poured by those winsome servants, and Wulfhere and Cormac kept their hands and remarks to themselves.

"Fetch the crock of ale from 'neath the floorboard," Zarabdas said, and when that had been done: "Become scarce and deaf, Zenobia and Odainata; we have business and did you hear it you would be in terrible danger."

The woman and the girl, whose names Zarabdas had surely been pleased to give them himself, made themselves scarce.

"Terrible danger?" Cormac said.

"Only some. We do border on treason, keeping matters from the king whilst we decide what to tell him. But such words, and we being who we are, ensure that my pretty little girls will not try to listen far more than would a closed door."

231

"Excellent!" Wulfhere said. "Suberb wine! I'd think ye'd merely put a spell of sleep on them." He eyed the jug of ale.

"I do not spell," Zarabdas said quietly, "save at my king's command. I am a man of another people, far from here; of a city smashed into ruin by the Romans two centuries agone so that now it is but a shadow of the Palmyra of Odainath and that great queen Zenobia. Here I am welcome, and well treated, and honoured. An my loyalty and restraint make me a strange mage, so be it. I do not seek to be like other men . . . any more than do you two, who slay so few on captured ships."

"The barge—" Irnic prompted.

"Is gone," Cormac said. "Smashed and sunk. Those who crewed and accompanied it are dead, to number half a hundred."

"Accompanied—"

"Half a—"

Cormac and Wulfhere told them of their activities this night, with Wulfhere discovering and declaiming the while that Zarabdas's crock-sealed ale was the best this side of Dane-mark. Irnic and Zarabdas listened closely, and asked questions. Disbelief was neither considered nor possible.

"By Arawn's horns!" Irnic grunted at last, challenging the Dane for the large glazed pot of ale. "What foulness! And the kelp?"

"Guided by them," Cormac said. "Sent by them, only to stop the beacon so that theirs could lure men to death . . . doubtless that barge grew in size with each ship they seized! The seaweed is only seaweed. Without its masters to send it, it is no menace to anyone—but can be excellent in a stewpot with pork!"

"Foulness indeed," Zarabdas said. "Cthulhu is a god not of this earth! We may be sure that what your men

232

interrupted tonight, Commander, was a temple to that
same tentacled god who hates humankind. And . . . now
I suppose I suspect something else, though we may never
know, unless she's found. Ah, fool that I've been! Wise
Zarabdas, never to have suspected, much less guessed!
Yet it's from a flower in the desert called Palmyra I
come, far from the sea. As for Lucanor . . . a native of
Antioch that one is, close to the cultish Levantine lands.
There is the ancient home, ye see, of such as the
Phoenicians and Philistines . . . seafaring peoples. Aye,
and we may be sure that the Philistine sea-god Dagon is
no other in truth than Cthulhu from . . . elsewhere. Off
this very earth. As for Lucanor—who can doubt that he
studied in Levantine cities? Was he brought the cult
here, and was he moved swiftly to bind to him certain
peasants he treated . . ."

"*And* nobles," Irnic said. "Or a noble: forget not Lord
Unscel!"

"*And*," Zarabdas said, "the queen."

And they were silent with thoughts none of them
liked.

Cormac broke that silence: "Suppose Lucanor came
here because he divined the location of Cthulhu's
keep . . ."

"R'lyeh," Zarabdas said. "And you are convinced it
is just off our shores."

"Aye. Fathoms down, where once plains rolled. I
know."

Irnic and the mage stared with knitted brows at the
Gael.

"Dispute him not," Wulfhere said, with a most
unusual quietness of voice. "When my battle-brother
says he *knows* something such as that, we other men may
merely accept. A god has touched this son of a noble of
Eirrin," the Dane solemnly told them, ignoring the fact

that he was wont japingly to call his Gaelic sword-brother a pig-farmer's son. "He knows better than any that some life-forces return again and again, for—"

"All," Irnic said.

"All souls return in the Endless Ring," Zarabdas said.

"Well, we Danes don't hold so, though Cormac's experiences have troubled me with frowns on this happy face. Yet who would question our skalds—and who'd dare give the question to the All-father and his thunder-bringing son!" He gave three unbelieving foreigners a mildly truculent look. "At any rate, Cormac *remembers*. It comes on him like a dream, and him awake. If he says that once the Sueves were green with purple hair, believe him. If he says I was once Alexander of the Greeks, I believe him. If he says we slew Cthulhu's servants just on the doorstep of his undersea keep—*believe*."

"Never am I after telling ye it's Alexander ye be, Wulfhere."

"No, but it's a pleasant thought, a great conqueror and all—and he *was* red of hair, wasn't he?"

Cormac made a face and waved a hand impatiently. "Ye've heard our tale. The sea and Brigantium Harbour are clear. Now what of your activities this night, Breaker of Axen?"

"Some time I must tell you how I came by my sobriquet," Irnic said, but no smile lighted his face. "Was a dark cult we crushed this night. Nor did we invade that hellish temple soon enow. A peasant child—a sweet little thing with fine parents I'd night with—was sacrificed in a foul rite this night, the way we have not done for centuries! Aye, and still in Lucanor's hand was that bloody knife when we broke in, in force, and in his other hand her . . . her dripping heart. All the members of that cult he presided over are . . . being detained. Three fought like demons, but we took them alive;

including the noble Unscel—my own wife's cousin! Others were there, though, as guards: those wore weapons and mail under their muffling cloaks, and gave battle. Sore was the shield-clashing for a time, and more blood than an innocent child's now splashes that place. My men were taken by surprise, and slow to draw steel and fight in a *temple,* until one was down bleeding. I lost that man. Another bears a wound will keep him down for months. As for the cult-guards: all are dead save one. Him we persuaded to speak, as he liked not the prospect of a candle's being prodded into his wound and therein turned."

Wulfhere and Cormac showed teeth, though the Dane's grim grin was broader.

"Not Suevi, those armed men," Irnic went on, "but of Cantanabria our neighbour. They represented only themselves. Of that we made sure—we have no official quarrel with Cantanabria. Was they, Cormac, who sought to do murder on ye, that day in the meadow. On Lucanor's orders."

"Gladness is on me to know that," Cormac said, for he'd liked not the thought that some of Galicia abhorred him for a reiver so much as to try to do murder on him. "And what of Lucanor himself, Irnic?"

Irnic lurched up from his seat and paced away. He whirled to face them, his back to a multi-hued eastern tapestry. His face worked.

"Lucanor escaped. He *vanished.* Nay, wait and give listen. There were—there *are* but two means of entering and leaving that temple. We entered through both at once, and left men outside, too. Yet Lucanor stabbed my man who sought to arrest him, there beside the very altar where the child's blood still dripped. Then he whirled and fled into a dark niche behind the altar, with his damned blood-red robe and black cloak flapping like a great bat. And then he was not there. Nor did he leave by either door, for men waited outside. They could not have missed the emergence of a mouse."

"Did ye sound the walls of that niche?" Wulfhere asked.

"Of *course*. We 'sounded' them—with hammers! Solid stone, like the rest of that temple. And ask me not about the floor; it contains no trap door."

Cormac gritted his teeth. Lucanor gone, escaped, and he had surely initiated the cult and roused the creatures of Cthulhu and . . . more? He wondered, for a question remained unasked. Meanwhile, he rearranged his mind. Zarabdas, with his strange name that seemed sinister to western ears . . . a friend and good man who practiced his magicks only on his king's command. Lucanor, healer with the name of that healer who was said to have followed the Dead God . . . he was a black magician, a priest or helpful servant of a foul god from off this plane; a murderer of children and misleader of peasants; a practitioner of foul arts who had recruited —

"Ah. And . . . what of . . . that woman of whom we spoke earlier, Irnic?"

"Zarabdas knows, Cormac."

Wulfhere said, "I fault ye not for telling me, Wolf. But I too know of Queen Venhilda's peregrinations-by-night."

"Well, what of her?" Cormac demanded without patience. Yet he feared the reply, for he liked Veremund, for all that he was a king.

Irnic heaved a mighty sigh and spoke without pride or happiness.

"She was *seen* to leave the King's Hall. She was *seen* to enter the old temple. And she did *not* depart. Yet she was not among the cultists, nor of course is she now."

"By the Morrighu—not with Lucanor, in Behl's name?"

Irnic shook his head. "Nay, Cormac. I said it: she was not in the temple when we entered. But there, before the altar, the cloak she had worn . . . was."

After a long while of brooding silence, four unhappy men began to discuss sadly how much should be told the king. All, they eventually decided.

The reactions and emotions of the King of the Suevi-become-Galicii were mixed. Others were joyous at the news; Veremund was of course pleased at the removal of the murdering sea menace, and even at the discovery and crushing of the cult, for he was king and the tower of death become only a light-tower again. Yet he was skeptical of the full report, and silent.

Cormac knew the man was fearful of the answer that must be a loud voice in his royal brain: Where was Queen Venhilda?

Mac Art slept, and alone, and wondered if Veremund, alone, slept.

Whether or no, the king was up and looking the king on the morrow, with congratulatory words for Cormac and Wulfhere. Too, he would insist on riding down to the shore with them to see what remained of their triumph, and to survey coastal waters made safe for his realm and its visitors.

So they did. The tower now seemed bright and cheery, container of a beacon to guide seamen in to a shore eager for trade. Yet they found that which was far from pleasant.

Of craft or creatures there remained no sign asea, as though that god from another plane had sucked all down to his drowned kingdom, even in sleep. Yet the tide had brought in an ugly reminder of the battle, and proof of all.

The sea-creature lay on a spit of sand, washed in and abandoned by the tide. It was as hideous in death as it had been in life, and the spear Cormac had hurled still transfixed it. Nor was there any preventing Veremund from seeing: this frog-fish-human creature wore two pieces of jewellery.

Around its almost nonexistent neck glittered a chain supporting the figure of an anthropomorphic yet hardly human creature whose head sprouted tentacles. Though less exotic, the other piece of jewellery, a ring, was more spectacular. Above the joint of a claw-tipped finger, the ring bore a fine prodigious stone that glittered and winked in the morning sunlight. A huge opal it was, besprint within by many flecks of a half-dozen colours.

Veremund stood slump-shouldered, though Cormac knew that the king had known no love for his changed, pallid wife for a year or more, and had no love of her. And too, he had lately consoled himself with Clodia, probably the finest event to befall him since his coronation.

"This . . . *thing,*" the king mumbled, "slew my beloved Venhilda and wears even her own favourite ring."

That she had of Lucanor, Cormac thought, *who could not cure her . . . of a "disease" he brought on, seeking to create a changeling queen of monsters?* But he saw the tense faces of Zarabdas and Irnic, and their eyes bright on him, and he sighed . . . and nodded.

"Aye, so it must have been. Pride is on me to have taken vengeance for yourself, lord King."

Cormac did not believe his own words. Vengeance? In a way—but Lucanor was gone, alive, escaped—and the queen was surely dead, of Cormac's hand.

Though he could not be certain, it seemed hideously likely that Lucanor, while he "tended" the queen, had used his magical wiles and connection to a monster-god of old on her. The result was this ugl ⁄ creature lying dead on the sand. *She never blinked,* Cormac mac Art remembered. *Because she was changing!* Losing her humanity; taking on fishlike qualities and traits. And last night, her cloak alone remained of her in the temple. Perhaps because with a final arcane rite and blood-sacrifice, Venhilda had been fully transformed . . . only to die among other monsters at the hand of a man in her husband's employ?

Standing beside the king in the bright sunlight, mac Art could be certain of none of his surmising. But he knew that all of it was probable.

Unconsciously touching the bit of jewellery out of Egypt that he uncharacteristically wore for some reason he could not name, Cormac gazed at another sigil on its chain. It circled the neck of the dead monster he and Irnic and Zarabdas and Wulfhere knew full well had been Queen of the Galicians.

"Kraken," Wulfhere said, staring at that same sigil with its tentacle-sprouting head.

"Nay," Zarabdas of Palmyra said. "This is a representation of the ancient demon in the world since its birth . . . Cthulhu, he who awaits asleep in his house in sunken R'lyeh." Almost dreamily, Zarabdas spoke on: "When last this demon stirred in his sleep, the world shook and rocked and the oceans drowned land-masses larger than all this Hispania we stand on. No nation but has tales left it of the Great Flood. The kraken . . . ah! The kraken are but his remote get, his time-enfeebled spawn. And if ever he should awake again, it will be horror on the earth again, and . . ."

"Ragnarok," Wulfhere muttered. "The twilight of the gods . . . and men."

If you enjoyed this saga of heroic fantasy, you won't want to miss the sequel to THE TOWER OF DEATH, the third book in the *Cormac mac Art* series: WHEN DEATH BIRDS FLY. Here's a small sample of what's to come . . .

"For these are the birds of death; the Owl, a predator of the night, and the Raven, presider over battlefields."
—*Alexandros of Chios*

Sorcerous evil swooped above Nantes on broad black wings. Hate and Evil slept fitfully in the nighted city below. Those two dark forces called to each other as land to restless sea. Black wings slanted downward, riding the wind. The warm summer's night seemed to shiver around the ragged edges of swooping night-wings spreading broader than a man's height.

Sigebert of Metz, more lately called Sigebert One-ear, stirred in his bed and muttered. Much strong wine without water had gone down his throat earlier this evening, more than one cup drugged by his physician, a man tight-lipped against his patient's cursing. The wine brought Sigebert no peace, him most men would have said deserved no peace.

A recent sword cut had caught and torn one corner of his sensuous mouth, plowed messily along his cheek, and shorn off the ear on that side of his head. The raw pain of it came into his dreams even through the fiery fumes of drugs and drunkenness. Even so, in Sigebert the hate was stronger than the pain. Through his villainous brain burned visions of a sinewy, tigerish Gael of Eirrin and a huge ax-wielding Dane.

"Death for them," he mumbled, and he panted. "By Death itself—death, death for them! Death slow and awful! Death!"

Sigebert awoke to the drumbeat of his pain.

His skin was cold with fevered, nightmare-induced sweat. The coverings of his bed pressed suffocatingly on his limbs and athletic form. Was difficult for him to be certain whether he slept or woke, and in truth Sigebert hardly cared. He lay gasping and sweating, hating.

Of a sudden he went rigidly still. Eyes invaded his chamber. Eyes—yellow as topaz, lambent, blazing— were fixed on him from the foot of his bed. Something —not someone—was there, staring.

Am I awake? Surely this too is dream . . .

His horror-stricken gaze could discern no more than a blocky and indistinct shape that was like a short thick log, or a man's head and limbless torso. Black as the heart of midnight it was, indistinct in the darkness of Sigebert's draped night-chamber. Yet it gave a strong, foul impression of deformity and distortion; or perhaps that was in Sigebert One-ear's mind, weighted by pain and alcohol.

In his terror he thought that some goblin or hellish fiend had come for his soul, which was admittedly damned.

The thing moved. Grotesquely, it seemed to shrug and expand. Vast wings flexed and their tips reached nigh from wall to wall. Their spread was more broad than the height of a tall man. Black feathers ruffled.

The thing spoke . . . or did it speak? Sigebert heard words . . . or did he feel them?

Do not cry out, Sigebert of Metz. An you do, I shall be gone, the which will be to your detriment. I bring news of your enemies.

Night-spirit, Sigebert thought wildly. Some demon in the form of a gigantic *bird* . . .

"Who are you?" he said, and heard his own voice croak.

I am the soul of Lucanor Magus the Physician. Far—

Something surged in Sigebert. Relief, preternaturally sent? Blinking and with sudden hope he said, "Physician?"

Aye. And mage, Sigebert of Metz, and mage!

"You—have you come to help me in my agony?"

Sigebert received an impression of mirth, which angered him even while it despoiled his shaky foundation of hope. *Against your enemies*, he was told. *Is not your hatred for them as much a part of your agony as your physical hurts?*

This time Sigebert was unable to speak, and the bird continued, voicelessly.

Far to the south, in a village of the seafaring Basques, my fleshly body sleeps. All of me that is significant has winged hither, to aid you to destroy those you hate whom I also hate—yea, and for greater reasons than yours! Yet it is known to me aforetime that you will not heed my advice . . . this time. On the morrow, in day's bright light, you will believe this was merely a dream, gendered by your hate and pain. You will ignore it.

Sigebert's thoughts moved in slow, murky channels. Already he had gone from fear to disbelief to fear to hope to shattered hope and wonderment—and curiosity.

Half drugged and but partly wakeful, he yet put a shrewd question.

"You know this? Then why trouble to come to me, physician, mage . . . creature?"

For reasons that you will learn from your folly, and heed me when again I come to you. You know those enemies I refer to; you well know them and their inhuman prowess and luck! They are Cormac mac Art and Wulfhere the Skull-splitter of the Danes—those bloody devils of the sea!

At those names Sigebert came wide awake, and hatred pulsed in him more strongly than the pain that rode his heartbeat. "Ah."

They live, and thrive. They have taken refuge in the Suevic kingdom, ruled by Veremund the Tall, that whispery voice went on, that was not a voice. *He now employs them. Even now they prepare to leave Hispania, those bloody pirates. They undertake a mission to the land of the Danes for this same Veremund. Once I served him. I, Lucanor Magus, served him, and served him well. Now he has exiled me and, could he lay hands on me, would have me die slowly. They are to thank for this—Cormac mac Art and Wulfhere the Dane of their ship Raven. May they be accursed and accursed to world's end and Chaos to come, and the Black Gods of R'lyeh devour them!*

Sigebert One-ear laughed hoarsely. "I know not your gods, mage. But I share your wish!"

Then attend. Three days from this, these pirates leave the port of Brigantium in Galicia, and will sail east. For a short time they will lie to in a sheltered bay below the Pyrenees. Though they know it not, I await them in that same region. I shall incite my . . . hosts to slaughter them, for these Basques are a folk who love outsiders not at all.

An I am successful in this, you will not set eyes on me again, Sigebert One-ear, for I shall have no need of you.

*Should the Basques fail me, these pirate scum will doubt-
less run by night up the western coast of Gaul. Past
Burdigala, past the Saxon settlements—and past your
own city of Nantes. Beyond that lies Armorica, called
Lesser Britain. There they two have friends and can find a
measure of safety. An you are vigilant, you may entrap
them ere they reach that haven. In your hands will it lie
then, agent of Kings!*

Sigebert strained to pierce the darkness with his stare.
It seemed to him that the creature crowding his
bedchamber with its presence was an immense, malefic
owl. God's Death! The musty stench of its feathers was
choking him!

Yes, an owl. He could distinguish the bizarre shape of
its evilly wise head, the blazing eyes and hooked beak.
Though he saw them not, he sensed too the taloned feet,
ready to drive inward-curving claws with merciless
power through live flesh. An owl; a black owl! The bird
of Athena. Silent-winged predator of night. Terror of
those more timid night-creatures it fed upon. Emblem of
death and occult wisdom from ancient days. And vaster
than an eagle, this one!

So. A wizard's soul gone out from the body in tan-
gible form.

In the dim Frankish forests, Sigebert's people knew of
such things, for despite his Latin education and manners, Sigebert One-ear of Metz was a German: a Frank.
His own people called this sort of sorcerous messenger
Sendings, or *fylgja*. He could not doubt that this owl
was real; Lucanor's *fylgja*.

Lucanor.

The name was strange to him. Greek, was it not? No
matter; the names of Cormac mac Art and Wulfhere
Skull-splitter were very, very familiar indeed. Pirates.
Too recently, whilst they sought to dispose of their

sword-won gains ashore, Sigebert had acted in his official capacity as representative of the king. He sought to take them into deserved custody. Was then that a sword in the hand of one of their men had butchered his face.

"Be sure that I will act," he promised, who had been called the Favoured, for his good looks, since he was first able to walk. No more.

Laughter?

I am sure that you will not! In the light of day you will believe that none of this occurred, and put it from your mind. You are not the Count of Nantes, nor will you go to him with a tale so doubtful. The more fool you!

Sigebert gritted his teeth and his nostrils flared in an angry breath. He'd like to meet this Lucanor as a *man,* and see how sneery he was then!

His visitor saw. Despite its haughty tone, the thing that was Lucanor knew well that it might need this Frank for an ally. As chief customs assessor of Nantes, Sigebert held some power, and was well informed of all goings and comings within the city. More, he hated the huge Danish pirate and his dark henchman even as Lucanor did. Yet Lucanor's physical body lay far indeed from northward Nantes. It had not been possible for him to travel so far, swiftly enow to give Sigebert this warning in the flesh. Nor would he place himself physically in the power of this clever villain until he had shown the Frank his value.

Besides, his spirit double, his Sending or *fylgja* as the barbarians called it, must return to his body ere dawn, for the sun's direct light could destroy it. They were no friends, Sendings and sunlight.

You will remember, the black owl said, or whispered, or thought harshly. *You will not believe, Sigebert Oneear, Frank, of Metz and now of Nantes . . . but you will remember, and in my time I will come to you again.*

With a horripilating rustle the great fell bird hopped to the window and was gone on spectral wings. Sigebert felt the air stir. The thing's shadow was an evil splotch that flowed over buildings and dark streets of Nantes. Watchdogs and alley curs across the city cringed and whimpered softly at its passing. None dared bark.

—From *When Death Birds Fly,* copyright © 1980 by Andrew Offutt & Keith Taylor

WHY WASTE
YOUR PRECIOUS
PENNIES ON GAS OR
YOUR VALUABLE
TIME ON LINE
AT THE BOOKSTORE?

We will send you, FREE, our 28 page catalogue, filled with a wide range of Ace Science Fiction paperback titles—we've got something for every reader's pleasure.

Here's your chance to add to your personal library, with all the convenience of shopping by mail. There's no need to be without a book to enjoy—request your *free* catalogue today.

CONAN

ANDRE NORTON

WITCH WORLD SERIES

☐ 89705 **WITCH WORLD** $1.95

☐ 87875 **WEB OF THE WITCH WORLD** $1.95

☐ 80806 **THREE AGAINST THE WITCH WORLD** $1.95

☐ 87323 **WARLOCK OF THE WITCH WORLD** $2.25

☐ 77556 **SORCERESS OF THE WITCH WORLD** $2.50

☐ 94255 **YEAR OF THE UNICORN** $2.50

☐ 82349 **TREY OF SWORDS** $2.25

☐ 95491 **ZARSTHOR'S BANE** (Illustrated) $2.50

Available wherever paperbacks are sold or use this coupon.

ACE SCIENCE FICTION
P.O. Box 400, Kirkwood, N.Y. 13795

Please send me the titles checked above. I enclose $_____.
Include $1.00 per copy for postage and handling. Send check or
money order only. New York State residents please add sales tax.

NAME_____

ADDRESS_____

CITY_____STATE_____ZIP_____

A-03